Elin Gregory

Eleventh Hour

Manifold Press

Published by Manifold Press

ISBN: 978-1-908312-76-1

Proof-reading and line editing: Two Marshmallows twomarshmallows.net

Editor: Julie Bozza

Text: © Elin Gregory 2016
Cover image: © TfL, detail of a poster from the collection of London Transport Museum (see the back pages for the full illustration)
Cover design: © Michelle Peart (and Julie Bozza) 2016
E-book format: © Manifold Press 2016
Print format: © Julie Bozza 2016
Set in Adobe Caslon

For further details of Manifold Press titles both in print and forthcoming: manifoldpress.co.uk

Dedication

This book is affectionately dedicated to the best bits of early 20th century adventurous fiction, which is so awful in some ways and such a delight in others.

Also to the numerous people who provided oodles of advice and support over the rather long time it took to write, revise and edit *Eleventh Hour*, and to the Manifold Press team for giving it a chance – you all rock, I love you to bits, thank you SO much.

Chapter One

Briers Allerdale paid off the cabbie with a half crown and a smile. "Keep the change," he said. As he turned towards his destination, the man's grunted thanks faded into the clip-clop, rumble and growl of the morning traffic. Briers had last visited London on leave in '25 – good Lord, was that really three years ago – and had enjoyed the soft June sunshine. Now, the chilly October breeze driving across St James's Park reminded him that his business was most urgent and he should be on his way.

He jogged across the road, dodging another cab and giving an apologetic wave to a coal man who had to rein in his horses. His destination could have been a bank or the chambers of a particularly well-heeled firm of solicitors. However, beside the door, a discreet brass plate with the address, Broadway House, and a portcullis marked it as an official establishment of His Majesty's Government. Briers shrugged off his trench coat as he entered the lobby, folded the wet sides together and draped it over his arm. Hat in hand he approached the desk. "Good morning," he said. "My name's Allerdale, Belgrade office. I have an appointment."

"Right on time, sir." The man at the desk made a careful note in a ledger. "If you would take those stairs, sir, and the corridor to the right on the second floor. Ah, I see Mr Naylor has come to meet you."

"Thanks." Briers strode to the foot of the stairs and bounded up them to join the man who was waiting on the half landing.

"You made good time." Naylor turned and led the way to the next floor. "Sir James is in a meeting but will be with you shortly. In here, Allerdale, if you please." Naylor opened a door to an office with a small waiting area. "Would you care for some tea?"

"No, thank you. I had coffee on the train," Briers replied.

Naylor hung Briers' coat and hat on the coat tree while Briers took a seat. As waiting rooms went, it wasn't too bad. There was a fine oak desk with matching filing cabinets standing on a patch of carpet that, from the gloss of the pile, might have been Persian. The chairs, while hard, were of good solid construction and the soft glow of the gas lights, necessary in this windowless room, gave a suggestion of warmth. Opposite the door by which they had entered was another, double the width, highly polished, with ornate brass knobs and push plates. Briers watched Naylor seat himself at the desk then folded his arms, crossed his legs at the ankles and settled down to wait.

He had been there no more than five minutes when there was a quiet knock and the door to the corridor opened again.

"I so sorry, Naylor, I only just got your message. Am I late?" The man who entered glanced once at Briers but directed his apologetic smile at Naylor.

"Only a minute or two, Mr Siward." Naylor's deadpan expression eased a little. "But Sir James has been held up. If you would be so good as to take a seat?"

"Of course." Siward settled two chairs along from Briers. He fixed a pair of gold *pince-nez* on his nose and opened the blue covered folder he had tucked under his arm. Briers, who had been beginning to get bored, closed his eyes and reviewed the appearance of both his companions. He prided himself on never forgetting a face – in fact, it was thanks to that skill that he had been recalled to London. Naylor: medium height, brown hair receding, a little heavy around the waist, well-kept hands with no rings. His would be a hard face to remember, apart from a small white scar interrupting the bristle of one eyebrow and a single pock mark high on his left cheek. The other chap, Siward – had Naylor really said Siward, because there was quite a story attached to that name – could have been the office boy if it hadn't been for the official stamp on the front of the file he was perusing and the quality of his excellently-cut morning suit. A gold signet ring with a worn heraldic device hugged the third finger of his left hand, a discreet pearl pin gleamed in his tie, and a plain silver watch chain arced across his waistcoat. His blond hair was slicked back, darkened by the brilliantine, from an unlined, clear-skinned face. Briers opened his eyes to take another look, wondering if his imagination had improved upon the original. He cast a casual glance in Siward's direction, his eyes sharpening. No, it hadn't been his imagination. Short straight nose, long lashed eyes, excellent bone structure and that mouth!

Dear God, he thought, *what I wouldn't give to have that wrapped around my* ....

Siward's colour rose. Briers cursed himself as he reflected that he probably wasn't the only one in the room with good peripheral vision.

He cleared his throat and reached into his pocket for his pipe and tobacco pouch. "I don't suppose you have a match. I've run out, worse luck."

Still a little pink, Siward turned another page in his folder before replying. "I'm sorry, I don't smoke. Perhaps Mr Naylor … ?"

"I can let you have a box of matches when you leave," Naylor said. "But Sir James prefers his guests not to indulge."

Sir James' word was law, obviously, so Briers thanked him and put his pipe away. "I suppose," he murmured to Siward, "that there's not much chance for the smoke to escape. Being kippered wouldn't improve Naylor's looks."

Siward shot him a disapproving glance but Briers could see the tension around his mouth that meant he was trying not to smile.

"My name's Allerdale," Briers said turning a little in his seat to offer his hand. "Briers, with an E, Allerdale."

"With an E?" Siward shook his hand. "Miles Siward, with an I."

If he would have offered any further intimacies, and Briers could think of a few he would have preferred, he was prevented by the faint chime of a bell from beyond the far door. Naylor got up. "Gentlemen," he said, "Sir James will see you now."

"Both of us?" Siward-with-an-I said as he followed Briers towards the office door. He was shorter than Briers had thought.

"Sir James will explain," Naylor said and announced them as they entered.

Inside, Briers had to bite back a nervous laugh. Long windows lay splashes of watery light to brighten the carpet and furnishings and glint on the gold embossed spines of the books on the many bookshelves. It reminded him strongly of his old headmaster's study and he felt the familiar tremor of uncertainty – was he going to be caned, carpeted or congratulated? Possibly Siward felt the same frisson. If anything, he looked even more apprehensive.

"Gentlemen." Sir James Lorimer looked like a headmaster, too: pale and austere with calm, weary eyes that had seen all the follies of the world. "Thank you, Allerdale, for making such a difficult trip so quickly. Your help will be invaluable. And Siward, I have made arrangements with your departmental head – as of now and until further notice you are on secondment, answering only to me or Naylor. The paperwork has already gone through."

"Active duty, sir?" Siward's back had straightened, bringing him up to – oh, probably five feet five. Briers who topped six feet one in his socks, couldn't help but smile.

"Active duty," Sir James said. "Your familiarity with London will be an asset, likewise your linguistic skills. And Allerdale – I have had a glowing recommendation from the embassy in Belgrade and your record speaks for itself. I can't promise danger, gentlemen, but I can't promise safety, either."

They both made the expected eager murmurs. "Might I ask, sir, which languages in particular?" Siward added, with enthusiasm born from complete innocence, Briers judged.

Sir James nodded to Briers. "Allerdale can tell you that. Also give you a more complete idea of what we're up against. I understand that the recommendation that we take the threat seriously was echoed at the highest level."

"As it should be, sir." Briers took the chair indicated by Sir James and turned a little so he could keep an eye on Siward. Briers let him settle on the edge of his seat, poised like a robin on a particularly prickly twig, before speaking again. "I'm sure Sir James is aware of a – let's call him a patriot – called Andrija but have you ever heard of him, Siward?"

"I don't believe I have." Siward coloured, lips tight.

"He is a Macedonian," Sir James said, shifting a paper on his desk an inch or two and peering at it. "A ranking member of IMRO and has been a terrorist since before the Great War. Of anything other than that, I too am disturbingly ignorant. How did you come to know him, Allerdale?"

Their eyes met and Briers raised his eyebrows. The report he had wired had been concise but covered all the basics. It could only mean that Siward was of more importance than he had assumed if Sir James wanted him spoon-fed the necessary information. And if this Siward was a connection of the other then, Briers decided, it might be worth his while to take some trouble over the briefing.

"You've heard of the Pritich Incident?" Briers waited until Siward's eyes lit up with amusement. "Yes, that ludicrous business over a dog straying

4

across the border from Greece into Bulgaria that lead to an armed invasion and the intervention of the League of Nations. Pure tomfoolery. Buchan couldn't have made up a story like that. Well, there was no dog. The situation was engineered by Andrija as a distraction while he got his operatives across the border into Greece, about 20 miles further north. I was following, trying to get some idea what they were up to, and caught up with them on the outskirts of a village. I got spotted and they shot me."

"Won't it be a problem if Andrija can identify you as readily as you can identify him?" Sir James frowned.

"I'm prepared to stake my life that he wouldn't recognise me." Briers gestured to his chest. "I had a beard down to here and was dressed local style. I think they just put a round into me on principle. I was left coughing blood and counting myself lucky to be alive. It set back our operations in the Balkans by six months. Half a dozen villagers came out to see what the shooting was about and that bastard – my apologies, Sir James. Andrija's not an impressive looking man, you'd pass him by in the street, but I'll never forget that calm voice and the shrug as he said, "Oh, kill them", then he turned away and didn't even wait to see it done. To make it look like bandits, they set fire to some houses, looted the rest and took a few girls with them. We never found out what happened to them, poor things."

Briers glanced at Siward and noted that the edge of his keenness seemed to have dulled a little. That was good. The boy wasn't stupid. He gave him an approving nod and continued. "Since then, we know that Andrija has stoked the fires under any number of seething pots. He may have started out as a true blue patriot –"

"Red and gold surely," Siward murmured and Briers grinned.

"Yes, Macedonian to the bone, fighting for his country's freedom, which is something I think we can all understand. But somewhere along the line, we think he realised that there's very good money to be made by a man who puts himself in the right place at the right time and isn't too fussy what he does once he's there. For instance, you may recall the manner of the assassination of the Bulgarian prime minister?"

"Stamboliyski?" Siward grimaced. "That obscenity with the severed head in the box of biscuits?"

"Very good. Yes, according to our informants, that was Andrija's suggestion, though he did not wield the knife himself." Tiring of the history lesson, Briers decided to bring them all up to date. "Since he prefers to keep his hands clean, he has drawn in some followers of particularly repulsive habits. We do our best to keep tabs on them, and I was lucky enough to obtain information that Andrija and his most trusted lieutenants were about to embark on a journey to London to join Josephine, his paramour. She's a Serb, we think, and she's damn near as clever, and certainly as vicious, as he is. If she and Andrija and the rest of his crew are coming to London, it means something big is about to happen. Something potentially very damaging."

Sir James nodded. "Indeed, and her present location, which we have discovered, suggests a particular target. If this man is killed, at the right moment, it could destabilise the whole of the Balkans. Luckily, we have been able to find the ideal solution for keeping an eye on the woman, while other operatives try to intercept the men.

"You will both be under cover." Sir James produced two files from a desk drawer and passed them over. "Due to the comparatively short notice, we have had to improvise but I think you will be comfortable enough. Siward, I know we are asking a lot, but I am convinced that you will be able to carry it off."

"Sir!" Siward's face had fallen, his cheeks pale. "I understood that it had been decided that I should not have to do this again."

"Needs must," Sir James said briskly. "And your previous assignments were a success, despite your feelings on the matter. King and country, Siward. We all serve according to our talents and abilities. Now, run along. I need to bring Allerdale up to speed, and you need to get yourself over to Resources. They will be expecting you. Ring your man and tell him to pack for at least a week. As of this afternoon, the official story is that you are attending a refresher course. Naylor will give you the details."

"Sir," Siward said, chastened. He inclined his head to Briers in an abrupt little bow of farewell and left the office with his shoulders drooping.

"Tea?" Sir James said, as soon as the door clicked closed. "No? Very well, let's get down to business. I don't need to tell you what a serious situation this is."

"I know how dangerous they can be, sir, but the presence of Josephine is particularly suggestive. Andrija would never risk her unless the situation was particularly delicate or particularly lucrative. Intelligence about who else he has brought into his organisation may provide a clue about his intentions." Briers frowned down at the new identity in his folder. *Brian Carstairs* – it had a ring to it. "Forgive my bluntness, sir, but you mentioned other operatives. It's important my back-up should be both capable and experienced. That young … clerk strikes me as being neither."

Sir James' lips pursed for a moment – thought or annoyance, Briers couldn't decide which – before he answered, confirming a guess Briers had made earlier. "Mr Siward comes from a family devoted to the welfare of the British Empire. His father is currently the British consul in Bucharest and his brother, George Siward, should be known to you by reputation at least. Miles Siward is anxious to follow the family tradition. When we recruited him, he was under the impression it was purely on account of his family connections and his impressive grasp of Balkan languages but," Sir James nodded to the file in Briers' hands, "it was also due to his ability as an amateur actor."

Brian Carstairs, Briers read, turning the pages, *and his wife …*

"Mildred," he said.

"Millie," Sir James said with a smile, "chosen because it was Siward's nickname in college, just as we chose Brian for its similarity to Briers. You haven't time to get used to completely different nomenclature."

Briers leafed through the file of papers, noting addresses, distances, possible targets, and began to nod. "I see," he said. "But, sir, surely an actual woman would have been more suitable? I can assure you I can be trusted to treat her with the proper courtesy and there would be far less risk of discovery."

"Trust in you isn't the issue." Sir James' smile was chilly. "Constrained as we were by time and circumstances, the sole suitable lodging only accepts married couples. We have few female operatives, and none with the language skills Siward has to offer."

"I'm not quibbling about his language skills, sir, but his ability to pass himself off convincingly as a respectable married woman."

"I can assure you Siward makes a very convincing female; not at all music hall or pantomime but quite unremarkable. We have used him thus on previous occasions in more exposed circumstances and he has carried out the deception with great success. In addition, though necessarily limited in his abilities by his – er – type, he can be counted upon to be discreet. My apologies for putting you in an awkward and distasteful position but, as I said, King and country. Even those who otherwise might not be trusted in any situation requiring the manly virtues may serve at a pinch."

Briers tilted his head, studying the papers in the hope that his lowered lids would mask the anger he was feeling, and merely cleared his throat by way of reply.

"Yes, indeed. Let us change the subject." Sir James took his half-hunter watch from his pocket and frowned at it. "I have another meeting shortly. If you would be so good as to return to Naylor? He will give you instructions about your immediate future. Siward will have been instructed to meet you in the lobby." Sir James cleared his throat. "God speed," he murmured, "and good luck."

"Thank you, sir," Briers said and left the room.

'Manly virtues'? he thought. *Good job you don't know the truth about me, you sanctimonious old prig!*

As promised, Naylor provided Briers with a passport, carefully aged, with visa stamps for France and Switzerland. He also handed over a bank book and an envelope with expenses. As Briers retraced his steps to the lobby, he flicked the envelope open and calculated the amount in notes inside. If the largesse was commensurate with the size of perceived danger, someone must be scared stiff of Andrija and his nasty band of cut throats. With good reason, too. Briers had to admit to an uneasy feeling in the pit of his stomach at the thought of facing some of Andrija's nastier henchmen backed only by a professional pen pusher in skirts.

On the half landing, Briers looked over the bannisters to see Siward waiting close to the doors. Rarely had Briers seen a man who looked more miserable. He was watching over two large suitcases and a portmanteau, with a bowler hat in his hand and a very fine cashmere paletot coat over his arm. A much taller, somewhat beefy man in tweeds was puffing on a meerschaum pipe and chatting to him while Siward made terse responses, his knuckles whitening as he gripped the brim of his hat. The beefy man grinned and leaned a little closer, murmuring something that brought blood flooding to Siward's pale cheeks. Briers scowled. There was something threatening about the way the other man loomed over Siward, who Briers assumed he should begin to think of as his partner. Briers had no particular affection for him, but if anyone was going to bully the poor little clerk, it would be him and nobody else. Briers hurried down the stairs and strode across with a cheery, "There you are, Siward. I hope I didn't keep you waiting."

"No, not at all," Siward replied, his tone polite rather more than relieved, so perhaps this bullying was routine.

"No need to fret. Siward's good at waiting." The other man thrust out a hand. "Mortlake. Siward tells me you two are off on a course."

"Yes, Ukrainian." Briers took the proffered hand and wasn't surprised when Mortlake attempted to crush his knuckles – the secret handshake of the society of obnoxious asses. Briers applied equal pressure and Mortlake freed his hand with a jerk.

"You language wallahs do a useful job." Mortlake's tone managed to be both derisive and patronising. "It wouldn't suit me, of course, but we field agents appreciate your back up."

"Wouldn't know what to do without us, at a guess." Briers grinned at him. "And it warms my cockles to hear how much you cherish us."

Siward's bland expression didn't waver as he said, "Indeed, that makes it all worthwhile. Allerdale, our cab is here. Sorry, Mortlake, no time to gossip."

Mortlake ignored Siward, nodded to Briers and strolled across to the desk.

"Let me guess," Briers murmured. "London-based and has never been east of the Channel?"

"It would be unprofessional of me to comment." Siward's stoop to pick up one of the cases wasn't quite quick enough to hide his smile. "Where did you leave your luggage?"

"Charing Cross," Briers replied. "I got in on the nine o'clock from Dover."

"We can fetch it on our way. I need to drop in at home first. If you could bring the other case? The trunk will be sent on."

The journey was short and they had no real time to talk before the cab pulled up in Castle Lane, almost opposite the chapel. A portly gentleman in the black coat and pinstriped trousers of a servant trotted down the steps from an attractive town house and opened the cab door to bow Briers out.

"Welcome, sirs," he said. His accent was roundly Welsh, overlaid with the acquired plumminess befitting his station. "I have packed most of your things, Mr Siward, and there's tea on the hearth. I will have the baggage taken round to the mews directly."

"Thank you, Pritchard," Siward said, paying off the cabbie. "Come, Allerdale. I won't keep you long but you may as well wait in comfort."

The comfort was considerable. Siward's rooms took up the whole first floor. He led Briers into the flat, then nodded towards the scuffed chesterfield couch and the table by the fireplace.

"There will be tea presently," he said.

"Never touch the stuff," Briers said, "but I will read your paper, if I may."

"No tea, good grief." Siward gestured to the couch. "But in any case, make yourself at home."

Brier hung his coat and hat on the stand by the door and made himself comfortable on the couch with the *Times*, snorting as he read of the success of the hare-brained German scheme to fly a Zeppelin to New York.

"Tea, sir?" Pritchard had entered and Briers scowled, not liking it one bit that he hadn't heard him approach.

"No, thank you," he said and forestalled Pritchard's comment with a smile. "I only drink coffee. I've spent too much time on the continent."

"Indeed, sir?" Pritchard didn't smile back but a crease at the corner of his eye deepened. "Then I will be certain to add some and the necessary brewing equipment to Mister Siward's luggage. Excuse me, sir." He picked up the tea tray and carried it through a doorway at the back of the room. When he didn't return, Briers got up to indulge his curiosity.

The painting above the fireplace was a watercolour landscape with a large house nestling amidst trees in the middle distance – the Siward family home? – and painted with a fine deft hand. The book shelves were crammed with all the titles Briers would have expected from a man of Siward's age and class: Dickens, Trollope, all the classics plus some more modern and somewhat racier titles, all of which had been well-read apart from a few nearly-new volumes. Briers picked up Maugham's *Ashenden* stories, read a page and snorted.

"If you'd like to borrow it, feel free," Siward said.

Briers turned to meet him, again irritated he hadn't heard the man approach. He imagined Siward and Pritchard constantly making each other jump, and grinned. "Signed, I see."

"I exercised all my cheek and lionised Maugham at the opening night of *The Letter*. He was restrained in his enthusiasm but quite gracious." Siward had changed into a lovat tweed jacket and well-cut cavalry twill trousers, and had a soft cap tucked under his arm. His hair was slightly rumpled. It suited him. He smiled at Briers. "Feel free to borrow the book. One assumes we won't be working all the time and we'll need something to do."

Briers pocketed the book. "Thanks," he said. "This sort of job can get very tedious. I get through a lot of books."

"Then I'll bring a pocket chess set as well." Siward stooped to open a drawer. "We can take turns in watching as we play."

Briers took a moment to admire the swell of Siward's arse as the flannels pulled tight, but turned away when Pritchard cleared his throat.

"I already took the liberty of packing the chess set, sir," the valet said. "Plus a couple of decks of cards. Shall I bring the car round?"

"No, thank you, Pritchard," Siward said. "We'll go to the mews ourselves."

"Enjoy the course, sir," Pritchard said with a smile. "Ukrainian – who'd have thought it, eh?"

Siward laughed. "If HM decrees we need to learn it, who am I to argue? I'm sorry you can't come but I understand we'll be roughing it. Just like college, eh, Allerdale?"

"Yes, that's it," Briers said. "Thank you, Pritchard."

Siward picked up a small leather bag and led Briers out of the back of the building into a cobbled court.

"Nice car," Briers said, admiring the vehicle's powerful lines. "Armstrong Siddeley?"

Siward opened the dickey seat and crammed his bag down into it. "Four-Fourteen Tourer, Mendip model. It was George's," he said as he got into his seat. "He only drove it twice. I'm keeping it in tune while he's convalescing."

Briers waited until Siward had turned the car and driven it out onto Buckingham Gate before he spoke again.

"How *is* your brother?" he asked.

"As well as can be expected." Siward drove carefully, without much dash, content to follow a coster's cart until sure it was safe to pass it. He glanced at Briers and smiled – a polite but unconvincing grimace. "Thank you for asking. He's walking now, at least, and is his cheerful self, but we don't know how long it will be before he can get back to work. He misses it."

Briers expected he did. He didn't know the details – all very hush-hush – and hesitated to embarrass Siward by asking. "Your brother's a brave man. He could have cut and run. He didn't owe his informant anything."

"Yes, he did." Siward's reply was sharp. "The man was risking just as much as George was, if not more. And he got George to the border, injured though he was. I hope … I hope if ever I'm in a similar situation, I have half the courage. In comparison with that, anyone should be proud to do what they can, even if it's not what they expected to be asked to do."

"I see," Briers said. Once Siward had taken the turn into Victoria Street he broke their silence again. "So – this business. Mildred?"

"Dear God in Heaven." Siward sighed. "Don't think I'm doing it because I like it. I just happen to be very, very good at it."

"And how did you discover that?" Briers asked. "No, honestly. I'm genuinely curious, not poking fun." He turned a little on the broad seat and studied Siward's profile. "We're going to be in close quarters for a while and I like to know a bit about the people I work with. Was it at school?"

Siward's flush was immediate. Even the narrow strips of skin visible between his cuffs and his driving gloves went pink. "I didn't go to school. I had rheumatic fever when I was six and again when I was nine, so I stayed with my parents and we hired a local tutor wherever we happened to be. Hence all the different languages, I suppose. No, it was when I went up to Cambridge. I read English and wasn't doing too well. My supervisor – dear me, even he was a war hero – suggested I join the Shakespeare performance society. He felt it might give me more insight. I'm not sure it worked as he intended but, over my time there, I think I played all the main female leads – Viola, Ophelia, Rosalind, Beatrice, even Lady Macbeth. I enjoyed the challenge but that was Shakespeare, with all the weight of tradition of men playing female roles. Out in the street, it's something else entirely."

"We all have to play roles in this business," Briers said. "Just remember you are doing something unique. Something I most certainly couldn't do."

Siward replied with a peevish snort. "Well, no, because you are a proper stalwart type. You don't get people sneering at you barely behind your back. I bet you played rugger and boxed for your college."

"Good guess." Briers chuckled. "Rugby League was the big thing in my house. Pa was a follower of St Helens and when I was born, the week before they played in the Challenge Cup, he named me after the entire front row."

"Briers?" Siward's tone was sympathetic.

"Briers Winstanley Allerdale," Briers said. "Actually it should have been *Winstanley* Briers Winstanley, because the brothers were playing, but even Pa wouldn't go that far. Being Brian Carstairs for a week or two will come as something of a relief."

Siward chuckled. "So your father was a Rugby League enthusiast. What about your mother? Are they still with you?"

"Yes, bless them. Pa is a country doctor, with a practice outside Eccleston. Ma – well she organises things, mostly Pa. I've got a younger brother who's in the practice with Pa and a sister who's courting."

"Someone suitable, I hope?" Siward said. "Do they know what you do?"

Briers shrugged. "I think Pa has guessed. The others think I'm something to do with steel production, which I am some of the time."

"That must be difficult," Siward said. "At least when I write to my family I can tell them a little of my daily life. A clerical post with the government is close enough to the truth."

"Just how many languages do you speak?" Briers asked.

"Five usefully." Siward's tone was matter of fact. "One picks them up easily as an infant and my nursemaids were a mixed bunch. I could speak Czech and Serbian by the time I was three and learned this odd kind of dialect mixture of Macedonian and Bulgarian from an Embassy driver who had the most wonderful pet ferrets."

Briers laughed. "So if ever I need someone to give a talk to the ferret fanciers of Skopje … ?"

"I'm your man," Siward said. Their eyes met for a moment and both grinned. "Charing Cross." Siward nodded to the turn ahead. "Why don't you nip in and get your baggage while I turn the car around?"

Chapter Two

"Too tight?" Throckmorton asked, and Miles shook his head.

"It's fine," he said, and eased the frock down over the light padding they had applied to his hips. It was a good frock from a great Parisian designer and less than a year old. Just the thing for a well-bred Home Counties miss to have worn on her honeymoon. In two-tone grey wool, with long sleeves and a high collar, and a pleated skirt that skimmed a little below his knees, it fitted well, but then Miles had expected nothing less from Resources. Racks of clothing lined the walls of every room in the disused music hall, a casualty of a Great War Zeppelin raid, with shelves of boots and shoes, crates of equipment, and sets of tools. Everything the ladies and gentlemen of the Secret Intelligence Service might need to pass themselves off convincingly as someone they were not. There were guns somewhere, too, though Miles had never been in a position to need one of those. Many of the rooms had an unpleasant stench about them – oil, sweat, animal dung – but this, the star dressing room, was kept clean and aired out. Here, the real quality clothing was kept and here, for the past hour and a half, Miles and Throckmorton had effected what Miles hoped would be a complete transformation.

Miles knew he was keeping Allerdale waiting and didn't much care. He also knew it was unfair to blame the man for his present plight but he needed – really needed – to direct his ire somewhere and Allerdale didn't look as though he would be bothered by a little professional terseness. No, Allerdale could take it. His shoulders were broad. He was probably outside now, drinking coffee and sniggering over Maugham's book of Secret Service stories, having performed feats himself that made Maugham's hero look like a village bobby. Allerdale's transformation had only taken a change of clothes and an adjustment in attitude. Miles refused to feel guilty for taking the time he needed to achieve exactly the right effect.

"There." Throckmorton gave the skirt's hem a final tweak and got up. "What do you think?"

Miles tilted his head and studied his reflection. He – she – Millie looked good. Smart. Miles adjusted one of his spit curls and let out a long calming breath. He deliberately lowered his shoulders and felt the first easing of tension as he began to relax into the role. The excitement would come later. "How is that cut?"

Throckmorton – who had been in the flickers before the Great War spoiled his looks – pursed his lips and lifted the hem away from Miles' calf. "Fine," he said. "The styptic pencil stopped the bleeding. Tonight, when there's time, do your thighs and the rest of your chest. You can't be too careful. And for pity's sake, buy a safety razor. That sabre of yours is only fit for cutting throats."

"It cuts closer than anything else," Miles said, "and then I don't have to wear so much slap."

"All I can say is, thank God you're blond." Throckmorton grunted and grabbed Miles' chin, turning his face towards the light. "Shall I do your eyebrows?" he asked.

Miles groaned. "All right. But not too thin. I'm supposed to be a not-too-bright, provincial lass, not Theda Bara."

Throckmorton grunted again. As well he might, because Miles had to admit he looked nothing like Theda Bara. Elissa Landi, perhaps. Millie would be a handsome girl if not conventionally pretty. He closed his eyes and tried not to wince as Throckmorton plied the tweezers.

"How much do you know about this Allerdale chap?" he asked after a few moments. Resources got all the best gossip but could be relied upon to pass on only what one really needed to know.

"Not much," Throckmorton replied. "And what I do know is classified as 'most secret'. But I can tell you he's sound. You'll be fine. All you'll have to do is watch and keep notes. Allerdale will do any of the active stuff. You'll come to no harm."

"That wasn't exactly what I meant," Miles snapped.

Throckmorton clapped him on the shoulder. "Well, I don't want you to come to any harm. You're the only person who fits that set of clothing and it cost a pretty penny. Take care of it. You'll need these too." He offered Miles a leather-bound case, and Miles snapped it open and nodded glumly. Adam's apples were inconvenient things but a pearl choker would camouflage it in the evening. By day, a scarf would do.

"If you're serious about this, you should have your ears pierced." Throckmorton flicked one of the accompanying pearl drops with a fingertip. "Clip-ons give one the most frightful headache."

Miles shut the case with a snap and slipped it into his handbag. "I'm not contemplating having to wear them for long," he said.

Once his tamed eyebrows had been darkened, ditto his eyelashes, Miles applied powder and a little discreet lip colour.

"Pinch your cheeks," Throckmorton advised.

"You pinch yours," Miles growled. He got up, gave himself a little shake to settle his pleats, then picked up his hat and set it carefully on his head. With a scarf – silk printed with peonies in the Chinese style – snugged up under his chin, he draped his coat over his elbow and picked up his handbag. He looked into the mirror, catching Throckmorton's reflected and approving eye, and turned to the left and to the right. Millie looked good. She looked *really* good. Mrs Carstairs, blonde but nobody's moppet, gave them both a cheeky grin.

"I'll do, then?" Miles asked. He coughed and repeated the phrase in a softer tone.

"You'll do. One last thing." Throckmorton gave Miles a squirt of Arpège, then tucked a smaller bottle into his handbag. "Break a leg, darling."

Miles chuckled, pressed a kiss to Throckmorton's scarred cheek and turned on his three-inch heels.

As Miles entered what had been the old stage door reception, Allerdale glanced up from the book he was reading. He frowned, then shut his book with a snap and his mouth opened in a way Miles decided to believe was genuine surprise rather than meant satirically. Allerdale had changed, too, into a well-cut suit from a second-rate tailor. His collar was starched, his tie brightly patterned. He looked well-off but slightly flash – newly come into money, perhaps. His hair, in need of a cut and inclined to curl when Miles had first seen him, had been pomaded down to a smooth sheen. As they studied each other, Allerdale's ready smile didn't waver but Miles saw exactly the look he had expected in his eyes. Amusement coupled with a wary respect. Society had very strict expectations and often displayed a profound distrust of those who did not conform. Miles understood it, but couldn't help his feelings of hurt. Millie, luckily already a strong presence, rolled her eyes and told him to buck up.

16

"Well?" He stepped forward, skirt swirling about his calves, and well aware of the challenge implicit in his tone.

"Mrs Carstairs!" Allerdale nodded. "Let me see. A twirl, if you please. I admit I had my doubts but now … Very nice, indeed. Smart and fashionable, but not too eye-catching."

"Thank you. That was the effect I hoped to achieve. Are you ready?"

"Car's packed," Allerdale said. "What about the Armstrong Siddeley?"

"Throckmorton will take it back to the mews and drop the keys in for Pritchard. He'll store your bags until you need them." Miles glanced at his watch, squinting a little at the tiny gold figures. "Hadn't we better go?"

Allerdale nodded, slipping his book into his coat pocket, and then he took Miles' coat, shook it open and held it for Miles to put on. "May as well start as we mean to go on," he suggested. "How long have we been married? Eight months? Pa still holds Ma's coat for her after thirty-five years."

Miles fastened the buttons and took his gloves from his pocket. "Good point," he admitted. "Though I'll assume you would prefer me not to see you off to work each morning with a peck on the cheek."

"If it gets the job done …" Allerdale chuckled. "You look very convincing." He offered his arm.

Leaving Throckmorton with their thanks, they went out to the Austin Seven that had been provided for their use and settled their cases into the back seat. It was a flashy little vehicle, the new model with the electric ignition, painted maroon and cream, and very much in keeping with Allerdale's persona as a car salesman. As Miles opened the driver's door, he reflected that, between the warnings provided by the car and the suit, he wouldn't buy an evening paper from Allerdale … who was leaning on the bonnet and grinning at him.

"So Mrs Carstairs drives, does she?"

Miles felt his colour rising again and hoped the powder might mask it. "I see no reason why she shouldn't," he said. "However …" He allowed Allerdale to open the passenger door for him and seated himself, tucking his coat around his legs.

Once the car was moving, they went over their story again. Both were used to taking in information quickly and had all the basics by heart already, but the little details of Brian and Mildred Carstairs' life together needed to be established.

"Your birthday is on the fifteenth of May," Miles said at one point. "What would you like?"

"Dunno," Allerdale said with a grin. "Socks? Don't expect me to remember when yours is."

"You'll be in trouble if you don't," Miles warned him, surprising Allerdale into a laugh.

"All right, what would you like? Diamonds? A sable tippet? The vote?"

Miles snorted. "I'm not sure if you've been following the news but I've had that since July, thank you very much. Not before time, either. And I don't think we're flush enough for furs or jewellery, so you can buy me something racy in the novel line."

"I know where I can get a copy of *The Well of Loneliness*."

Miles fixed him with a steely eye. "If you think that's racy, you obviously haven't read it. Don't believe everything you see in the *Sunday Express*. It's shameful the things they are saying about the book."

Allerdale mouthed, "Sorry," and turned back to the road.

Miles consulted the map.

"Ah, I think we need to turn left here."

"Are you sure?" Allerdale – Brian – asked.

"What do you mean? Of course I'm sure." Miles shot him an exasperated glare that turned into a scowl when Allerdale chuckled. "I'm not going to play one of those fluffy dimwits who can't read road maps," Miles informed him. "The way I see it, Brian Carstairs can't have married Millie for her good looks, so it must be her intellect."

"Maybe you're really good in bed?" Allerdale suggested as he made the turn.

Miles felt his cheeks heat. "That was uncalled for." He folded the map with a snap and tucked it into his bag. "There's a crossroads up ahead. Turn right and the house is maybe fifty yards down on the left. I hope we'll be able to park nearby so you don't have to carry the bags too far."

Allerdale shot Miles a heavy-eyed look. "If I do, you can make it up to me later," he said.

"I'll run you a cold bath, Brian, dear," Miles promised. Allerdale chuckled again and Miles smiled too. It was such a ludicrous situation.

Allerdale was probably as worried about it as he was.

The house was unremarkable, part of a Georgian style terrace of equally handsome buildings. It was double fronted behind black painted railings, four stories not counting the basement level, with a white stucco front broken by well-proportioned windows. The street was broad and quiet. The car stuck out like a sore thumb.

"We have to find somewhere else to park it," Allerdale murmured. "It's too obvious."

"That could be good," Miles pointed out. "There's a bus stop at the end of the street and we're five minutes' walk from the Tube. Anyone seeing the car here will assume you're here, too. Let's keep our options open."

Allerdale nodded to another building across the road and along a bit. "There's our target," he said. "I hope we have a better view from upstairs."

Out of the car, Miles smoothed the creases out of his coat and adjusted the set of the scarf around his neck. Then he left Allerdale to deal with the bags and climbed the steps to tug the bell pull. The jangle came from below his feet so he wasn't surprised by the wait before the door was opened. A very small maid blinked up at him before asking him his business. He was surprised by the smooth way Allerdale spoke over his introduction.

"Mr and Mrs Carstairs to see Mrs Merrill. Chop, chop, sweetheart, it's perishing out here on the step."

The maid giggled and opened the door. "Oh, come in, do," she said then called back into the house. "Missus M – the new folks 'ave arrived."

"Show them in, Lizzie." The order was delivered in a cracked voice with a thin veneer of gentility overlaying a strong London accent.

They piled their bags beside an enormous mahogany hall stand and hung up their overcoats at Lizzie's request, then she guided them through the hallway with its faint aroma of cabbage, carbolic and floor polish to a room at the back of the house. "The new tenants, mum," she said as she opened the door fully.

Miles stepped into the kind of room that had gone out of fashion with the demise of the Old Queen. Knick-knacks abounded, layered in order of height on every flat surface. Chairs adorned with lacy arm covers and antimacassars packed a lot of the floor space. In the one closest to the fire sat an elderly lady who levered herself to her feet, tipping a large tabby cat and a fat dun pug from her lap onto the floor. Her dress was black, the bosom draped in gold chains, a locket and no less than three cameo brooches.

"Come in then," she said. "Let me get a look at you."

The room smelled of cat, dog, coal dust and gin. Miles stepped across the threshold with a smile.

"Mrs Merrill?" he said. "I'm Mrs Brian Carstairs and this is my husband."

"Indeed?" Mrs Merrill gave them both a searching look. "Married, I understand. I suppose you have your marriage lines? Because this is a respectable house and I'll have no goings on here."

Miles did his best to summon up a blush as he turned to Allerdale. "I believe you have them, dear," he said. "In your wallet."

"No," Allerdale gave him a beaming grin. "Last time I saw them they were in your little case. Honestly, Millie, you might have thought to get them out."

Miles glared at him before sending Lizzie to fetch it. Crocodile, well-worn with his own MS monogram, it was a more suitable piece of luggage than anything Throckmorton had been able to offer. Miles unlocked it and fished the battered envelope from one of the side pockets.

It was astounding the difference a suitably-aged forgery could make. Mrs Merrill peered at the paper, nodded and smiled as she returned it.

"One can't be too careful, can one?" she said. "As I said, this is a respectable house."

"A comfort to hear it." Allerdale leaned past Miles to offer his hand. "When I am away at work, I would hate to be worrying about Millie. But here you'll be safe enough, won't you, old girl?"

"Why yes, Brian, dear." Miles agreed and stooped to pet the pug.

"You will join us for dinner, won't you?" Mrs Merrill urged. "But for now, you must make yourselves at home. Lizzie, show Mr and Mrs Carstairs to their room."

On their way, Lizzie pointed out such amenities as the trunk room where Allerdale could store the suitcases and the passage that led down to the back door and the yard. "There's a laundry service that picks up twice a week," she said, "but if you want to wash stuff by hand, there's a laundry in the cellar next to the kitchen."

"You can show Millie later," Allerdale said. "She knows how particular I am that my collars be properly starched."

Miles bit back a comment to the effect that he could starch his own damned collars and followed Lizzie up to the first floor.

"First floor front. Best room in the 'ouse." Lizzie unlocked the door then passed a set of keys to Miles.

Allerdale set the cases down and laughed. "Come on, old thing," he said and Miles was unable to suppress a yelp as Allerdale swept him from his feet.

Miles clutched his hat with one hand and his dressing case with the other. Under the circumstances, Miles felt proud that he remembered to squeak. "Brian, for goodness' sake!"

"A man has to carry his bride over the threshold, doesn't he?" Allerdale asked Lizzie, who giggled and pushed the door open. "Thanks, m'dear. I think we can find everything ourselves now."

Inside, with the door closed and his feet on the ground, Miles was able to get his bearings. "Very funny," he said. "Now, let's see what we've got."

"Wardrobe, chest of drawers, washstand. Chaise longue. Table and chairs. Oh, there's a gas ring so you can make my coffee. But most important ..." Allerdale went to the huge brass framed bed and bounced on it. "And it doesn't squeak either."

Miles paused in removing his hat and went to the chaise longue. "Neither does this," he said, "And I think it's just about long enough for me to sleep in comfort."

Allerdale sighed. "You're a hard woman, Millie Carstairs."

Chapter Three

Miles snored. It was nothing untoward, just gentle snuffles, interrupted by the occasional sigh, but Briers had to restrain himself from throwing a boot at his head. After their dinner, which was as uninspiring as Briers had feared boarding house fare might be, Miles had undressed inside his flannel nightgown and had gone to bed on the chaise longue, the epitome of chastity. It was just as well – Briers couldn't afford complications, not with this job – but if Miles had deigned to share the bed, at least Briers could have relieved his feelings and stopped the snoring by elbowing him sharply in the back.

The following day, his opinion of the man began to improve.

"Have you finished with the shaving water?" Miles asked. "I can't ask for more. They might wonder why."

Briers had to concede that was a good thought, even as he ground his teeth in frustration. Miles in only a towel was a sight to gladden the heart, amongst other things. Willowy was the word, almost wasp-waisted, with a delightfully pert behind. But most importantly, untouchable, Briers decided, and he averted his eyes while Miles lathered his face and shaved, then continued to scrape the cinnamon coloured hair from the parts of his body he hadn't had time to see to the day before. Not that he was hirsute, but what little foliage he had was ruthlessly cut back until he was smooth everywhere Briers had seen, which was everything apart from the small area from navel to thigh concealed by the towel.

"Have I missed anything?" Miles demanded, holding the towel in place with first one hand then the other as he twisted and turned, trying to see the backs of his calves.

"I don't think so," Briers admitted, and turned away abruptly to look out of the window.

His experience with women had been limited the occasional fumble when it had seemed rude not to, and one heart-breaking affair in Prague when it had been assumed he would be willing, if not eager, to seduce the lonely wife of an Italian chargé d'affaires. He had hoped to keep it to hand-holding and promises of more, but his masters had insisted he at least show willing. Easy for them to say. Still he had done what was necessary. The dear lady had put his reticence down to inexperience, bless her, and couldn't have been kinder. Once the incriminating photographs had been taken and the damning letters had been exchanged, he had caught a train back to Belgrade. The woman would be approached with the evidence and encouraged to pass on any little scraps of information her husband might let slip. Everyday business for the SIS, but this time it had left Briers feeling even dirtier than usual. The worst thing had been that he had truly enjoyed the woman's company. She had been tall, slender, and opinionated with a bright smile, very much like Millie Carstairs.

And hadn't that been a surprise? Small, diffident Siward, fussy in his formal pin-striped suit and *pince-nez*, had given way to forthright Millie. Miles had seated himself as though afraid of taking up too much room and had spoken softly. Millie stretched out her long legs, crossed them with a slither of silk, snapped her little gold glasses onto her nose with much the same air as a guardsman presenting arms, and told Briers what was what.

Briers found the steely glint in her big blue eyes and the challenge in her conversation as stimulating in their own way as he had found Miles' gentle smile. There had been a youth – or girl he should say really, he supposed – some years back in Belgrade. Draga had been petite and blonde and utterly beautiful, and Briers would have passed her by without a glance if it hadn't been for the particular bar he had seen her in. Curiosity had paid off and they had spent a very satisfying week together. Briers couldn't help but wonder if, given the right encouragement, Miles would be as voracious. But he kept his back turned and his eyes on the window. In part, this was to conceal his interest – his sudden vivid image of himself yanking the towel away and tipping Miles up to inspect every recently shaved inch had caused him an embarrassment in the trouser department – but partly to keep an eye on their target.

Just across the street and one door down was another house very much in the same style as their lodgings, only a storey shorter. Next door but one was another grander dwelling. The first was inhabited by Mr and Mrs Crane, their infant child and a servant. This attractive young woman was Colette Fornier, according to her papers, but was better known to Briers and the SIS as Josephine. Briers had never been able to work out which of the two was more dangerous, Josephine or her lover Andrija.

The second house, outside of which a uniformed chauffeur ran a chamois gently over the windscreen of a Bentley, was occupied by the Honourable Evelyn Ingram. An ex-captain of the Guards from a family of career diplomatists, he had entered politics after the Great War as a staunch supporter of the Labour Party. Briers supposed that could explain why he was slumming it in Camden Town rather than the family home in Mayfair. But whatever his address, he was now one of the rising stars of the Foreign Office with a particular interest in the Kingdom of Serbs, Croats and Slovenes. To have any connection of Andrija's in such close proximity to Ingram could only be bad news. Sir James Lorimer had instructed Miles to keep as close an eye on both houses and inhabitants as he could, while not doing anything out of character for Millie. Briers had his own list of tasks.

Standing back from the window, he watched the chauffeur hurry to the back door of the car and open it, standing to attention while Ingram paused on the doorstep to exchange a few words with his footman. Silk hat, black Benjamin overcoat, pinstriped trousers, spats. From this elevation, Briers couldn't get a good look at Ingram's face and decided to remedy that. He checked his watch – five to eight. Tomorrow, at that time, he would be at street level to get a better view.

"Can you fasten this for me?"

Millie was back. A handsome if slightly gaunt young woman with a fashionable short bob set off with a spit curl on her left cheek. Briers hooked the back of her gown, then settled the skirt on Miles' hips.

"You look as though you've missed a few meals," he commented as he gave Miles' back a pat. He would have liked to pat his arse, remembering the taut swell of it under the towel, but suspected the accolade would not be appreciated. "Still, your legend covers that pretty comprehensively."

"A sanatorium stay on a diet of goat's milk?" Miles snorted. "At least I know how that feels, and it does explain the lack of – um." He glanced down at the slight swell of his falsies.

"It's a fashionable look," Briers said. "Gamine, that's the word. Come on Millie, old thing, we'll be late for breakfast."

Meals were taken at a long table in the dining room where empty spaces indicated early rising tenants had already eaten and departed. Briers dealt briskly with a pair of kippers, scrambled eggs and plenty of decent coffee.

"I should be back by six," Briers told Miles as Lizzie cleared the table. "Why don't you go out and explore?"

"I'm a little tired," Miles said. "Perhaps later. I have letters to write."

By the time Briers seated himself in the Austin, Miles was at his station, spectacles on his nose apparently writing his letters but actually watching the houses across the road.

"A bit of a change from the office for you, my boy," Briers said and grinned up at the window, giving Miles a wave. Miles, in character, Briers assumed, waved a hanky in return.

Briers parked the Austin in a residential street in St John's Wood and returned to Broadway House by a circuitous route involving the Tube and two buses. A word to the reception staff and Briers was invited to proceed to an office on the third floor where he found Naylor and a jolly rotund Scot who introduced himself as MacGregor.

"It was quite a task," MacGregor said, "but we think we may have a result." He fanned a sheaf of photographs across the table. "Your descriptions were good and knowing past aliases was a boon. One of them hasn't bothered to make himself a new identity, so we have a firm identification in his case. We've narrowed the choices down to a couple of dozen for the others."

Briers flicked through the pictures, which were grey, grainy and still slightly tacky, discarding some and scrutinising the remainder. Eventually, he selected two. "This is Nemanja," he said, "I'd recognise that nose anywhere. Broke it myself. And this is Javor Béla. Both truly nasty pieces of work. I'd guess it's Béla who's using an old identity. He always was lazy."

"Travelling as an academic called Bronski." Naylor nodded. "We had the name on file, so picked him up when he got on the boat. Nemanja is travelling as Leontin, a representative for a company making agricultural machinery. So that's two. Are there any more?"

"I'm still looking," Briers pointed out. "I can't see Andrija and that's a bad thing. Give me the other photos. Andrija is a small man but I suppose he could be wearing additional lifts." He shuffled the photos again, tilting them towards the light and peering at the faces. "Too fat, too thin, no, the chin is real, that beard – possibly fake?" Briers paused, taking a closer look at the passenger standing partially obscured by the bearded man. Not

Andrija, but just as worrying in a different professional and far more personal kind of way. Falk Behrend, witty, handsome and fulfilling a similar role as Briers' but on behalf of the German government, was dressed quite differently from how Briers had last seen him. Then, strolling down a street in Belgrade, he had been in the shabby genteel suit of a clerk. Now, from his silk hat to the silver-topped cane under his arm, he could have been a cabinet minister or the son of an earl. Once noticed, he could not be mistaken. The silver cigarette case open in the long pale hands was another giveaway. Briers drew a breath, allowing himself a moment for the memory to sweep over him – of the cool weight of the case on his chest as Falk opened it and read the inscription, and the exquisite thank you that followed. Falk's presence could be coincidence but Briers doubted it. He put the photograph to the back of the pack and subjected the next to the same minute inspection.

"Could Andrija have travelled separately? Or changed his plans?" Naylor frowned at the photos. "He might have got word of our interest. The man is a professional."

"He's an arrogant murdering bastard." Briers spread the photos out on the table again, scowled at them and felt for his pipe and tobacco. "But yes. I suppose he might. Dammit." He lit the pipe and puffed, glaring at the images. "Crew? Where are the pictures of the crew?"

MacGregor spread his hands. "Customs assured me that it was the regular bunch. All vetted, all familiar."

"Well, if Customs say so …" Briers sighed out smoke, his teeth gritted on his pipe stem. "At least we have a clear idea of where Josephine is and what she's doing."

"As long as Mr Siward is playing his part, of course?"

The question was barely to be heard, but Briers nodded and gave Naylor a reassuring smile. "Playing the game gallantly with barely any idea of the rules. Maybe he'll have beginner's luck?"

That comment came back to him when he parked the Austin in Albert Street and spotted Miles peering down at him from their window. He looked more anxious than a quiet day spent observing warranted.

"Oh no, what have you done?" Briers muttered and hurried inside.

Miles met him on the stairs with a bright smile with a touch of hysteria about it.

"Brian, dear, I've had such an interesting day. Come up and let me tell you about it before dinner."

"Let me get my coat off, old thing, then I'm your man," Briers assured him and they walked up the stairs arm in arm.

In their room with the door closed, Miles turned to him. "I think I may have completely destroyed your operation," he whispered. "Oh God, I'm so sorry."

Briers tossed his hat and coat onto the bed and sat down. "Tell me." He reached for Miles' hand, missed and got his wrist and used it to tug him down beside him. Miles wrenched his wrist free and picked up Briers' hat, to smooth the brim and tweak the shape of the crown.

"I went out," he admitted. "Mrs Merrill asked me down to take tea with her. I didn't see how I could refuse politely but that was all right. We were in the parlour rather than her own room and I had a good view of the street from where I was sitting. Then she started quizzing me about my family and your family and – oh Lord – everything. I made notes, we'll have to memorise them –"

"Miles." Briers spoke firmly. "What did you do?"

"Mrs Merrill asked me to go to the shops to buy her a paper of pins and a spool of thread. Lizzie was black-leading the stove, apparently, and it would take too long to clean her up. I didn't see how I could say no."

"That's quite reasonable," Briers assured him. "Nobody is expecting you to keep your nose to the window all day. It's just a pity you may have missed some action."

"That's it – I didn't. I found the haberdashers all right, it's a couple of doors down from the Tube station, but as I was leaving Josephine rammed into me with the pram. I swear I didn't know it was her, Briers. We both apologised – the way one does – and she told me she was meeting her employer off the Tube and while we were chatting, Elsie Crane turned up and I had to introduce myself."

"Still not the end of the world," Briers said, hoping sincerely it wasn't. The thought of Miles speaking to Josephine was excuse enough, he thought, to be anxious.

"Yes, but when Mrs Crane realised where I was staying, she was delighted and said we must have tea with her and dear Sidney on Saturday afternoon. I said I'd have to see if you were available, but the damage is still done. Josephine has seen me, so how much use am I going to be following her?"

"It's a setback for sure." Briers tried not to let his irritation show. "But maybe it will be all right. I can sound Sidney Crane out, see what kind of man he is, while you coo over the baby and distract the missus. We might get some idea of Josephine's movements. For instance, does she mix with the Ingram staff? Access to the Ingram household must be why she's here. Andrija is strictly political."

Miles grimaced. "If we must … but no, you're forgetting. I might just about pass as a woman casually in the street, but how am I going to cope socially? They are bound to suspect something."

Briers took a deep breath, reminding himself that Miles was only a couple of days from the calm and safety of the cipher and translation department. The edgier aspects of field work were probably only just coming home to him.

"Listen to me." He twitched his hat from Miles' fingers and took both his hands to still them. "You look terrific and if you can fool a wily old bird like our landlady, I reckon you can fool the Cranes. Josephine is another matter, but she's playing the maid. There's no reason for her to be alarmed by you, and none at all for her to be joining in the conversation. If you're still worried, you can impress them with your blue stocking credentials. A suggestion that only your illness prevented you from attending – I dunno – Girton, maybe?"

"Girton." Miles' hands were warm in his and the panic had faded from his eyes to be replaced with the bright self-confidence Briers had come to associate with Millie. "Yes, yes I think I could do that."

"You're certainly well-read enough. Talk about literature and politics." Briers grinned. "Then they might overlook any traces of five o'clock shadow."

"Oh God, not again." Miles darted across to look in the mirror, hands running across his smooth cheeks, then shot Briers a glare of pure irritation. "You – ratbag," he muttered.

Chapter Four

The following morning, getting out of his blankets, dressing and making small talk with the other tenants over the breakfast table expended as much of Miles' nervous energy as he had available. Despite his assurances to Allerdale, the chaise longue was not a comfortable bed, and the change in routine had made him feel on edge and irritable. Also, Allerdale snored – not loudly but steadily – and it was a constant reminder that there was a bed a few paces away with a large warm exciting body in it. Miles had been lucky enough in the past to share a bed on a regular basis and missed the closeness, that feeling of welcome and safety, rather more than he missed his departed lover. They had known it couldn't last, and when Tommy had headed off for a diplomatic posting in Lisbon, they had parted with affection but no anguish. That was just the way things were for men like them.

Married couples don't know how lucky they are, Miles thought as he joined in the conversation at breakfast. The Joneses, second floor front, were a middle aged couple from Wales who communicated more in meaningful looks than words. The Bassetts, second floor back, were younger and he suspected they were playing footsie under the table. Miles tried to imagine showing affection for Allerdale in public, but his imagination failed him. Millie, on the other hand, would have no problem. Recklessly he stirred in his seat and leaned to allow his shoulder to touch Allerdale's arm. Allerdale picked up the cue with admirable speed, and looked into his eyes with a smile, then asked if he would like more tea.

Not just tea, Miles thought as he accepted the cup. *Come back to bed with me and hold me for a while. Let's make the pretence real for a week or two. How likely are we to have a chance again?*

Once he had seen Allerdale off to work for the day, it was a great relief to go back to his room, kick off Millie's fashionable shoes, and sink into the chair by the window. Another day of boredom awaited, but he could use the time by brushing up on local and national news to give himself something to talk about in the evening.

Accepting the invitation to take tea had been madness, but Elsie Crane had been so insistent and so relieved when he had accepted, he wondered if something was upsetting the woman.

Josephine had surprised him. She was tall, with an unfashionable mass of soft brown hair, and a pretty face that smiled readily. She looked the ideal nanny until one caught her face in repose and saw the chill in her eyes. That she made no attempt to conceal it while he chatted with Elsie suggested her contempt for her employer, or perhaps the belief that Miles' glasses meant he wouldn't be able to see her.

Miles opened the *Daily Herald* he had picked up from the hall stand and made the resolution to have the *Times* delivered. He might be in disguise but a man needed his newspapers, and he saw no reason why Millie shouldn't read them as well. Dividing his time between observing activities in the street and reading accounts of the works to repair flood damage in Millbank and the flight of the Graf Zeppelin, he passed a quiet morning.

At lunchtime, he obeyed a summons from Mrs Merrill to join her, as she put it, in a light repast.

"A nice bit of boiled haddock," Mrs Merrill said with relish as Lizzie brought the plates in. "That shouldn't do your belly any harm."

Miles agreed and diverted her from more enquiries about his health by encouraging her to gossip about her neighbours. Most of it he ignored, but he did pay attention when she mentioned Ingram.

"Such a gentleman, and regular as clockwork in his habits. Mrs MacDonald, his housekeeper, is a particular friend of mine and she says his linen cupboard is a sight to behold. And his shaving water has to be ready at sixty-thirty on the dot. A three-egg omelette, no more, no less. Oh yes, any woman can tell you that a man of regular habits is to be prized."

"I can imagine," Miles said, imagining passing on these nuggets of information to Allerdale. "And Mr Crane? Is he regular, too?"

Mrs Merrill sniffed and set her fork down. "Well, not at all the same kind of thing as Mr Ingram but yes, he's a decent sort." She picked up her fork again. "But as for that new maid of theirs …"

Ah ha! Miles looked an enquiry but realised Mrs Merrill was playing hard to get. "So she joined the household recently?" he asked. "You see, I met her and Mrs Crane yesterday. She seemed very pleasant. Attentive to her mistress and the baby."

"Attentive?" Mrs Merrill nodded. "Attentive to the whole household, if you ask me. I've no word to say against her professionally –" she pronounced the word with relish, lingering over the syllables "– but it never did no good to a marriage to have a servant in the house what's prettier than the mistress." She fixed Miles with a severe stare. "Just my opinion. Elsie Crane has fluff for brains, otherwise she'd know that colour hair makes her look cheap. Again, just my opinion."

Miles raised a hand to his own blond locks, pushing a strand back from his forehead and Mrs Merrill chuckled and said, "Oh my dear, no need to worry on your own account. I can see there's nothing false about you."

Miles looked aside modestly – actually to hide a grin. "I would by far prefer to be dark," he said. "There's something about this shade of hair that encourages people to make assumptions."

"I don't think you need to worry too much about that, either," Mrs Merrill assured him, casting an eye over his bony shoulders and fashionably flat chest.

Miles returned to his room with the feeling he had passed a test with reasonable marks, and continued to record such events as the presence of a road sweeper, the delivery of a telegram to a house further down the street and, high excitement, one of Ingram's servants walking a Cairn terrier. He had a game of solitaire almost completed when the Crane's door opened and Josephine eased the pram down the steps. Miles made a quick note of the time – twenty to four – and grabbed his hat and coat to follow her. Allerdale had cautioned him it was better to risk losing Josephine in the crowds than to get too close and alarm her. So he stopped on the way out of the house to ask if Mrs Merrill needed anything, and let Josephine get well ahead. The perambulator was a large one, so he felt safe in assuming she'd be unlikely to hop on a bus or grab a taxi while in charge of it and its occupant. She was still in sight as he left the house, and Miles strolled up Albert Street, followed her into Camden Town and browsed shop windows on the other side of the street while she fussed with the pram outside Camden Town Tube station. He could see her clearly in breaks in the crowd as he pretended to adjust the set of his hat. One moment she was stooping over the pram, the next she was smiling as a man in the dark cap and pea coat of a sailor approached and spoke to her, cigarette packet in hand. She shook her head in apology. He smiled, his shoulders easing as though relieved as he put the packet away, then they turned and began to walk down the high street.

"Sign and countersign, by Jove," Miles muttered and followed, shopping list in hand.

Josephine parted from her admirer on the pavement near the entrance to Mornington Crescent Tube station. There was nothing unusual about a sailor taking the opportunity to talk to a pretty girl with a pram, but they didn't usually get off at one Tube station only to walk half a mile to another. Miles had shadowed them every step of the way, scared to approach any closer but unwilling to lose sight of them. At the gates of the Tube, they paused to say their goodbyes. They made no attempt to embrace but the man patted her shoulder, then stooped over the pram. Miles couldn't be sure – the road had widened and traffic had picked up – but he thought the man's hand had darted into the perambulator, delving under the covers. As he straightened up Miles saw a flash of white before he put his hand into his pocket. Josephine spoke to him, chin up and he smiled, turned and disappeared into the darkness of the Tube station.

Feeling he had seen all he was likely to see, Miles hurried home and went to prepare for the evening. He even ironed a shirt for Allerdale, braving the kitchen and Lizzie's company so she could show him how to use the ferocious-looking gas-powered iron that was her pride and joy.

"So much better than them old flat irons," she said. "And much gentler on good linen." She eyed Miles' day dress and added, "That could do with a press, if you don't mind me saying."

Miles glanced down at his skirt, which was somewhat crumpled and made a mental note to take more care in sitting down.

"It will have to do for now," he said. "I'll wear another dress for this evening."

"Ooh, what colour?"

"I – er – haven't decided," Miles said. "I'm not sure how formal to be. Does Crane keep a very formal table?"

"I dunno." Lizzie giggled. "If it was up to Mrs Crane, it would be all Hollywood an' stuff. She really wants to be Mary Pickford, Mrs Merrill says, but she acts more like Theda Bara."

"Oh, Lizzie. Don't repeat things Mrs Merrill has said. Even if they are true, Mrs Crane might hear and be upset. You wouldn't want that would you?"

"No, miss." Lizzie sighed and continued to flick water onto the shirt as Miles moved the iron. Steam wafted up, and he breathed in the pleasant smell of clean linen combined with the faint scent of lavender hair pomade that clung to Allerdale's clothes and person. It was a good smell and Miles found himself smiling as he pushed the iron across the snowy fabric. Millie would smile, he assured himself, because she would be thinking of her husband, maybe even remembering the firm body that would soon warm the linen. Since it was in character, Miles saw no reason why he shouldn't indulge his memory too. Not that he had seen Allerdale's body, or not much of it, but what he had seen had made his pulse race. Strong and big-boned with wiry muscle rather than bulk, large hands and feet, enticing wisps of curling hair in the open neck of his shirt – Allerdale was everything Miles preferred in a lover and it was tragic he seemed to be no more than an open-minded work colleague.

Because I think I could make you happy, Miles thought. *Happy? I could make your eyes come out on stalks!*

"Oi, watch it, miss. You don' wanna singe it."

Miles whipped the iron away from the shirt and got his mind back on his job.

When Allerdale got home that evening, he seemed to appreciate the care Miles and Lizzie had taken with his shirt, but appreciated the news about Josephine's naval swain even more.

"Quick, what did he look like?" he demanded as Miles was fastening his collar studs for him.

"Chin up, please." Miles nudged his jaw with the back of his hand. "You must realise I didn't have a very good view and for most of the time I was on the other side of the street. He seemed short, shorter than Josephine, but quite broad in build. What I could see of his hair seemed to be light brown, perhaps a little long, it touched his collar. He was clean shaven. Couldn't see his face very well because of the cap he was wearing. It was pulled forward to shade his eyes. I got the impression his teeth were rather prominent – rabbity."

"Hah, Andrija!" Allerdale nodded, dislodging the collar stud again. "I knew he'd turn up. I don't suppose you managed to follow him into the ticket hall and find out what line he got onto?"

"No, I didn't," Miles said scowling. "I thought I'd done as much as I could without Josephine spotting me. I didn't want her to, perhaps, get the idea I was following her and get scared and lace our tea with strychnine this evening."

Allerdale snorted then gave Miles a gentle push. "I was joking. You did well. And now we know Andrija definitely *is* in town and Josephine is gathering information for him. Did she talk to anyone else that you could see?"

"She stopped at a newsagent on her way back and bought a magazine – but that was the Radio Times off the rack. I don't see how anyone could be using it as a letterbox – not safely."

"I'll have the place checked out." Allerdale picked up his tie and began to fasten it.

Miles took a step back and studied him, once again feeling a wistful twinge of attraction. Allerdale looked superb, filling the shoulders of his well-cut suit to perfection. "You have a little lint," he said and picked it off Allerdale's lapel.

"Thank you." Allerdale grinned then nodded to Miles' attire. "Turn round," he ordered. "I want to get the full effect."

Feeling somewhat foolish, Miles revolved on the spot. Elsie had eyed his clothing avidly, so he assumed she followed fashion. He hoped his frock, simple in shape but swirled from throat to hips with tiny hand stitched pin tucks, might please her. From Allerdale's intent expression, it didn't please him.

"Stop, your hem's uneven."

Miles closed his eyes as Allerdale tugged at his clothing. The brush of his knuckles on the back of Miles' silk clad calf was very distracting. Not at all the thing to be thinking about when he was about to give the biggest performance of his life.

"There." Allerdale gave him a playful swat on the hip. "Mrs Carstairs, you look a treat. Elsie Crane's eyes will drop out in envy. Are you going to wear your pearls?"

"Just the earrings." Miles knew he was flushing and knew Allerdale

34

could see it, so his reply was more terse than polite. "I thought the necklace might be a bit much. I have a scarf that will do."

"Well, get it then and we'll be off. It wouldn't do to be late."

It seemed hardly worth putting on coats to cross the road, but the night was icy and there was a breath of rain in the air. Josephine opened the door to Crane's house with another of her pretty but cool smiles, greeted them politely and took their coats and Allerdale's hat in the hall.

Her French accent added an attractive edge to her husky voice but it didn't ring quite true to Miles' practised ear. There was an edge to some of her consonants that would have located her origins much further east, but he doubted either of the Crane's would have doubted that she was a true Parisienne. He was so intent on placing her accent, he forgot to worry about her seeing through his disguise until after she opened the parlour door and announced them.

"Mister and Mrs Brian Carstairs," she said.

Of all the things Miles had expected, he had not expected to like Sidney Crane on sight. Crane bounced from his chair to greet them, beaming with pleasure.

"Come in, come in. Take a seat. Elsie, won't you introduce us?"

Elsie, baby in arms, stood up and came forward with the self-conscious welcome of a woman who knows herself to be the most attractive female in the room. "Sidney, this is the young lady I was telling you about. Mrs Millie Carstairs. Mrs Carstairs, my husband, Sidney."

"A pleasure to meet you," Crane said and stooped a little as he took Miles' hand. Miles realised he was bowing and wondered what Elsie had told him.

"Grand to meet you, too," Allerdale said with a grin and grabbed and pumped the man's hand. "No need for formality, is there, Millie old thing? Brian and Millie Carstairs, and very pleased to find ourselves in such decent lodgings."

Miles smiled as he was guided to a seat on the sofa by Elsie, and Allerdale took a chair close to Crane.

"The maid will bring tea in shortly," Elsie said. "Unless either of you would prefer coffee?"

"Oh, absolutely not," Miles assured her, ignoring Allerdale's stare. "Tea would be wonderful. Young Lizzie makes a fine brew but it does tend to be a little stewed."

"Ah, Lizzie," Elsie chuckled, "but at least she's not as bad as Mrs Merrill's last girl."

As he had hoped, Miles was able to sit back and make agreeable noises as Elsie told horror stories about uncooperative or incompetent servants. Miles had heard his mother and her friends chat for hours on such subjects, and nodded and smiled while Allerdale extracted as much information as he could from Sidney Crane without appearing to be ill-mannered.

"And your current maid?" Miles asked when Elsie's fund of stories seemed to be dying down.

"Oh, Colette is a marvel," Elsie said. "When Mary, our previous maid, had to leave in such a hurry – a death in the family, poor dear – we were at our wits end what to do. But Mary had contacted an agency on our behalf, and they sent Colette round the next day. She's been a true godsend. Wonderful with young Georgie, and she cooks too."

"A paragon," Miles said. "It must be such a relief to have someone trustworthy."

"Yes, it is," Elsie said and lowered her voice. "And she's good company, too, for when Sidney is working. His promotion, you know, was well deserved but it does mean his hours are much longer."

"And what does Mr Crane do?"

"He works for the Water Board," Elsie said. "He's in charge of all the … water pipes and … and things. And reservoirs and the like."

"I see." Miles controlled his voice with an effort as something very alarming occurred to him. "A very responsible position."

As tea was served, Miles eyed Josephine and tried to imagine what she and her cadre could do to the water supply of London. Poison was the obvious suggestion. Or maybe some kind of sabotage? What if Ingram was not their target? What if Sidney Crane and his knowledge of the "water pipes and things" was?

As soon as they had taken their leave of the Cranes and had got back to their room, Miles offered this idea to Allerdale for consideration.

"Possibly," Allerdale agreed as he undid his collar. He sighed with relief and opened the neck of his shirt. Miles looked away from the glimpse of soft skin and wisps of dark hair. "I don't think anyone has got a poison potent enough to kill or incapacitate everyone in London, but it's possible. They are doing terrifying things with chemistry on the continent and there's no point trying to tell ourselves there are weapons too horrible to use. We learned that lesson the hard way in the last lot. But still, I talked to Crane a little about his work and his responsibilities are far more administrative than Mrs Crane implied. Forward planning, amongst other things, for all the suburban developments for the next twenty years. Andrija plans ahead, but not far. I can't help but feel Crane's house is just a convenient location. Ingram is by far the most likely target. Dammit." Allerdale's stomach had rumbled. "How long is it to dinner? Cucumber sandwiches and a cup of tea. Why on earth did you say we didn't need coffee?"

"I didn't want them to feel we were troublesome," Miles lied, not prepared to admit he had also been paying Briers out for his comments about Miles' inability to follow Andrija. "And besides, if I'd lost my head and mentioned you'd got the taste for it abroad, it might have made Josephine curious."

Allerdale grunted. "The things I do for King and country."

Chapter Five

Briers wished the case was progressing more quickly. Not that he wasn't enjoying Miles' company. Far from it. He found the man's quiet observations on life in the Merrill household to be both shrewdly observed and witty, and he was impressed by the poise with which he handled the Cranes.

Several times, Miles' terse warning came back to him – *"Just because I'm good at it, doesn't mean I enjoy it"* – but Briers wondered how true the assertion had been. Miles did seem to take a nervous satisfaction in the play-acting, but his care and attention to his appearance seemed to Briers to be more than caution. As the layers were applied – padding, lace, beautifully-cut clothing, hosiery, the soft hairstyle that curled around his ears, and finally the merest hint of lip rouge – so Miles' natural diffidence faded to be replaced by Millie Carstairs' sharp-tongued and witty self-possession. Small, delicate, unimpressive Miles Siward was a pale shadow of Amazonian Millie, and the more Briers saw of them, the more he felt Miles was really enjoying the freedom.

What was more frustrating was that he was unsure whether Miles was of a lavender persuasion or not. Sir James Lorimer had dropped the strongest and most contemptuous of hints, but Briers was inclined to put that down to bigotry. Briers had spent many years on the Continent, where opportunities for expressing one's less conventional desires were more plentiful and where, if one moved in the right circles, such things were understood. Not so in Broadway House. There, certain standards were demanded and assumptions would be made about even those who were coerced into breaking them. Miles' talents would mark him out. No wonder the poor child was on edge. And even if, Briers reminded himself, Miles did enjoy dressing in ladies clothes, it meant nothing. One of the toughest, most woman-hungry men Briers had ever known had been wearing lace under his tweeds when they stripped his body before disposing of it.

So, rather than making advances, Briers had enjoyed watching Miles strip and had entertained some lurid and arousing thoughts of what they might do together should time and opportunity allow. Much better, much safer to keep his mind on the job and find Andrija.

That Andrija had entered the country as a crew member rather than as a passenger had been confirmed by their office in Calais. The discovery of a steward floating face down in the dock might have been passed over as an accident, but that the man had been engaged to sail on the same ship as Béla and Nemanja was too much of a coincidence. Once in London with his luggage reclaimed, Andrija could have gone anywhere, but the fact that he was still wearing the garb of a sailor suggested a few places where Briers might track him down. And if he did, he promised himself, he might save the country the cost of a rope and arrange a quick and fatal accident. Andrija was too dangerous a man to be moving around able to do as he pleased. And not just Andrija. Briers had made discreet enquiries about Falk Behrend, who would be, Briers was sure, up to no good. That he should have turned up at the same time as Andrija was very telling.

Briers scoured the East End, Limehouse, Wapping and Deptford, asking leading questions but mostly relying on his eyes. His greatest advantage was he knew Andrija by sight but Andrija did not know him, and he was confident he would spot the bastard even if he was disguised. There was something about being shot at that fixed a face in one's mind.

But it was frustrating. Day after day he left for work, changed his clothing into rough workman's wear, then roamed the back streets and alleys. It was boring and lonely, but familiar. Having someone to go home to was unfamiliar but oddly enjoyable. But for now, he decided he needed a little rest and recreation, mostly to prevent himself from reliving his constant imaginings of Miles, warm at his side in bed, or better yet, hot, under him in bed. And there was one place above all where he knew he would find what he sought.

The Grange Road Turkish baths in Bermondsey were not the largest or most salubrious but they catered well to a certain clientèle. Briers paid his shillings, collected his towels and a locker key, and set about relieving himself of both his clothing and some of his frustrations. Ten minutes or so in the steam room got some of the stress-induced kinks out of his shoulders and at least one promising approach, but Briers had never been one for public performance. He murmured a polite refusal and suggested perhaps later might be better and they parted without rancour.

Shampooing and massage left Briers relaxed and a little sleepy but still eager to see what diversions offered themselves. He ordered light ale from a steward and took a rattan chair to read a Daily Mirror someone had abandoned on a table. There was nothing of note in the paper, but the view over the top of it was pretty as half a dozen chorus boys between engagements posed and bickered, casting long glances in his direction to ensure he was appreciating them. A couple of businessmen, pale and paunchy, wedding rings glinting, pored over the same copy of the Financial Times. They ignored everyone apart from each other and Briers wasn't surprised to see them go into the same cubicle and draw the curtain. The steward brought his ale. Briers sipped it, wondering if one of the chorus boys might be brave enough to do more than look. There was a blond one, willowy and sharp-faced, who turned and allowed his towel to slip a little. Briers grinned, enjoying the flash of pink flesh and damp dark hair, and the boy smiled at Briers taking a step in his direction.

"I'm sorry I'm late." A chilly hand on Briers' shoulder made him start. "The meeting went on forever. Is that beer? Steward – two more, please."

Briers glared. "Behrend," he murmured.

"Oh please." Falk lay back on the next chair, crossing his long legs at the ankles. He smiled at Briers and continued his conversation in Czech. "The current name is Bauer. Conrad Bauer, though you may still call me Falk for old times' sake. Cigarette?"

The silver case glinted in the dim light, half filled with Turkish cigarettes, the inscription partially obscured. Briers remembered buying it and the time he had spent trying to think of a suitable sentiment – one that would express his feelings while not giving too much away if it was seen. Falk hadn't changed much: still fine-boned, still smiling, his blond hair damped close to his skull, his eyes amused and acute, his nipples still the exact same shade as his lips.

"No, thank you." Briers reached for his tobacco pouch.

"Ah, you still smoke that terrible pipe. Well, no matter." Cigarette lit, Falk licked his lips and blew a smoke ring towards the chorus boys.

Gritting his teeth, Briers waited until the steward had brought their drinks and endured Falk's chaffing when the man asked if he could get them anything else.

"A sense of humour, perhaps?" Falk suggested. "And some privacy. We have a lot to discuss and," Falk dropped his voice to a murmur, "I'm sure my friend would prefer to do that in private."

He got up offering a hand to Briers, who ignored it and stood, casting a regretful glance at the chorus boy.

The cubicle was small, dark and dank, a reasonable reflection of Briers' mood. Falk put his glass on the table and turned smiling. "You don't look very pleased to see me," he murmured.

Beyond the partition curtain, Briers could hear the regular creak of a bed and occasional moans.

"Not displeased," he insisted. "Not if you're in London just to sightsee and enjoy the baths."

Falk snorted. "As if men of our profession are ever anywhere just for pleasure. Though I admit it did give me a frisson when I saw you again."

He pushed sweat-dampened hair back from his brow and took a pace toward Briers. "I'm here on the same business you are – Andrija. For the same reason – to kill Andrija. And to find out why certain persons of interest have left home."

"Who?" Despite himself, Briers was interested. Intelligence had been slow coming in from the continent.

"Hmmm, I'll do my best to remember. But in the meantime I see no reason why we can't have some fun."

Briers looked Falk over, from the knowing smirk to the dusting of hair across his chest then down to the rise at the front of his towel, and sighed. Every night he had spent listening to Miles' soft breathing had been filled with heated imaginings. Now here was Falk, heat personified, and a huge temptation, apparently intent on exchanging information for personal services.

"Briers? Remember the coffee house in Belgrade. That upstairs room. Pulling the mattress onto the floor so we could really spread out."

"Oh, Christ." Briers groaned and closed the space between them. Falk's mouth was open even before their lips touched, grabbing greedy kisses as they pushed the towels aside and Briers took a double handful of Falk's arse. Falk hummed with pleasure and slid his hand between them taking both hot hard pricks in a firm grip. "How do you want it?" Falk grinned. "Standing or kneeling? Or I can bend over the bed."

Briers looked down and ran his fingertips over both prick heads, smearing the slickness. "Bend over," he ordered.

It was fine. It always was with Falk, who knew exactly what he liked and how to get it. Since what Falk liked fell in line with Briers' needs, they did well together.

This bath was well provided with 'hand lotion' for the masseurs and Briers spent a few moments massaging Falk where it would do the most good. He was a feast for the eyes, leaning forward with his arms folded on the thin mattress of the couch and his long smooth back arching to Briers touch. "Yes, there," he murmured. "Oh, God yes."

Briers entered him with a sharp thrust, one hand holding his hip and the other gripping the nape of Falk's neck, because he knew Falk liked it and because he felt better with a firm grip on the slippery bastard. The familiarity of the position reminded him sharply of their room in Belgrade and the fury Briers had felt when he realised he had been played. Seduced by an enemy agent, the worst possible mistake to have made. But all the same, he couldn't help but recall some of their encounters. Falk sprawled on the floor, barred with sunlight pouring through a crack in the shutters. Falk laughing and feeding him bits of pastry dipped in the strong coffee they sold downstairs. Falk shaking him awake with a scowl demanding he fuck him again.

Falk moaned, pressing back onto him and Briers muttered a curse and leaned down to bite Falk's shoulder, just as Falk liked.

"Did you get my message?" Falk murmured. "Mmm, that's good."

"Message?"

"No, don't stop. I left a message at the coffee shop. I hoped they might forward it."

"I was transferred for a while," Briers admitted, his voice muffled against Falk's shoulder blade. On one level, he was intrigued by what Falk was saying, on another he wished Falk would shut up so he could concentrate on getting them both off. "And I never went back there."

"Well, it wouldn't be the same without me, would it?" Falk's voice broke from its smug tone as Briers reached round and gave his balls a squeeze. "Ah! Same old Briers. So physical."

"I'll show you physical," Briers growled and stood up, hands on Falk's hips, to give him the strong rogering he deserved.

"That's it." Falk stifled a laugh, bracing his hands on the edge of the couch. "Oh – it's been a while for you, hasn't it?"

"Shut up."

It was important not to make too much noise. Also important, not to make the couch rock into the curtains around the cubicle.

"I say," the voice on the other side of the curtain spoke sharply. "Steady on, chaps."

"Foreigners," the other sounded even more irate. "I heard their jibber-jabber. It quite put me off."

Falk's mouth opened in a silent howl of laughter that turned to a gasp as Briers pushed him down to the floor. On all fours, he gave his arse an inviting waggle. "Well, come on then. I have places to be."

"Bastard," Briers hissed in his ear and went back to work with gusto. He sank his fingers into Falk's hip, gave his nipple a sharp pinch then squeezed his prick in time with the pump of his hips. Normally, Falk would have been shouting, but here he hissed his pleasure until the final moment came and he threw his head back biting back a groan. Briers hung on until Falk's taut body began to relax, then his own coming was equally restrained.

"Well, that was fun," Falk said as he pulled away and reached for his towel.

They looked at the mess they had created and laughed. "Don't worry," Briers said. "Once we've gone, they'll come in and swab the place down with carbolic. Thanks, it was much appreciated. You said something about a message?"

"It was a while ago," Falk admitted. He put the towel on the couch and sat down, his hands on the thin mattress either side of his knees. "After you left, I gave the matter some thought and decided, enemies or not, we had worked well together and it would be a pity to part on bad terms."

"It was a bit late for that." Briers decided he preferred to stay on his feet. "Anyway, I was given another assignment."

"Me too." Falk swung his feet gently and smiled down at them. Briers looked at them too. Falk had long and flexible toes with, as he recalled with delicious clarity, a remarkably dexterous grip. "But there's no need for us to be enemies now? Not when we have a common enemy? If you recall, I had some names for you."

"I hadn't forgotten," Briers said, "and they are … ?"

Falk's smile broadened but he answered when Briers took a step towards him. "Václav Radoslav and Ričardas Sašo dropped out of sight last month. Gregor Tamarkin was seen on a south bound train from St Petersburg but didn't get off at any stop we were monitoring. Marjan Havel hasn't been seen for two weeks."

"Havel took a whack at me in Zurich so I dropped the bastard off an Alp." Briers paused to accept Falk's bow of approval. "I can't see Tamarkin lowering his principles to work with Andrija. He loathes his guts."

"As do we all. So, that leaves Radoslav and Sašo. Both have worked with Andrija before. Do you know them by sight? I do. I could probably find them for you. Now, do you have any information for me?"

"Technically, no, because I know I can't trust you. However, we know where Josephine is and are keeping tabs on her." Briers shrugged. "I know you will be working for your country's best interests, as I will for mine, and that means I can't be as open with you as I would like. Besides, I already have a partner."

Falk stared at him. "You do? Does he know?" His gesture took in Briers' nakedness and the spread of wetness on the floor.

"Yes, I do and no, he doesn't. Though I think he might be one of us, he's far too nervous to show it."

"A nervous spy." Falk turned on the couch and lay back with one arm behind his head. "He won't last long and then you'll know where to find me."

"Oh, I think he'll do. But, just in case, where *would* I find you?"

"You can use this place as a letterbox. Just leave a message for me at the desk here." Falk grinned. "C. Bauer, care of Mr Rosenberg. Fold the top left corner of the envelope so I know it's from you."

"For old times' sake, eh, Mr Bauer?"

Falk smiled. "I'm not really going by the name Bauer."

"I never thought you were." Briers stooped to retrieve his towel from the corner and fixed it around his waist again. "I need another bath before I go home to the wife."

Falk stared again, only this time he looked genuinely shocked. "I thought the ring was a prop."

Briers held up his hand to let the gold glint in the dimness. "Not this time," he said, aware he was being petty but not much caring. "Sorry,

Falk."

"Well." Falk slid off the couch and hooked a finger over the top of Briers' towel. "The offer – both of my help and my arse – is still open. There are some things even I couldn't fake for my country. You're a better actor than I thought."

When Falk offered his mouth Briers took it, but this time the kiss was gentler. The goodbye they hadn't managed to find time for in Belgrade? Briers didn't know but as he made his way homeward, he found himself smiling.

His good mood lasted all the way to Albert Street. He parked the Austin and looked up, expecting to see Miles at the window as usual, but the room was dark. Not particularly concerned, he locked the car and entered the building. Lizzie met him in the hall with a big happy smile.

"Oh, Mr Carstairs, Mrs Carstairs rang on the telephone. She says she's gone up West to see Uncle Charlie and could you call to find where they'll be."

"Uncle Charlie," Briers said, his heart sinking. "I'll call now, if I can use the phone?"

Lizzie watched as he unhooked the receiver and dialled. He desperately hoped she'd go away but watching someone make a phone call was probably the most exciting thing she had done all day. "Charles Naylor, please," he said. "He's expecting my call. Brian Carstairs."

Naylor answered almost immediately. "Hey, Uncle Charlie," Briers injected as much enthusiasm into his voice as he could. "Where are you? Are we going to a show?"

"Ah, you have company." Naylor sounded peeved. "Yes, it's possible you are. I will do my best to join you but for now, Mrs Carstairs is on her own. She says she has found where – Cousin Andrew is staying."

Chapter Six

Miles watched the half inch of lemonade swirl against the sides of his glass, then realised what he was doing. He put the glass back down squarely in the centre of a beermat and linked his hands in his lap. He had been sitting in the pub for an hour and was regretting his impulsive behaviour, and dreading what Allerdale might have to say about it.

Josephine had left the house a good deal later than usual that day, prompted, Miles was sure, by the presence of Ingram's chauffeur who had the bonnet of the Bentley raised and was fiddling with the engine. Miles had grabbed for his coat and hat, preparing to follow the pretty woman who casually rocked the pram as she flirted with the chauffeur. The young man seemed flattered by her attention, first pointing at something under the car bonnet, then laughing and moving closer. She asked a question and he pushed his hat to the back of his head and grinned. Miles wished he could lip-read. Had that been something about Ingram? Their hands touched. Had he passed her something? Then they made their goodbyes and Miles left the house in pursuit.

Josephine took her time, going from shop to shop, pausing in one establishment to try on hats, of all things, and then buying a cup of tea from a roadside stall. Miles, who was beginning to get thirsty himself, cursed her reflection as she took it to a bench and sat down to drink it. Time passed, the early November dusk began to draw in. He was feeling even more frustrated and annoyed when Andrija finally appeared. After their usual question and answer with the cigarettes, Andrija greeted her with a kiss on the cheek and an arm around her waist. They strolled down Camden High Street. Knowing the routine, Miles hung back, checking his watch. Quarter to five, so he had rather more than an hour until Allerdale was likely to be home.

It was gone five before he saw them taking their leave. Today, Josephine didn't accompany Andrija right to the doors of Mornington Crescent Tube station but stepped into a grocer's shop. At once, Allerdale's gibe about Miles' failure to discover which Tube line Andrija used popped into Miles' head. He fished his purse from his handbag and stepped out to join the queue at the ticket office. Luck was with Miles and soon he was able to follow Andrija to the southbound platform. At the entrance, a strongly built man with a stubbled chin and loud tweeds stepped away from where he had been leaning against the wall and tapped his watch. Andrija laughed and shrugged and they pushed their way through the crowd together.

"So who the devil are you?" Miles muttered and followed them as closely as he dared.

While he waited, Andrija took papers from his pocket and opened them to read. Handwritten sheets, with copious notes arranged around some diagrams, sketched in pencil. Miles couldn't make head nor tail of the crabbed writing. He tucked himself in behind a group of uniformed schoolgirls and edged a little closer, peering over their shoulders. A map, hand-drawn and not particularly well executed. Andrija traced the lines with a finger and nodded. When the train arrived, Miles tagged along with the girls and was a little shocked at how closed he was to Andrija when they settled in their carriage. Andrija had put the papers away and he was sitting beside the man in tweeds. They murmured to each other and Miles pricked his ears. That had sounded familiar – Slavic. A word here and there, a phrase as he got used to picking out their voices from the babble around him. It was going well, on schedule. Problems but nothing insurmountable. They were blending in. Different gangs. A muttered joke in poor taste about Josephine's employers. Then, quite clearly, something about a farm, a day or two, hopes for success, timing being crucial, something spoiled by damp.

The train slowed and stopped at Charing Cross, and Miles followed Andrija and his companion onto the platform. The two men took the tunnel for the District line, paused to slap hands in the tunnel, then Andrija headed off for the east-bound trains and his friend headed west. Dare he risk it? No, not with the other man watching as Andrija walked away. Miles waited until he moved, fiddling with his bag as though he had mislaid something, then followed the man onto his train.

When the man got off at Westminster, Miles followed him to Millbank where the signs of January's catastrophic flooding were still obvious on the walls, despite a half-hearted attempt at whitewash. The stocky man headed for the most derelict area, where ruined houses were being demolished, and disappeared into a building with boarded-up windows. Miles made a note of the address and headed off to find the nearest place with a telephone that might allow him to use it. A pub, unfortunately. Not at all a place for a gently brought up young lady like Mildred Carstairs, but needs must.

Before entering Miles thought of the saddest thing he could bring to mind – the embassy cat that six-year-old Miles had loved so much until it met an untimely end under the wheels of a Russian charge d'affaires' car – and let the remembered grief wash through him. As he stepped into the beer and tobacco tinged warmth and closed the door behind him, Miles met the disapproving glare of the barmaid with wet eyelashes.

"I'm so sorry," he quavered. "I wonder if I might use your telephone? I was supposed to be meeting my husband – I was *sure* he said Millbank but – but maybe it was Millwall? And I fear I'm most horribly lost and when I tried to find my way back to the Tube there was this – this *man* and …" Oh yes, a quivering lip and suppressed panic was doing the trick nicely.

"Come through into the snug, miss," the barmaid said with a pitying smile. "We'll get you sorted out."

Five minutes later, call made, reasonably warm and with a demure glass of lemonade in his hand, Miles was left with nothing to do but wait and worry.

Had Miles really found where the anarchists were operating? Or was it a wild goose chase? While he was cooling his heels in this awful little pub, was something terrible happening in Albert Street that he might have been able to stop if he had followed his orders and stayed at his post?

If he peered through the cracked pane of the window, he could see the cordoned-off areas where the demolitions were still going on. The whole area was ruined, dotted with houses whose foundations had been weakened by the force of the floods that had swept the parish. Miles recalled the pitiful accounts of the survivors who had scrambled for safety as Father Thames made an unwelcome visit to their bedrooms. Tragic and horrible. And it was here Andrija's men were lurking, picking the place over like crows on a carcass. Miles hoped he was right. Hoped that when Allerdale came, they would be able to stop them, now, stop whatever foul plans they had made and see them safely into custody.

"Another drink?" The barmaid looked tired but she had been kind to

Miles. "I don't suppose he'll be much longer."

"Oh yes," Miles said and passed her his glass. "I don't suppose you could put a gin in there too please. And one for yourself."

He was halfway through the drink when he heard a stir in the public bar; Allerdale's clipped voice and a laugh from the barmaid. As the snug door opened, Miles stood. Allerdale darted in and gave Miles a wholly exasperated glare. He put his hands on Miles' shoulders, gripping tight. "Millie, for God's sake, I said Millwall not Millbank. I've been worried sick."

"She's been all right, sir," the barmaid said and raised her glass to Miles.

"I have, honestly, Brian," Miles said, shrugging Allerdale's hands away and feeling for his handbag. "But I am glad you are here. Did I miss the speeches?"

"Yes," Allerdale said. "You did, but I'll tell you all about it on our way. Many thanks, my dear." Miles was glad to see him press what looked like a ten shilling note into the barmaid's hand, then they hurried to the door and into the foggy street.

"Filthy weather," Miles remarked as the smoky air caught his throat.

"Weather!" Allerdale gripped Miles' arm above the elbow, steering him across the street with rather more force than Miles felt was necessary. "What the hell do you think you're playing at?" Allerdale growled. "I spoke to Naylor and he said you found Andrija's hideout. I want to know why you were anywhere near him. Did you miss the part where we told you he's dangerous?"

Miles freed himself with a yank and stood his ground. "I didn't miss a thing. For a start, you can do me the courtesy of not jumping to conclusions, and secondly, you're going in the wrong direction. We need to go this way." Allerdale couldn't have looked more surprised if Miles had kicked him in the shin, but made no objection when Miles turned east towards the river.

Arm-in-arm they walked further into the derelict area, noting the empty buildings and the ones where families still clung to their homes and what normality they had been able to find after the flood. As they walked Miles described his afternoon and made what he hoped was a suitable defence of his actions.

"It was too good an opportunity to miss," he said. "I took great care.

Andrija didn't look in my direction, not once. And the other man picked up a newspaper and was reading the sport."

"Sport." Allerdale's comment was a barely heard growl.

"Yes, sport," Miles snapped. "Maybe he's a rugby fan, too? He looked like he could be a storming flanker. Big, a bit on the heavy side. Bushy eyebrows."

"That sounds like Béla. There really is a god that looks after small kids, drunks and idiots. He's nearly as bad as Andrija."

"There's no need to be offensive." Miles took a deep breath, controlling his temper with an effort. "Do you want to hear this or not?"

"I'm all ears. Carry on." Allerdale's tone had a weary note that suggested he expected all manner of foolishness from Miles.

"I followed him from the Tube and saw him go into a house in the next street. Three stories, boarded-up windows. The lamp post outside has been smashed but the next one along is still working. If you step around the corner, you'll see it."

"But I'm not going to step around the blasted corner because I might meet Béla coming back the other way," Allerdale grated, "and he is one person I do *not* want to meet when I've got an unarmed amateur at my back."

"That's hardly fair. If it wasn't for me, you'd still be wandering the streets on the off-chance you might spot one of them. At least now we know one of their bases. Andrija said something about a workforce."

"All the more reason to stay well away, then." Allerdale freed his arm and edged up to the corner where an empty shop offered a deep doorway for cover. He peered around the edge of the boarded-up window and nodded. "There are half a dozen men outside, taking a smoke break by the look of it. You didn't go any further than this, did you?"

"No," Miles snapped. "No, I didn't. So, what happens now?"

"We go home, picking up a meat pie on the way. I'm famished." Allerdale stepped back around the corner, looked past Miles and his eyes widened in alarm. "Dammit. Béla."

Miles looked too. There were two men heading for the corner, heads close in conversation, carrying a beer crate each. He had just time to notice that before Allerdale grabbed his wrist and drew him to the doorway.

"Dammit dammit dammit," Allerdale muttered, as the heavy footsteps approached. "What to do … How good an actor are you, Siward?"

"Excellent," Miles assured him.

"Time for an excellent performance then," Allerdale whispered and pressed him back into the corner.

"Oh God." Miles blew out a breath, part shocked, part amused, as Allerdale dropped his head as though mouthing at the side of his throat. He wrapped one arm around Allerdale's waist and put the other hand where it would be seen on the back of his neck, holding him close.

The footsteps paused, then there was a chuckle. Miles' skin prickled with the knowledge he was being watched, and especially with the knowledge he was being watched while doing this, though it was so dark surely all they could see were shadows and the paleness of face, hands and the light silk of his stockings. Allerdale must have thought the same because he pushed Miles' coat aside. Allerdale's knee pushed between his thighs and he clawed at Miles' skirt, hooking his fingers behind Miles' knee to draw it up exposing more flesh as the silken pleats of his skirt slid high. The watchers gave an appreciative mumble.

"Kiss her, then," one of them advised.

Allerdale tilted his head, still keeping his face in shadow. "Only," he said, his voice a gravelly cockney, "if you two fuck off. 'Cause frankly, you're putting me off and I don't want to waste me shilling."

"'Ere, you cheeky bastard," Miles squeaked. "It were 'alf a crown."

"Yeah, but I ain't 'ad thruppence worth yet."

The two men laughed. One was an everyday sort of tough, shabbily dressed with huge muddy boots. The other, Béla, bulky in his tweeds, was a chilly eyed gent with a snub nose and a loose lower lip. His eyes were fixed on Miles' thigh.

"Well, go on then," Miles said and tilted his head. He expected Allerdale's mouth to touch his cheek or chin, but no. Their lips met with increasing pressure and Miles tilted his head still further. *In for a penny*, he thought. *I'll show you how good an actor I am.* He opened his mouth, smiled as he heard Allerdale's sharp surprised gasp, then their tongues slid smoothly over each other.

Kisses – he had missed kisses. He had missed touches like the one on his thigh where Allerdale had pulled it still higher, his fingertips tracing the most sensitive spot where thigh met buttock. Despite his annoyance,

Miles didn't even try to suppress his moan but wrapped his calf around the back of Allerdale's thigh, pulling him close. That he was no longer acting but was thoroughly in the moment didn't occur to him until Allerdale grunted against his lips and pressed closer still. Heat and hardness pressed against his belly. Allerdale's finger tips traced the crease of his arse down to stroke his balls. Miles moaned again.

"Give her one for me," one of the watchers said, his voice barely heard over the beating of blood in Miles' ears. Their footsteps had faded into silence before Allerdale tilted his head to press his forehead to Miles' and let out a long sigh. He stroked down Miles' thigh, pressing it and the skirt back into place. Miles' lips felt cold. He bit them together to try and warm them, tasting again the tang of their kisses.

"So …" Allerdale murmured.

An innocuous word, said with a slight rising inflection that could easily be the prefix to an equally innocent sentence. Just a word that, to those not in the know, would mean nothing but to the initiate posed a question that begged an answer.

"Well, yes, as it happens. And you?"

"Christ, yes." Allerdale tilted his head again feeling for Miles' mouth. The man was a judgemental menace, but by God he could kiss. They kissed until Miles was dizzy and his hands had found a warm place under Allerdale's clothes, his palms flat against the smooth skin above Allerdale's arse.

"No. We should go home," Allerdale whispered. "Otherwise – no, a shop doorway isn't the place. Home."

"Stopping for a pie on the way?"

"No." Allerdale's voice was rough and the heart pressed to Miles was beating fast. "The only thing I plan to eat tonight is you."

Chapter Seven

They didn't talk much as Briers directed the Austin through the busy streets of central London. Once on their way, Briers tried again to impress upon Miles the hideous risk he had taken in getting close to Béla, of all people. The thought of Miles in Béla's hands still made Briers feel nauseous, so while he tried to show how much he approved of Miles' cautious shadowing, he also impressed upon him the very real risks he had taken. He felt he had succeeded pretty well as Miles' comments petered out to a reflective silence, and those wonderfully soft and responsive lips tensed into a grim line.

"You did well," Briers said, "but – how would Naylor put it? You exceeded your brief. I'm the one who is supposed to tackle those crazies. I'd be happier knowing you were out of danger." He glanced across at Miles and when there was no response, he reached out and gave his knee a squeeze. "Soon be home. And I think an early night would be in order, wouldn't you, Mrs Carstairs?"

Miles neither twitched away nor yelped a protest, so Briers put Béla and Andrija out of his mind to concentrate on his driving and picked up the speed a little.

The street was deserted when Briers parked outside their lodgings. The only other vehicle was another Austin, parked on the opposite side a dozen doors down. Briers spared it a glance then scanned the street before leaving the car and rounding the bonnet to open the door for Miles.

"Mrs Carstairs." He bowed him out, grinning to see Miles' dignified nod. So poised, so sure of himself. Briers took his arm and escorted him up the steps, wondering if he was a screamer. Ah well, if he was he could always get him to bite the pillow.

Miles' latch key was in his hand and he opened the door onto a powerfully enticing smell of liver and onions, and the muffled sound of opera.

"Think we can sneak past?" Briers asked but the parlour door was already opening.

"It's Carstairs!" Jones grinned at them both and glanced over his shoulder to add, "And Mrs Carstairs. We missed you at dinner."

He moved across the doorway to let Mrs Jones squeeze under his arm. She gave him a merry smile, slipping her arm around his waist then darted a glance at Miles. "Come and join us," she urged, "and tell us about your evening out. We've got the radio on but can turn it down a bit."

"Yes, do." Mrs Merrill was out of sight but her reedy wheeze rang clearly over the carolling of the soprano on the radio. "We don't see much of you."

"Ah, perhaps we should …" Miles began but Briers cut smoothly over him.

"It's been a long day, Millie old thing, and remember what the doctor said." He put his arm around Miles' shoulders. "Early to bed, early to rise." He caught Jones' eye and was pleased to see a spark of humour.

"Oh quite." Jones gave his own smiling partner a squeeze. "Another time perhaps?"

"Absolutely." Miles' smile was even brighter but Jones took half a step back. "The sooner the better."

"Goodnight, all." Briers turned them both about, raising his free hand in acknowledgement of their good wishes, and accompanied Miles to the foot of the stairs. Behind them the door closed but not before Briers heard Mrs Merrill's laugh and someone say, "Ah, newlyweds!"

Miles hurried up the stairs. Briers followed, admiring the play of muscle in Miles' silk-clad calves and contemplating his memories of smoothly-shaved thighs and the pert swell of his arse. Two weeks he had been following that delectable morsel around, and finally tonight he might get a taste of it.

The door unlocked onto slightly chill dimness, but that didn't matter. Briers would put on the lights and maybe a bar on the gas fire later. For now, he had better ways of bringing warmth into their lives.

"Mrs Carstairs," he murmured and caught Miles around the waist, pressing him back against the closed bedroom door. This time, the brim of Miles' hat got in the way and Briers' mouth found his jaw rather than his lips. Briers bit gently, hands parting the folds of warm woollen cloth to find the silk frock over still silkier skin beneath.

"Allerdale." Miles' voice was a bare breath against his cheek, and Briers grinned at the press of Miles' hands on his hips.

"Right," Briers whispered. "Why do it against the door when there's a perfectly adequate bed. Come on, get that coat off."

"I'd prefer not to."

Briers raised his eyebrows, brushing a kiss across Miles' ear. He'd thought as much. The lovely little Draga in Belgrade, had preferred to at least keep something lacy on in bed. He could play along. It might be fun. It would certainly be a relief, because he'd been half hard ever since the shop doorway and now he was positively uncomfortable. "Millie," he breathed and slid one hand up Miles' side to cup one of his falsies as the other reached under his skirt.

"No!"

It was as though Briers had stepped on a mine. Miles exploded out of his arms, knocking him back against the fireplace and catching him a glancing blow across one cheekbone with one elbow as he fled. They stood facing each other across the width of the room, Briers able to hear the harsh whistle of Miles' breath.

"You aren't listening." Miles voice was a deep growl with no trace of Millie's softer tones. "You don't bloody listen. I said I'd prefer not to. I might have to put up with you talking to me as though I'm an idiot, but I don't have to go to bed with you. Because, in case you hadn't noticed, I'm not your fucking wife."

"Keep your voice down and be a professional," Briers snapped. "If you didn't behave like an idiot, I wouldn't have to remind you. And if you weren't interested, what was that stuff in the shop doorway?"

"Me being a professional." Miles went to his usual spot by the window. He set down his bag, stripped off his gloves and removed his hat, every part of him vibrating with anger. But by the light of the street lamp, Briers caught a good look at his face and was shocked at his pallor and the stress around his mouth. "Me doing what has to be done for King and country as requested by our master. We kissed, that's all. It was a reasonable method of dealing with a dangerous situation. And just because we kissed, it doesn't mean you have any right to anything more."

"We didn't just kiss. That wasn't a bloody peck on the cheek. You were as hard as I was. I could feel it and I don't think you're that good an actor. I think that, if you'd wanted, I could have had you right there in that doorway and it would have been great."

"*You* could have had *me*?"

Briers had the barest split-second warning but managed to avoid the coffee pot Miles shied at his head.

"Out!" Miles spat.

Since Miles looked as likely to break down sobbing as continue the argument, Briers saw no point in hanging around.

"If this is what married men have to put up with on a regular basis ..." He shook his head and headed for the stairs.

Had he misjudged the situation? At one point there had been the barest break in Miles' voice that in another less controlled man he might have called fright. Miles surely wasn't that virginal. At the very least he'd had a lot of practice at kissing. Maybe Briers had been a little pushy but Miles had seemed so eager.

Briers' wallet was in his pocket and he had never had a chance to take off his coat, so he decided to do what he always did when annoyed and frustrated and possibly a little regretful because he had a feeling that somewhere along the way he had made a miscalculation. At the top of Albert Street was a pub. A pint or two should put things into perspective.

He had only covered a couple of dozen yards before he heard the slam of a door behind him and glanced back. Jones was following, a cheerful grin on his broad face.

"You look like a man with a mission," he said. "Would you mind company? The missus thought you might need someone to talk to, but I can easily go back again if you'd rather not."

"And what made her think that?" Briers asked, moderating his pace to Jones' shorter legs.

"Who knows what women think?" Jones shrugged. "She seemed to think Mrs Carstairs wasn't feeling too well and when I said she'd looked fine to me, she gave me one of those looks and sent me to fetch my coat."

Briers snorted. "Well since we've been officially let off the leash, how about a pint and a pie and – do you play darts?"

"It's dominoes up at the Spread Eagle," Jones said. "But otherwise it sounds like a good plan."

Pies consumed and on their second pint of a very fine dark stout, Briers felt in a much better frame of mind and was more amused than resentful when Jones insisted on sharing his experience of women with him.

"It's more than likely, see –" Jones' Welshness had increased as the level of beer had fallen, "– you'll never find out what it was upset her in the first place. But what I found works is to let her calm down, then she'll decide it's her fault and she'll apologise."

"She will?" Briers chuckled. "And you accept graciously."

"Damn no, boy, you say it was all your fault and you beg for forgiveness even if you did nothing wrong. Flowers never go amiss either."

"But it's November."

"All the better. She'll know you haven't popped over the wall into the park." Jones raised his glass. "Here's to hothouse roses and compliant wives. May one lead to the other."

Jones was good company in an innocent and undemanding sort of way, and by the time they got home, Briers felt up to dodging all and any domestic utensils and being good-humoured about it into the bargain. After a trip to the bathroom to unload some of the magnificent stout, he let himself into his dark and silent room and paused by the door to hang his coat and hat.

Miles was almost invisible on the chaise longue, just a faint curve delineating his hip, and his breath was quiet and even. Too quiet and even. Briers decided the best thing to do was to go along with the pretence he was asleep, because it was late and he was tired. Tomorrow would do for a heart-to-heart.

Despite all his worries, Briers slept well. He woke to the usual sound of clip-clopping in the street below as the milk cart made its rounds, and wondered if Miles was awake yet. But when he looked, the chaise longue was empty, the covers neatly folded. Briers got up, made himself decent and was on his feet when the door opened.

"Bathroom's free." Miles gave him a tense and somewhat shamefaced smile. He looked awful, pale and strained but his tone was friendly. "And I brought your shaving water. Get it while it's hot!"

A joke they had made on other, happier mornings. Briers pasted on a grin and thanked him and went to start his day with a quick bath.

Over breakfast, Miles could not have been more pleasant, the very picture of an affectionate young wife who was still clearly not in the best flush of health. Briers played up to him for all he was worth and got an approving nod from Jones through the steam off the porridge.

They were finishing their breakfast when the doorbell rang, and a few moments later Lizzie entered the room with a telegram. "Ooh sir, I'm so sorry," she said offering the envelope to Briers. "The boy's waiting. Wants to know if there's a reply."

Briers took the envelope and read the terse message.

"It's from Uncle Charlie," he told Miles, well aware of other interested listeners. "Um – I can barely read this writing. Can you make it out, Millie love?"

Miles took the paper and peered at it through his little specs. "Of course, dear. It says – um – 'Show went well. Drop in noonish if poss'."

"I can do that. No reply, Lizzie, but please give the boy this." He pressed a penny into her hand and turned to Miles. "Would you like to come?"

Miles turned to him with a lift of pencilled eyebrows. "Not today," he said. "But thank you for asking."

There was such warmth in his voice it would have seemed odd not to acknowledge it. Briers gave his shoulder a gentle pat and returned to his coffee.

There was far less warmth in Naylor's voice as he filled Briers in with their decisions about the house in Millbank.

"We have not been authorised to divert men from our other responsibilities." He turned over papers on his desk with an irritable ruffle. "Sir James feels we have already committed enough resources to the matter and we are better served by protecting our potential target. He has added to the number of operatives watching Ingram and is relying on Siward for warning if Josephine appears to be on the move."

"On the face of it, that's a wise decision. He only has my word for what I found out."

"We've done more on less information," Naylor growled. "By the way, congratulations are in order for the piece of work yesterday. Please let Siward know it was appreciated. He seems to be doing well."

"Better than he thinks, which is probably my fault, sir," Briers admitted. "I gave him a bit of a rocket for overstepping the line. He is only supposed to be an observer, after all. But my – er – language was a little immoderate." Briers grinned and added, "If you get a request that he be reassigned, please ignore it."

"I've already had such a request this morning and sent an immediate reply to the effect that he'll be reassigned when the job is done. However –" Naylor shot Briers a chilly look over the top of his specs "– it would be appreciated if you could use a little more discretion in your critique?"

"Thank you, sir, and I will endeavour to do so." Briers felt a little shocked because he had been joking, and hadn't even considered Miles might have been so angry he would try to get out of his responsibilities. "So he's to continue with the observation, and I presume I should carry on trawling the depths to see if I spot anyone I know?"

"Indeed. It's not an exact science, I know, but I feel you'd be of more use on the move than staking out the house in Millbank." Naylor picked up a sheet, partially typed with scrawled notations. "Also, there's been a development. We've had word from Berlin that one of their better agents has been moved to London. Remember that business in Belgrade? You knew him as Ritter, I believe, but Lord knows what name he'll be travelling under now."

Briers grimaced to cover the urge to grin at the memory of the smooth curve of Falk's bare back and his moan of pleasure as Briers' hands fastened on his hips. "That slippery bastard?"

"His presence may have absolutely nothing to do with Andrija but as a coincidence, I don't like it."

"Neither do I. I'll keep both eyes open for him, sir," Briers promised and, after a few more exchanges of general information, took his leave.

He spent the rest of the day visiting his usual places, left a message for Falk at the bath-house and paused on his way home to buy flowers.

As he left the car to mount the steps, he was hailed and paused to wait for Jones. The Welshman strode towards him, bowler hat at a jaunty angle and swinging his briefcase.

"Flowers, eh? Good job, my lad. Oh and scented ones, too. Very good."

Briers glanced down at the small but pricey bouquet of pinks and white rosebuds and shrugged. "Never let it be said I can't take advice from an expert," he said and they entered the house together.

Inside, Briers wasted no time in mounting the stairs. As he had unlocked the door, a comment to Jones about getting a vase from Lizzie had been met with the advice to 'let the missus do it'. Apparently, that way she'd have the pleasure of showing off her gift to the rest of the household. Briers rather doubted Miles would be won over by a bit of foliage, but pretended to take the advice to heart and went up to crack the door and put the hand holding the flowers round the jamb. There was a stifled snort of laughter.

"Oh Brian, come in – do." Miles took the flowers from Briers with a wry smile. "A very public peace offering?" he suggested.

"Thought I better had, since apparently it was obvious we were at odds last night." Briers grinned and touched one of the delicate pinks, sniffing the spicy scent with relish. "So much so that Jones followed me to the pub to offer advice."

"Oh good grief." Miles lifted the bouquet and pressed his face into it. "I miss the garden. Thank you. So I suppose this evening it's time for a united front?"

"If you've forgiven me, that is?" Briers tried not to look anything other than earnest.

"I'm sure Millie is one hundred percent over her megrims," Miles assured him. "Have you had a successful day?"

They passed the time until dinner firstly by going down together to allow Lizzie, Mrs Merrick and Mrs Jones to enthuse over Briers' choice of flowers. With them safely deposited in a vase and set for all to enjoy on the sideboard, Briers and Miles returned to their room for a discussion of Naylor's latest news and mutual disbelief over the recalcitrance of the Home Office.

"Honestly, if they can't be bothered to act upon accurate information they don't deserve to get it," Miles said.

"Treasonous!" Briers grinned and gave him a gentle shove so he toppled back against the headboard of the bed.

"Not so much treason as genuine annoyance on your behalf. So we carry on as we are, then?"

"You to watch and me to wander about at random? It strikes me we might be better off with the boot on the other foot now. At least you know what Bela and Andrija look like and you know London better than I do."

Miles cheeks pinked a little, but Briers judged that was from pleasure rather than embarrassment.

"Only the political bits and some of the clubs," he admitted. "And somehow I don't think any of Andrija's crew are what one might call clubbable."

"I'd club any one of them given half the chance. Preferably with a big stick with a nail in it."

Miles whooped with laughter and was still chuckling when they went down to dinner.

It was a pleasant evening. They joined the Joneses for a hand or two of whist while a concert played on the radio. Mrs Jones was very attentive to Miles until it seemed she was sure Miles and Briers were happy together. Briers wondered at her cautious support and the reason for it. Maybe that too was a female thing. He'd heard enough of his colleagues discussing their women but generally only to complain or in more basic carnal terms. Perhaps women discussed their men in much the same fashion, though presumably not in similar language? He couldn't imagine a woman as politely spoken as Mrs Jones complaining her husband was overly partial to a knee trembler against the kitchen door, but he supposed one never knew.

Later, he and Miles made their goodnights and left the room arm in arm. On the stairs, Miles shook him off and clumped up to their room with a slightly apprehensive look on his face. Briers ignored it, having decided there was a time and place for a deep discussion about the previous evening, and that on their feet where they could throw things was not a good choice.

They took hasty turns in the bathroom, got into their night clothes and agreed it would be pleasant to read. Briers had never before had so civilised a conversation with someone with whom he suspected he might be quarrelling in a short while. Maugham's Ashenden stories failed to occupy his attention for long and he put the book down, marking his place.

"Are you ready to turn in?" Miles asked. Briers could have seen him if he sat up but he didn't bother. "Because I am, too. You can put out the light if you wish."

Briers did so, reaching across to flick the switch, then they both settled back in their respective beds.

Briers listened to Miles fuss with the blankets for a few moments then took a deep breath. An apology first, he reckoned, and he'd see where they went from there.

Chapter Eight

On the whole it had been a rough day. First, Miles had spent a lot of the night awake pondering over whether he had overreacted or not. It had been close to 4 a.m. by the strike of the church clock before he decided he definitely hadn't, and that Briers had deserved everything he had got. But it still didn't rid him of the uneasy feeling that he might have damaged their working relationship beyond repair.

That led to the logical consequence of sending a telegram to Naylor requesting to return to the cipher division, since surely the discovery of one of Andrija's bases would be enough to be going on with. The response, a polite but firm negative, had returned before luncheon was on the table and quite spoiled Miles' appetite. He spent lunch miserably pushing unwanted peas around his plate until he was able to escape to his room again and the last thing he wanted to hear was a tap on his door. Expecting Lizzie with linen or some such, he was shocked to see Mrs Jones from across the hall, holding a length of fabric.

"I – er – don't want to disturb you, Mrs Carstairs," she said, her plump face creasing in a sympathetic smile, "but I wondered if I could beg a moment of your time to help me pin this up? Try as I might, I just can't get the hem straight."

Miles' initial urge to tell her to ask Lizzie died as he noted that she was standing deliberately back from the door and definitely not looking past him into the room. Tactful, and she looked genuinely concerned. If he sent her away wouldn't that just cause more speculation?

"Of course," he said. "Would you like to come in?" Thank goodness the room was tidy.

The fabric was a skirt and soon dealt with by the simple process of getting Mrs Jones to wear it inside out, stand on a chair and allow Miles to pin the material level.

"You've never done this before," she said after the first pin and showed him how to do it, after which it went very well. Then Miles made coffee for them both and they had, as Mrs Jones put it, a little heart to heart.

"Men can be such a challenge," Mrs Jones – Dilys – said, her tone just a little wary, as though she was afraid of saying the wrong thing. "My first husband, now, I could never quite manage him. You know what they say? Kipling, I think. A silly woman can manage a clever man –"

"But it takes a clever woman to manage a fool?" Miles smiled at his guest. "Excuse me, Dilys, but Jones doesn't strike me as a fool and you've never struck me as a silly woman."

"Oh, I was then." Dilys laughed. "If I'd been able to put my foot down the first time Lewis came home reeling with gin and with lip rouge on his face I'm sure that would have been an end to it. As it was he led me a terrible dance until the influenza carried him away. The thing is, even when he began to, well, be really unpleasant, I could have got some help. My Mam would have flattened him, big as he was, but I was too ashamed to tell anyone."

As a hint that was pretty broad and Miles' heart flipped over as he considered how obvious his distress must have been the previous evening and how sad it was that this kind woman had been – whatever she was implying. Beaten probably. Belief in the rule of thumb still hung on in some areas. He reached for and took her hand that wasn't holding her coffee cup.

"I'm so sorry that happened," he said. "And I hope that Mr Jones treats you with the proper respect. As I am sure Mr Carstairs will treat me, now that we've had a chance to – um – clear the air."

Their eyes met and they exchanged nods of mutual understanding then Miles glanced down at her hand and said, "Oh Dilys, what a pretty ring!"

"Jones' grandmother's," Dilys said with a beaming smile that lit up the room.

They exchanged a few more confidences before she went off to do her stitching and Miles took his seat at the window feeling a good deal better. What was the worst that could happen? He was convinced Allerdale would persist in his carping criticisms, even if he dropped the sexual advances. Miles had to be honest with himself. On their own, the sexual advances were not at all unwelcome, but Miles had no interest in being marked out of ten for competence on *that*, for goodness sake. But he was quite certain that the scene the previous evening would not be addressed in any conciliatory way so the flowers were a shock and a challenge.

I'll show you who can be most professional, Miles thought as he thanked

Briers and dredged up memories of his mother's reaction to his own floral gifts. A vase, pretty much immediately, and all the better if some other females were present to admire the gift and bestow their approval upon the giver.

Dinner was very pleasant. Playing whist with the Joneses was actually fun. Miles took Allerdale's arm at bedtime with a smile and no particular sense of trepidation. Civilised – that's what they would be. A sensible civilised working relationship already blessed with some success and perfectly able to meet future challenges with courage and fortitude.

With that reassuring certainty in the back of his mind, Miles read a few more pages of the latest Georgette Heyer. He could hear Allerdale occasionally turning the pages of his own book, which was the only sound to break the comfortable silence of the room.

Once the light was out, Miles pulled his blankets straight and said, "Good night. Sleep well." He expected a similarly terse reply – Allerdale didn't normally stay awake for long after lights out – so he was surprised when Allerdale said, "Thanks but, Miles, don't go to sleep just yet. I want to talk to you."

"Oh?" Miles turned over, eyes searching the darkness, expecting to see Allerdale looking at him but the man was still lying down. "What about?"

"Last night, of course. I wanted to say I was sorry."

"Well, so am I," Miles said. "Especially about the coffee pot. It was a mercy it was empty. We'd never get the stains out."

"Shut up about the bloody coffee pot," Allerdale said, but the laughter in his voice robbed the words of any sting. "I don't mind about the coffee pot. I deserved the coffee pot. Look – and if you could let me get all this out in one go I'd appreciate it – I want to apologise properly. Chaps … well, chaps like us … Well, the biggest hurdle is finding someone like us, then you need to find out who likes what you like, and if they want to do it with you, and I made the assumption we'd established all that in the shop doorway last night. I'm sorry for that. I'm also sorry because I clearly made a bad faux-pas by carrying on treating you as though you were Millie. I just thought you might prefer that when, correct me if I'm wrong, you'd have preferred it if I'd waited for you to change and approached you as Miles?"

Miles blinked into the darkness, picking out more details as his sight adjusted. "No correction necessary," he murmured. "Millie – playing Millie

– is important to me but she's not about bed. At all. And it didn't help that you'd been harping on about what an idiot I was all evening then, when we got back here, you pinned me to the door without so much as a by your leave. Anyone, male or female, in those circumstances, would have given you your marching orders."

"Ah. Yes, I suppose I did go on a bit."

"A bit?" Miles snorted

"A lot then. I was just concerned that you understand how bloody dangerous Andrija and his men can be."

Miles propped himself up on his elbow the better to glare in Allerdale's direction. "What do you think I've been doing here, day after day? Tatting doilies? While you and Sir James were having your heart to heart, Naylor was giving me some background reading to do. All right, I haven't seen any of their nastier action first hand but I have been thoroughly briefed. I knew I was taking a chance but I saw the opportunity to follow Béla and I took it. If I hadn't you'd have probably complained about that."

Allerdale groaned. "Yes, yes, you're right. I would. I'm sorry for that too. It's so frustrating to be out there day after day with no leads at all and then you just breeze into the best bit of information we've got so far. I … I was jealous and unprofessional. And it's also frustrating to be in here with you day after day when I fancy you like crazy. One can't help but think."

"Apology accepted again," Miles said. "And I must admit that my thoughts have strayed a time or two. The attraction is mutual."

"Thank God for that, otherwise what I was doing to you in that shop doorway would have been a bit much."

They both fell silent for a moment and Miles wondered if Allerdale, too, was remembering the drift of hands, the play of mouths. "That was probably also unprofessional," Miles said with regret.

"Oh dear God, Miles, I really, really, want to be unprofessional with you. Look, can we start again? I like you, you suggested that you like me, we don't have to do anything you feel uncomfortable about, but while we're doing this job we could be making it a lot more enjoyable."

Miles grinned and resumed Millie's ladylike but waspish tones. "After one lousy bunch of flowers?"

"You're going to make me work for this aren't you? All right then, if you're going to be like that, I'm going to court you properly."

"Court?" Miles couldn't keep the laughter out of his voice. "You want to court me?"

"Court, woo, spoon, whatever they call it these days. So what'll it be? Are you going to let me take you out tomorrow? Dinner and dancing? Or maybe the flickers and a dish of eels. I can't afford to take you up West too often."

Miles snickered and hitched himself up on one elbow. "Dinner and dancing would be most acceptable," he said. This time Allerdale was looking at him, a darker shadow against the curlicues of the brass bedhead. Miles even thought he caught a glimpse of a smile.

"Good, and if you play your cards right, I might even let you lead."

"Mr Carstairs," Miles said, "You really do know how to show a girl a good time."

It was a good time.

They had their usual sorts of days. After Allerdale left, Miles took his post by the window, dividing his time between his book and his view of the street. He stuck to his duty until Josephine took the baby out for an airing. Then he followed her with relish, even though the wind was gusty and the air was filled with drizzle. He followed her to the station, hung back while she chatted to Andrija and took some time to himself on the way home to get another book. He was getting short of cash and was determined that if Allerdale did carry through with the promise to take him out, he would pay for the treat. So he visited the bank as well and used one of his own cheques to withdraw five pounds. A sensible sum for a young woman of modest means, that could be explained away as payment for services rendered.

"Don't want a note," he told the clerk in an accent as close to Mrs Merrill's as he could achieve. "Three pounds, two ten bob notes and the rest in half crowns. Got to share it out with the rest of the staff, 'aven't I?"

The clerk, snooty bitch, sniffed and pushed the money across the counter. Miles, who had been hoping for that kind of reaction, left the bank smiling and was surprised, and somewhat flattered, to be whistled at by a costermonger.

"What an accolade," Miles said, recounting the event to Allerdale. "It made me feel quite full of myself."

"Well, why not make the most of it?" Allerdale said. "We could go to the Criterion? They won't care who leads there."

And they did, and it was wonderful. The Criterion was always a crush and the menu could be a bit hit and miss, but that evening, the goodtime boys were out in force and on the dance floor, as Allerdale had promised, you could get away with a lot. Allerdale wasn't a good dancer, but neither was Miles, so they avoided stepping on each other's toes and followed the music as best they could. It was fun. Miles felt relaxed and comfortable in the excellent frock Throckmorton had provided for such events, and he thought Allerdale was having an equally good time.

I could get used to being courted, Miles thought and wondered a little what would happen when they got back to Albert Street.

Allerdale was, as they say, a perfect gentleman and Miles was grateful for that because, though they had settled their differences, he felt he shouldn't be too quick to get back to where they had been in the doorway. Anyhow, as they entered their room they were both in a deep fit of giggles due to the gin they had enjoyed and the mood was further lightened by the rolling baritone of Jones who appeared to be singing hymns in the bath.

"As an accompaniment to fondling, *Oh God Our Help in Ages Past* is such a passion killer," Miles said as he finished brewing Allerdale's coffee.

"Were we fondling? First I've heard of it." Allerdale took the coffee cup, sat back against the head of the bed and grinned at Miles. "Thanks for this. Come and sit with me?" He sipped his coffee while Miles took off his shoes – the relief – then tossed a pillow so Miles could lean against the foot of the bed if he preferred. Miles decided he did and sat cradling his cup between his hands more for the warmth than wanting the drink. He was surprised at the subject Allerdale chose to kick off the conversation.

"Have you heard from your brother lately?"

"Not since I've been here, no. But if he'd needed to get in touch, he'd have found me."

"So goes his reputation," Allerdale agreed, "but I don't think I ever got round to telling you how we'd met?"

It was a good anecdote, filled with the type of professional detail that would be bound to enthral a novice agent. Miles might have thought Allerdale was buttering him up if he hadn't previously heard the other side of the story from George.

"So that was you." He laughed. "You were bloody lucky. George nearly shot you on principle."

"Not my fault. Blame our masters for sending two agents to get the same asset without warning us we had company. I nearly shot him. I thought he was a Bolshevik."

Surprised into a crack of laughter, Miles covered his mouth with one hand and they both glanced towards the bathroom. But Jones' spirited singing hadn't missed a beat.

"Is that another hymn?" Miles asked.

"I don't recognise the words. Do you think it could be Welsh?"

"Well, we know it's not any of the Baltic dialects. George speaks almost as many as I do." Miles smiled and set his empty coffee cup down. "Last time I saw him, he was being fitted for a new prosthetic and was making plans to get back to work."

"Good," Allerdale put his cup down, too, drew up one knee and linked his hands around it. "Rumour has it he has been missed on his station. It's always best if the locals have someone they trust."

The singing from the other side of the wall stopped abruptly and they listened for the clunk of the bathroom door.

"Time to turn in?" Allerdale asked. "Would you like the bathroom first?"

"I bathed this morning," Miles said, getting off the bed to fetch his sponge bag. "And I doubt there will be much hot water left, so I won't be long."

There was nobody on the landing, which was a relief. Miles was always concerned that Millie without her make-up and the trappings of femininity might be too obviously Miles. Once he had finished his hasty ablutions, he returned to their room so Allerdale could take his turn, and took the opportunity to change into his night gear and to check that the stubble on his chest and legs wasn't too obvious. Notwithstanding Allerdale's teasing, his five o'clock shadow was negligible today but he would have to be careful to shave closely tomorrow morning before breakfast.

As Allerdale re-entered the room, Miles grinned at him and said, "I haven't worn out my dancing shoes but I think I've worn out my feet."

"Blisters?" Allerdale peered over the end of the bed. "Ouch, that looks nasty. Slippers for you tomorrow. I have no idea how you do it. I couldn't."

Miles settled on his couch tucking an arm under his head. "Nobody would expect you to," he pointed out. "They wouldn't have asked George, either."

"You do realise it's because we'd be rubbish at it?" Allerdale asked. "You can do a lot of things we can't do. I don't have the patience for surveillance, not the way you're doing it. And I've heard the way you vary your accent and the way you move. You go from shop girl to Duchess in mufti in the blink of an eye. That's real talent."

"Thank you." Miles frowned. "I believe if you're going to do something you should do it well. I just wish I wasn't prone to panic."

Allerdale snorted. "I can't see that George would have done any different if I'd grabbed his arse. I am truly sorry, you know. I didn't understand."

"I didn't exactly give you any information to be going along with. Oh, it's all too hard to put into words."

"Do you want to try? Because I'll listen. I do want to understand." Allerdale sounded so sympathetic Miles' breath caught. "I think it might help you too, especially if Lorimer gets it into his head to make you do this again. And don't worry, I'm the bee's knees at keeping secrets. We sort of have to be in our profession."

Grateful for the darkness that hid the heat in his face and the agitated twitch of his fingers, Miles looked up at the ceiling and tried to ignore Allerdale.

"What do you want to know?" he asked.

"Well, how did it start? I assume it's something you've always felt? Like I always knew where my interests lay. There was never any doubt in my mind."

"Nor mine, not really." Miles searched for the memories. "I had crushes from the time I could walk. The gardener in our house in Yorkshire when I was very little. All perfectly innocent then, of course, but having a huge pash on our Macedonian driver when I was sixteen wasn't innocent at all. And the – um –"

"Cross-dressing, I think they call it," Allerdale prompted. "I've seen girls do it, too, and there was a lovely lad I knew once."

"Then you probably know more than I do," Miles said. "It was an accident at first. Just a silly bit of student ragging. We had been rehearsing the Scottish play and there's that bit with Lady Macbeth in her shift. Tommy said it looked like a tennis dress and challenged me to a few sets on the way home. Some of the other chaps said they'd buy all the beer for a week if I kept on my wig and make-up. I decided to go one better and made myself look halfway decent. Tommy was laughing so much I knocked him all over the court, then as we got back to our house one of the porters tipped his hat and held the door open for me." Miles chuckled. "And the following day one of the Fellows who had seen us from a distance asked Tommy how long we'd been walking out together."

Allerdale laughed and Miles did too. "It was fun and after I did it a few more times, for a dare. Tommy thought it was hilarious. But I – it took me a while to realise I was enjoying it for its own sake. Allerdale – it has never been about actually wanting to be a girl. Most of the time I'm quite content as I am, thank you, but just sometimes I …" Miles ran out of breath as a huge bubble of distress grew in his chest. Never before had he tried to tell anyone about this. He had tried not to think about it, shying away from the thought with fear and defiance. It was too big and important. Much safer to treat it as a laugh, unimportant, a joke; just something he did sometimes and would continue to do as long as, dear God, nobody ever found out how much he loved it. How much he *needed* it.

It was dark and he was certain he had made no sound, but Allerdale spoke again.

"I wish you'd come here, Miles. I wish I could hold you, just for the comfort of it, so I can show you that, whatever you say, it's all right."

He was being played. Miles was sure of it. Allerdale was a trained agent, adept at getting information out of his targets with his calm coaxing voice that encouraged him to tell all he knew. Presumably there was a way to withstand this awful urge to spill his secrets, to lay them out one by one to be pored over, derided and discarded or exploited. But Miles had no training, and the sheer relief of finally acknowledging this secret part of himself made him want to curl into Allerdale's arms and sob.

But Siwards didn't sob! George wouldn't sob, so neither would he.

Miles took a deep breath. "I think we are better off as we are. This is something I need to say. I need to admit there are times when I want to feel feminine. I want to feel pretty, to wear silk. It makes me feel calm and confident. When I look in the mirror, most days I see that Miles is a small, unimpressive person, doing a useful but under-appreciated job, always having to rush to catch up, always having to defer to bigger more manly men. But sometimes – sometimes when I look in the mirror, Millie looks back and she's brave and bright and doesn't take any nonsense from anyone. She can be Lady Macbeth, or Portia or Beatrice. She can be a shop girl or a débutante. I don't want to be Millie all the time, but it gives me such courage to know she's there if I need her."

"And that is fine." Allerdale's voice was as definite and matter of fact as if he was giving road directions or suggesting a solution to a crossword. "Miles, you do realise there is nothing at all wrong with it? Yes, I know people like Lorimer sneer, and use you anyway, but I don't feel that way about you or Millie. Millie is a great girl and is doing a brilliant job looking out for Josephine. I'm enjoying working with her but it wasn't really Millie I wanted to take dancing tonight. It's you I want, Miles, and thank you for such a great evening. It was good fun. I'd like to do it again."

"Again," Miles echoed and drew in a ragged breath. He had been braced for contempt, for malicious laughter. So why on earth would such calm acceptance make him feel so much worse? He knew what to do with malice, but how on earth could you combat kindness? "Yes, yes, that would be fun."

"But maybe not tomorrow. Got to let those blisters go down a bit first. Want to go to the pictures instead?"

"The pictures! Oh yes." Miles swallowed; his throat tight, eyes stinging. "That would be fun, too." He turned his face into the pillow and hoped Allerdale didn't mind when he didn't reply to his cheery goodnight.

Chapter Nine

If there was one thing Briers understood very well, it was pride. It had been pride that had made him cling to life in the burning village in Greece, with blood bubbling in his throat and a sucking chest wound.

"He will die," one of the village men had said, and Briers had thought, "If Alexander the fucking Great can survive an arrow through the lung in fucking India, I can survive a little thing like a bullet." He didn't remember much about the few days after that but he had survived.

And long before, out in Flanders, he remembered how terrified he had been of letting his mates down and how his pride had made him go forward, always forward, until the officers ordered them to retreat.

Pride could be an asset, but Briers cursed it as he listened to what Miles' probably believed was silence, all too aware of what the painful and ragged breathing actually meant. When it had been lovely Draga, in Belgrade, who had been upset, Briers had folded him in his arms while Draga poured out his problems – fairly mild ones to do with broken nails or a quarrel with one of the other boys – and Draga loved the attention. But he knew he couldn't do it for Miles, not without damaging the understanding they had, he hoped, reached. For Miles to have admitted all that was probably one of the bravest things Briers had ever seen, or heard rather, because he doubted Miles would have been able to do it at all if he'd been able to see how much Briers pitied him.

"You poor little bastard," he thought. "What you need more than anything else is a cuddle. Not a fuck, just a nice warm cuddle and someone to tell you you're all right. Just give me half the chance."

He was still pondering over how best to handle the situation when he drifted off to sleep. He woke to the scent of coffee and Miles sitting by the hearth with his book in his hand, glowing from his bath.

"Morning," Miles said with a smile, and turned the page.

Briers grinned to himself as he dressed. There was the pride again.

After breakfast he got his hat and coat and stooped to peck Miles on the cheek. "Should be back around six-thirty," he said, "so unless something drastic happens, are you still all right with a trip to the flickers?"

"Really?" Miles grinned. "There's something on I wanted to see up at the local flea-pit. I'll find out what time the showings are."

"That's the ticket." Briers grinned and took himself off to work. Miles was showing a resilience Briers was sure would surprise the office boys he normally mixed with.

He said as much to Naylor when he checked in with him during the afternoon. "Be prepared for problems getting him back into the cipher division," he said. "Blood will out and for all he's a half pint, he's Siward to the core."

Naylor raised his eyebrows and made a note on his jotter. "I'll see what I can do," he promised. "Meantime, I'd be grateful if you could find something – anything – else about Andrija's movements. We're under pressure to come up with results."

Briers rolled his eyes. "Do the powers that be know how many smallish, brownish, slightly rabbity men there are in London? I can't inspect them all, you know."

"Yes, I do know." Naylor scowled. "And you can find that bloody German spy while you're at it. We're assuming he's still in London."

Briers nodded and left the office, thinking of the envelope he had picked up at the bath house and the carefully-phrased message that led him to believe his good friend Falk was currently in Lowestoft, following up a lead of his own.

As requested, Miles was ready to go when Briers got back to Albert Street. They just had to endure the dinner Mrs Merrill had provided – lamb chops, cabbage and mash, aesthetically unpleasing but nourishing enough – before they could go.

Coated and hatted, for the night was cold, they walked arm in arm down the road.

"Show starts at seven-thirty so we need to step out a bit," Miles warned.

"I'm not sure I can step out after Mrs Merrill's plum duff and custard." Briers grinned as Miles squeezed his arm. He was setting a good place, blisters and all, and Briers fell into step with him. "What are we going to see?"

"There's a film called Wings," Miles said. "It came out last year and I missed it but it's doing the rounds again. I – um – it's a war film. I hope that's all right."

"Oh yes," Briers said. "I saw it in January in Belgrade. Terrific piece of work. I think you'll like it."

The Hippodrome was everything a picture house ought to be, and they bought a bag of nuts to share and took their seats as the lights went down.

Briers had been to see films with girls and was used to them leaning on his arm, and jumping and squeaking at appropriate moments. Miles must have done something similar, because he remembered to do it for the first ten minutes or so, but after that was so caught up in the story Briers may as well have not been there. Briers stored up that little criticism for later and waited for just the right moment to sneak his arm around the back of Miles seat and drape it over his shoulder. Miles did jump then and shot Briers a glare, but Briers grinned and nodded to a couple a few seats down the stalls from them who were openly cuddling. Miles rolled his eyes but leaned in, warm against Briers' side, and offered him the bag of nuts.

The film was every bit as good as Briers remembered and he was keen to see what Miles made of it. As they left, surrounded by chattering couples and a bunch of rambunctious youths, Briers nudged Miles and said, "Well, what did you think?"

"Stunning," Miles said and made approving comments on Clara Bow's hair, clothing and make-up, until they were out of the crowd then changed tack and got really enthusiastic about the flying and the stunt work. "I can't believe they didn't kill a few pilots making that," he said. "And the young actor who played the cadet will be worth keeping an eye out for."

"Fancied him did you?" Briers grinned and patted Miles' hand. "Don't worry I won't hold it against you. I did, too."

Miles fizzed with laughter and added, "The bit that surprised me most though was – well, they kissed. The two men, I mean. I know it was only a peck but – dear God."

"I thought you might notice that," Briers said. "I wonder how long it will be before they are able to show two men kissing properly. If ever."

"I know." Miles sigh was soft and Briers slung his arm around his shoulders again to give him a comforting squeeze.

"It's a bastard, isn't it? But at least they've stopped hanging us. Two years hard labour, disgrace and ruination are a little less final."

"It's not always that bad," Miles tilted his head to smile up at Briers.

"I knew a man who only got three months with time off for good behaviour. All right, he lost his job and had to move to Canada but ..."

Briers laughed and gave him another squeeze. "What was he arrested for?"

"Ah, sad story. He propositioned an undercover copper in a public lavatory. The judge was sympathetic when he heard the copper made the first advances, but the letter of the law still had to be obeyed."

"Damn." Briers shook his head. "Wouldn't it be smashing if they'd just leave us alone. It's nobody's business but ours what we do as long as it's in private. And believe me, there's so much we could do."

"As long as it doesn't scare the horses is what Mother always says." Miles chuckled. "There are no horses on – where are we? Arlington Street. We could try to scare some pigeons instead."

A few paces ahead was a shop, shuttered and darkened for the night. It had a nice deep doorway. Briers tightened his arm around Miles' shoulders. "If only you actually meant that," he sighed, "nobody would think twice about a nicely dressed young bloke stepping aside to kiss his equally nicely dressed girl. And how often do men of our persuasion get a chance like this?"

"Not often enough," Miles murmured. They were level with the doorway and he paused and looked up at Briers. "And it would be nice ... but if you wouldn't mind, do you think we could just go home?"

"Don't put on the light," Miles murmured as they entered their bedroom. He stepped across to the window to draw the curtains, his body silhouetted against the glow of the street lamp reflecting from the stucco of the Crane's house opposite.

Tonight, they hadn't had to run a gauntlet as they entered the house, but had sped across the hall and up the stairs unobserved. Briers could hardly get the door open fast enough but tonight he didn't make the mistake of grabbing Miles. No, tonight Briers would wait to see what happened.

"I'll light the fire." He took a shilling for the meter from his pocket. Miles didn't reply. As Briers woke the warmth of the little gas fire, he was aware Miles had removed his coat and hat and had retreated to his usual spot at the table by the window. Miles shifted the newspaper on the table, adjusted the set of his glasses on his nose then abruptly folded his arms, gripping his own elbows as though holding something in.

Or keeping me out, Briers mused. But he wasn't going to lose his nerve now, even if it seemed Miles had. *Nothing ventured, nothing gained.*

He hung up his own coat before approaching him, moving slowly and letting Miles see what he was about. Miles' shoulders squared as Briers put his hands on them, the fine bones sharp under his palms, and he turned his head, the glow from the fire warming pale cheeks.

"That's better," Briers smiled. "It's cold tonight. I don't want you cold, Miles."

"I don't want to be, either." Miles' eyes were wide, vulnerable behind the shield of those delicate little specs. Miles raised a hand to take them off, placing them with care on the table, then touched Briers' cheek, thumb sweeping across his lower lip. Briers could feel the slight shake of it – nerves, fright, lust? He wasn't sure – and decided to cut to the chase. Patience was all very well but honesty might work better.

Briers caught Miles by the wrist, turning his hand and pressing his mouth to the palm. "Remember," he murmured against the warm flesh, "I promised. Nothing will happen you don't want to happen but – Oh Christ, Miles." Briers pressed Miles' palm to the erection Briers had been growing ever since they had entered the room. "Millie couldn't do this to me. I've wanted you, Miles, ever since I saw you in Naylor's office, and I can't wait to get you out of those cami-knickers."

Miles gave an involuntary bark of laughter and his fingers flexed causing Briers to take a sharp breath. "Really? Are you sure?" Miles set up a gentle rubbing rhythm as he offered his mouth.

Miles was an excellent kisser and his nimble fingers made short work of Briers' fly buttons. But his hands were icy and so were his cheeks. "Wait," Briers muttered into his mouth. "Hang on. No, Miles. You're frozen. Let's not rush it. Go and see if there's any hot water – I want to taste *you*, not perfume – and get that slap and those falsies off, while I warm the room up."

Miles sighed out a breath and withdrew his hand after one last squeeze. "All right. I feel pretty grimy after being in the cinema." He reached for his robe, towel and sponge bag. "Be back in a tick."

Miles wasn't very long, but that was long enough for Briers to do what was needful. With the gas fire glowing orange in the hearth, they had all the light they needed. Briers had put the water in the jug on the washstand to good use, figuring a cold water wash was better than nothing, but put his trousers back on to give Miles something to work with. He moved Miles' pillows from couch to bed and turned back the covers right to the foot. All the while he had been enjoying the anticipation, the tightening in his groin as he imagined what Miles might feel like. Then the door opened and he stopped speculating.

There, locking the door, was the poised young man he had fancied in Naylor's office, only wrapped in Millie's floor-length kimono-style dressing gown rather than a morning suit. Miles placed his bundle of clothing on the chair by the door and stepped towards Briers. "Clean from top to toe," he said.

Briers sat up properly, feet on the floor and reached to hook a finger into the front of Miles robe. "Top to toe. Was the water cold?" Briers applied a little pressure bringing Miles swaying a step nearer, then another, until he was standing between Briers' knees. He smelled of clean warm skin, male arousal and just a little of Pears soap.

"A little cold," Miles smiled. "I was counting on you to – um – warm me up?"

"I can do that." Briers nodded and their fingers tangled as they both began to untie the bow to free the belt. Miles' skin was cool and slightly goose-fleshed; Briers could feel the chill of it against the backs of his fingers as he parted the robe. He stroked down his chest, smiling at the faintest prickle of stubble, and pushed the robe back and off his shoulders.

Briers sighed and shook his head. "Oh yes," he murmured. "This is better."

Miles was all sleek flesh over an elegant armature of bones, small pink nipples tight with cold or desire, and a slender prick rising from a nest of light brown curls that Briers longed to nuzzle into. So he did, pressing a kiss just below Miles' navel.

"Oh Lord." No hesitation there – Miles' hands were on his head, urging him down. Briers laughed and heard an answering chuckle.

"I promise to reciprocate," Miles murmured. "If, of course, you like that kind of thing."

"Who doesn't?" Briers grinned up at him for a moment then closed his fist around the warm length and applied his lips to the head, tongue delving. It tasted just grand, so Briers took more, sucking lightly – he had no intention of letting Miles come – while he put his hands to good use. Stroking down Miles' sides, he urged his legs apart to cup his balls in the palm of one hand while the other kneaded his arse. Miles wasn't idle. He was stroking what he could reach of Briers' torso, and giving soft little moans of encouragement each time Briers touched him in a way he particularly liked. Briers kept going until Miles' moans were becoming more demanding and he felt the balls tighten against his palm, then he sat back and hooked Miles round the back of the neck to draw his face down for a kiss. Miles clung to him, breath harsh but slowing as the peak receded and he calmed.

"Oh God," he whispered, his cheek against Briers'. "You are wonderfully good at that. My turn, I think. I want to see if I can heat you up as much as you have heated me."

"No doubt of it," Briers said and caught him around the waist, pulling him off balance to tumble him onto the bed. Miles laughed, sprawling on his back, then put his hand on Briers' prick, rubbing the bulge of it through the fabric. It was Briers' turn to stifle a moan as Miles unfastened his belt and buttons.

"Stand up," Miles ordered, and when Briers did and his trousers slid down, Miles caught his breath.

Briers grinned. "Something wrong, Siward?"

Miles' mouth opened, tongue touching his lower lip. "I – um – no! Not at all." Then he reached out to touch, fingers tracing lines and circles, thumb smearing across the slit. Briers grunted with the pleasure of it, kicked his trousers off and away then clambered over Miles, settling top to tail with his knees on the pillow. A quick heave and he had Miles, giggling, where he wanted him and he pressed his nose into the soft brown fluff, Miles' prick dabbing moisture against his throat.

"You smell good," Briers murmured and slowly drew one of his balls into his mouth.

"Oh God," Miles muttered, then began an exploration of his own with lips, tongue and fingers that soon had Briers puffing like a steam train.

Timing was everything. Miles was a mere stripling compared to Briers, so letting him spill now might not rule out another go later, but Briers knew he had to pace himself. Miles, bright, gallant, playful Miles, deserved time and care. *But no coddling*, Briers thought as Miles gave a throaty growl that made Briers' toes bunch.

Drawing away from his own delectable mouthful, Briers put his hand down to detach himself from Miles' maddening mouth. "Wait – stop."

"Hmm?" Miles rolled an eye at him. "Sorry, Allerdale, did you say something?"

"I just – look," Briers said with a grin, "after what we've just been doing, do you think it would hurt to call me Briers? I was going to say 'please just give me a moment'."

Miles chuckled and shifted round to rest his cheek on Briers' chest, his knee pushing demandingly between Briers' thighs. Side-lit by the gas fire, he was all shadows and apricot-coloured highlights. His tongue tip skimmed his lower lip. "Briers, then. Just say the word when you're ready to start again," he murmured and nuzzled into Briers' chest hair to find a nipple.

"You can do that as much as you like," Briers muttered, cupping the back of Miles' head.

"Mmm? And this?"

"Good grief." Pleasure spiked at the rhythmic pressure of Miles' fingertips behind his balls. "Where did you learn to do that?"

"Cambridge." Miles chuckled. "I didn't spend all my time reading sonnets in a punt, you know."

"Time well spent. Do it again, then."

Miles did, with a bright and delighted grin as Briers grabbed him to pull him down into a kiss. With Miles' body arched over his, their mouths working against each other, Briers gave himself up to the sheer relief of it. He hadn't been wrong about his room-mate, and Miles – well, Miles was proving to be a little tiger between the sheets.

Chapter Ten

Miles placed another card into his solitaire pattern and leaned back into his seat. Since that astounding night a week ago, they had fallen into a routine. By day, Miles maintained the persona of Millie by making occasional shopping trips for Mrs Merrill, helping Lizzie with small tasks about the house, but mostly keeping an eye on the houses opposite. Twice he had seen Josephine lingering on the pavement to chat to Ingram's chauffeur. Once, when he had followed her to the High Street, he had spotted her chatting to Andrija again. On another occasion, he had seen her meet with the loose-lipped chap who had watched him and Briers in the doorway. Neither had glanced in his direction. Nobody looked twice at a young woman with a shopping basket since there were just so many of them, but he had kept his distance.

Briers was saddened that the discovery of the house in Page Street had not lead to Andrija's capture, but was otherwise pleased with their progress. But then, as October gave way to November and the nights grew still colder, Briers seemed to be pleased with everything.

When Briers returned home from work, Miles made sure Millie gave him an affectionate greeting. They joined the other tenants for dinner, and sometimes for conversation and card games afterwards, but there would be a growing tension between him and Briers until it was a reasonable time for a young couple to make their excuses and retire.

And then, as soon as Millie's smart frocks and high heels were put away, they would tumble into bed.

Since his first awakening in the house at Albert Road, Miles had grown used to the bone-deep chill seeping in around the edges of his blankets and the stiffness of limbs cramped by curling into a too small a space. To wake up deliciously warm and sprawled on a comfortable mattress was a novelty. To wake up, as he had that morning, to the brush of a palm along his side and the tickle of whiskers behind his ear had been a delight.

The memory was sharp in his mind – of his smile and Briers' pleased grunt as he turned to face him, of the encompassing hand gripping them both, of their biting kisses as excitement increased, of their silent stillness followed by stifled laughter as someone passed their door on the way to the bathroom.

"Oh, good grief." Miles abandoned his cards and dropped both hands to his lap. Less than three hours and he was already making an exhibition of himself. All he had to do was remember the way Briers muffled his moans against Miles' shoulder when the pleasure got too much to bear quietly. Those guttural growls plus the sharpness of Briers' teeth ... The lining of his skirts slid easily over the silk of his stockings. The padded underclothing with its rigid modesty panel was a problem but not insurmountable. Miles bit his lip, smiling around the pinch of flesh as he wondered if pleasuring himself during office hours was a case for instant dismissal or if he'd be let off for a first offence. Of course, he could be really decadent about it and move to the chaise longue but then he wouldn't have such a good view of the street ... where a telegraph boy was pedalling towards the house.

Pleasure forgotten, Miles leaned forward in the chair, wondering to which address the lad would go. The boy slowed, stopped, propped his pedal on the curb and disappeared from sight as he began to mount the steps. A moment later, muffled by distance, the doorbell jangled. It jangled again and Miles heard Lizzie's sharp tones of complaint and the boy's equally sharp reply. It might not be for him, but there was no point in taking chances. Miles smoothed his skirt and went to the mirror to check his hair and make-up would pass muster. He pinched his cheeks, grinning at the memory of Throckmorton's advice and was certain he looked just the thing when he opened the door in response to Lizzie's knock.

"Message, m'm," she panted. "'E said 'e'd wait for a reply."

Dorchester Grill – one sharp – Uncle Charlie's treat – B

Miles chuckled, wrote a quick affirmation and sent Lizzie off with a sixpence for the reply and a penny each for her and the boy.

The Dorchester – time to wear the pearls.

Briers was waiting in the lobby when Miles arrived. He beamed at him and flicked one of his pearl ear drops.

"You look gorgeous," he said. "I've been thinking about you all morning."

"Ditto." Miles gave him a heavy-eyed look worthy of Theda Bara. "And I was just going to do something about it when your telegram arrived."

"That's so unfair," Briers whispered. "You say a thing like that and expect me to have a sensible conversation with Naylor?"

At the entrance to the restaurant, Briers accosted a waiter and they followed him to a table a little separate from other diners, unfashionably close to the kitchen doors but sufficiently separate from other tables that conversation shouldn't be overheard.

"Ah, there you are," Naylor stood to pull Miles' chair out and waited patiently while he seated himself and deposited his handbag on the floor. "So good of you to come. I took the liberty of ordering for you both. I have a meeting at two so time is, as they say, of the essence."

At his gesture, a waiter poured wine, a very decent claret, and another began to serve them rack of lamb with peas and redcurrant sauce. Once the food was on the plates and the waiting staff were gone, Naylor picked up the thread of his discourse.

"Time is of the essence because, in the light of slow progress – not yours, you have both been very effective in keeping tabs on the targets – the powers that be have decided it is time to arrest those members of the cell we can catch. Then –"

"They what?" Briers voice cracked with shock. "That's ridiculous."

Naylor glared at him. "This is their decision. We have to make the best of it. If it means Andrija goes free, it is to be regretted, but if we act swiftly enough, his colleagues may give us information that will lead to his apprehension."

Briers scowled. "They do appreciate how driven the man is? Also, just because we have found one of his lairs, one of his groups of operatives, it doesn't mean there won't be others? I've never yet known him to make any plan without having one or two alternatives."

"Shall we say, we have done our best to make them aware such a thing is possible." Naylor smiled. "And they have reassured us they are sure our security is such that, should there be another cell, it will come to light very soon."

Miles paused in raising his fork to his lips. "So, what they are saying is they expect results, they expect them now and if they don't get them they will grab what they can?" Naylor's eye brows rose and it occurred to Miles that Naylor had never seen Millie in full flow.

"And they are aware that, as yet, we have no definite idea of Andrija's target? Ingram is chairing a meeting with various Balkan ambassadors at the Foreign Office on the fifteenth. If *they* are the target, it leaves us six days."

"Six days." Naylor nodded. "A lifetime in espionage. Allerdale, MacGregor's department has been instructed to put all their resources at your disposal. Siward, I have informed Sir James Lorimer that your conduct in this case has been exemplary. Please continue to observe Ingram and Josephine, but do not put yourself at risk. We will do everything in our power to discover the 'farm' you heard mentioned. Six days, gentlemen. I trust we will accomplish a lot in that time."

They parted from Naylor with little to lift their spirits other than an excellent lunch at His Majesty's Government's expense, and took their leave of each other on the pavement outside the hotel.

"I need to see if I can find a contact," Briers said. He gave Miles shoulder an affectionate pat and said, "I should be home around five unless I get a lead. If I'm going to be late I'll try to telephone. Meantime, take care and have something hot waiting for me when I get home." He smiled the smile that always made Miles' heart beat a bit faster. "Give me something to look forward to."

"I can do that," Miles promised. "I'll shop on my way home. See if I can find something to make your eyes pop."

"You mean a garrotte?" Briers feigned alarm then reached up to touch the side of Miles throat in a gentle caress. "I'll be speculating all day."

There was a moment of hesitation as they looked into each other's eyes. Then, outside the Dorchester in full view of everyone, Briers stooped and kissed Miles' cheek.

"See you later, Miles," he whispered then they parted – Briers to head for his car and Miles to go home.

On the way, Miles made a detour to Derry and Tom's where he browsed the shelves for a while, contemplating gifts for Mrs Jones and Lizzie but, more importantly, something for Briers. He knew their association was a finite one. If duty called, they must answer. He would return to his work in the cipher rooms, Briers to his place in the Balkans. But their time together had been sweet, and he wanted to mark it in some way.

"Make the most of it and have no regrets," he reminded himself. That was about the most men like him could hope for. But while they were together, Miles intended to make as many happy memories as possible.

He bought an exotic fringed and embroidered silk shawl for Mrs Jones that, he hoped, would match the skirt he had helped her pin up, a fashionable cloche hat for young Lizzie he was sure she would enjoy wearing, even if it was a little old for her, and a dozen large silk handkerchief squares for Briers. He spent a pleasant half hour on the Tube contemplating how Briers might look with one tied over his eyes and two more on his wrists while he waited to find out where Miles would kiss him next.

Then home to Albert Street.

"Ah, Mrs Carstairs." Mrs Merrill met him in the hall. "Your brother is here. He is waiting in the parlour." She dropped her voice. "I gave him tea because I wasn't sure when you would be home. Such a handsome young man. Such a pity."

"Oh!" Miles' heart thumped as he contemplated the very few terrible reasons why George might risk breaking Miles' cover. "Thank you, Mrs Merrill. I – um – I will go straight in."

He left the packages on the hall stand, hung his coat on the rack and entered the parlour with as much poise as he could muster bearing in mind Mrs Merrill was hard on his heels.

"George, darling," he said, whisking across the room to press a kiss to his brother's cheek. "So nice to see you. I hope there's no trouble at home? Can you stay until Brian gets here? He was only saying last night he hoped to see his brother-in-law again soon."

George, who had been staring at him, closed his mouth and stood to take Miles' hand. "You're looking good, sis." He smiled. "Everything's fine, but I was in town and thought I'd drop by. Surprised to see me?"

"Delighted." Miles had no need to feign that. "And relieved to see you getting around so well. Come and sit and tell me everything. How are Mother and Father?"

"I'll leave you to catch up," Mrs Merrill said. "More tea? Well, I'll refresh the pot just in case. And bring another cup. And maybe light the fire? It's warm for November but still …."

Once the landlady had departed with the tray, Miles closed the door behind her and let out a long breath.

George shook his head. "She'll be back in a minute. Miles – I mean, Millie – I never expected this!"

His gesture took Miles in from natty hat to silk stockings, and Miles grinned and gave him a twirl. "There's this little shop in South Ken," he said. "Now, sit down, and I think we ought to be the picture of family friendship when Mrs M comes back with the tea. Once she's decided we don't need chaperoning, then we can *talk*. And I do want to hear your news."

Miles smiled as his brother, George, war hero and secret agent, took a deep breath and said, "Mother sends her love."

Sure enough, Mrs Merrill returned a few minutes later, poured their tea and promised to be within earshot if they needed anything. Miles thanked her profusely and they were chatting again – an account of the vet's difficulty in establishing what was wrong with the family retriever – before she was out of the room.

"A purse?" Miles laughed. "He ate Mama's purse. How did you find out?"

"Shall we say that after a day or two it made a reappearance? The change washed up a treat with a bit of bleach but the bank refused to accept the notes."

They both laughed, then Miles pressed his ear to the door. He listened a moment, then he nodded, having heard Mrs Merrill haranguing Lizzie in her own parlour.

"She's telling the maid off," Miles said. "Now, lovely though it is to see you, why are you here, George, and how did you get this address?"

"Throckmorton," George said. "He and I go way back. He'd got wind of who you were after and was worried, and so was I, so I made enquiries in the accounts department and this was one of two addresses where something had been set up in the past month. The other was in Surrey, so when you cashed a cheque at the Camden branch of Lloyds it was a bit of a giveaway." George laughed as Miles rolled his eyes. "Hey, I'm only getting back in practice."

"Back to active service soon?" Miles glanced at the stick propped against the arm of George's chair.

"It's been a year," George pointed out, "and it seems unlikely it's going to improve much if I sit around at home, so I'll start by doing some desk work while I get up to speed with what's going on. Then – well, don't you think a man with a tin leg might do good service as a courier?" He stooped to rap on his calf with his knuckles. "I'll have little compartments made. Gun, spare ammo, change of linen, hip-flask, plans for the sequestration of Lichtenstein."

"Not truly?"

"Lichtenstein? Not as far as I know." George shrugged and sat back in his seat, shifting to get comfortable. Miles stood to pack a cushion in behind George's back and passed him his cup and saucer once he had settled.

"So that's the how," Miles said. "Now what about the why? Andrija is formidable, yes, but I can't believe you'd come all this way and go to all this trouble just to check up on me when all I'm doing is watching the house opposite." He had a decent view of the Crane house through the window, having chosen their seating with that in mind.

"Well, Andrija is worth worrying about." George put his cup on the arm of the chair and reached to give Miles a gentle shove in the shoulder. "But this dressing up business is what brought me here. Throckmorton almost boasted about your disguise. He seemed to feel I would know about your talents in that direction. I didn't let on, but as far as I knew this nonsense ended when you left Cambridge, Shakespeare and all that. But this ... Miles, you look pretty damned convincing to me and that doesn't happen without a good deal of practice. Have they been making you do this regularly? Because, if so, I don't think it's on."

Miles heart had sunk as soon as George brought up the subject and he bit back a protest that, he knew, would have done him no good at all.

"There have been a number of occasions," he admitted. "Some more serious than others. The first was during that scare eighteen months ago. There was some concern about the American Ambassador's wife. She seemed overly friendly with a man who had a connection to another embassy, met him for tea at least once a week at the Savoy, but we had never seen her pass anything to him and those conversations we had overheard seemed innocuous. It occurred to the powers that be that perhaps he had a confederate who was collecting the information in the ladies' powder room. The regular operative was delayed one day so I went in dressed as an attendant. No information was passed but I earned more in tips that day than I did in my wages." He grinned, hoping George would appreciate the joke but his brother was still frowning.

"And the other occasions?"

"A few easy little surveillance jobs. Sitting on park benches seeing who approached whom, that type of thing. Only one that was more serious." Miles picked up his tea cup to give his hands something to do. "There's a night club in Curzon Street, a sleazy down-the-stairs kind of place with a … bohemian clientèle. The son of a Cabinet Minister had been observed in there and it was judged he might be open to blackmail. The man on the case requested a female partner, our masters refused to allow any of their young ladies to enter such an establishment and they decided to use me. It wasn't a pleasant assignment, mainly because the people we were monitoring were far more charming and far less aggressive to me than my colleague. In any of your assignments, have you come across an operative called Henry Mortlake? No? Lucky you. He was utterly obnoxious, and so busy sneering at me and everything else around him that his mind wasn't on the job." Miles grimaced at the memory.

"But what if you had been challenged?"

"A man dressed convincingly as a woman was nothing out of the way for that place," Miles assured him. "I don't see why you are so worried, George. You have had to do far worse things for King and country than wear a skirt for a week or two."

George scowled down at his well-polished brogue and the false foot within it. "I suppose so," he said. "But it makes me uneasy to think about what people might be saying. It's not going to do your career any good, you know."

"Honestly, George." Miles tried very hard to keep his voice even but Millie wasn't taking any nonsense. "I feel it would do my career far more harm for me to tell Sir James Lorimer that he can wear the frock himself, don't you? And I'm doing more good here like this than I would stuck in my office translating telegrams and letters. Now, are you here to help or hinder? If the latter, you may as well be leaving."

"Well, that told me." George grinned. "When you put it like that … How can I help?"

Miles relaxed, relieved George wasn't storming to the door. "I don't know," he said. "I don't suppose I'm allowed to talk about it."

"I don't suppose you are," George agreed, "but when has that ever stopped us?"

They were still talking about it over an hour later when they heard the front door open and Briers greeting Mrs Merrill in the hall. George straightened in his chair and Miles sat back on his heels in his place on the floor surrounded by road maps and Post Office directories.

"In here? Oh, no thanks, Mrs M. I'll get Millie to make me coffee later. Thank you."

"Brian!" Miles called as his lover opened the door. "Look who's here! I was just telling George that you shouldn't be much longer so he decided to wait."

"George, old man!" Briers shut the door behind him and strode across the room to drop an affectionate kiss on top of Miles' head before extending his hand to Miles' brother. George eyed it for a moment then took it with a wry smile.

"No need to maintain the fiction on my account," he murmured. "Miles has brought me up to date on what's going on and, while I think the service has a bloody cheek putting you both in this embarrassing situation, I agree that it must have made sense at the time."

"A lot of sense." Briers took the seat that Miles had vacated. "So, George Siward, eh? A pleasure to meet you formally."

"Formally?" George frowned at Briers then let out a laugh. "You! Hah! I never forget the face of a man who's tried to blow my head off. A pleasure to meet you."

"The pleasure's all mine. I've long been an admirer of your work."

George snorted. "That you know about it shows how unadmirable it has been. Now I, on the other hand, have heard only the merest rumours about yours." He nodded with the respect of one professional for another and Briers chuckled.

"What are you two up to?" he asked, peering at the spread of maps.

"Looking for farms," Miles explained. "Andrija mentioned going back to the farm and seeing Nemanja at the farm. We know that it's somewhere off the District Line East so we were making a list of possible places – street names, hotels, house names."

"Oh, good notion. And the maps?" Briers leaned to pull one towards him. "Suffolk? Surely not."

"It seems unlikely, I know," George said, "but Andrija won't have all his eggs in one basket and he won't have the two baskets too close together, either."

"I'm betting he's in town," Briers said. "That's the place to hide – where there's plenty of people and everyone is used to strange faces."

"I agree, if all you want to do is hide."

Briers stared at George. "A farm. Isolated, maybe deserted. You could get up no end of things. You could – I don't know – land a small aircraft."

George grinned at him. "Or sail a small craft right up one of the creeks in perfect privacy."

"And sail it right back out again when your job is done."

"Much to the excited speculation of the locals," Miles pointed out. "Come on, you two. You know what it's like in the country. You're never quite as unobserved as you think you are."

"Then near a port," Briers suggested. He got out of his chair and settled on the mat beside Miles. "What about Tilbury? The locals around there must be used to seeing strangers and there was quite a lot of green around there last time I looked."

"Or somewhere else with work," Miles peered at the maps. "Work where strangers come and go. It's too late for fruit or hop picking. Anyone know anything about potatoes?"

"I prefer them fried to boiled." Briers leaned in, his shoulder against Miles's. "The picking gangs are pretty fluid. Easy come, easy go. Could be anywhere in an arc from here to here."

George gave a peevish grunt. "Shift yourself, Millie. I can't see."

Miles laughed as a poke from George's stick pushed him over so that George too could see the map.

"I've had an idea." George pointed along the coast. "Andrija's gang in Millbank is staying in condemned housing, right?"

"Just off Page Street, yes." Miles arranged his skirts to cover his knees, ignoring Briers' smirk. "Bad flood damage, there, and half a block is going to have to come down. Lord knows what they will build on the site. But if he's using deserted and condemned property there ..."

"Why couldn't he be doing the same out in Essex?" Briers beamed at Miles. "Maybe we should make enquiries about flood damaged rural property? Young couple looking for a dead cheap house in the sticks. I could make a sweep of the estate agents tomorrow, see what's available."

Miles laughed. "Be sure to get one with a nursery, dear."

George cleared his throat. "Whatever you do, you need to do it fast. What is it now – November ninth? This needs to be cleared up quickly so you can get back to your real work."

There was a tension about George's mouth that Miles couldn't bear to see. Embarrassed, he began to clear the maps away until Briers put his hand squarely in the middle of them.

"This is Miles' real work, Siward," he said. "Translators aren't ten a penny, but I don't know *anyone* else who could have done what he has been doing for the past couple of weeks and done it with such good humour. You or I certainly couldn't."

"No." George sighed. "No, I couldn't. And I'm proud of what he has achieved, I just …" He gestured towards Miles. "It just looks so wrong. Mother and Father asked me to check up on you. How can I tell them about this?"

"Don't." Miles shrugged. "If I've heard you say 'I can't tell you that' once, I've heard you say it a dozen times when Mother has been asking about your work. Tell them I'm on a special assignment for Sir James Lorimer. Or better yet, stick to the cover story that I've been sent on a crammer to learn Ukrainian. They don't actually *need* to know how good my legs look in stockings."

"Now you're being perverse," George said, but he was smiling again.

Chapter Eleven

George was still smiling when he took his leave half an hour later. Briers had been surprised at his own need to defend Miles' professionalism but it seemed to have done the trick. The affection the brothers displayed for each other was obvious, even if George kept frowning at Miles's, or rather Millie's, mannerisms. But George played along and the three of them stood at the kerb, the picture of congenial family life, while Briers and George chatted about the Austin and Miles, from his tense expression, tried not to butt in with his own opinions.

"No, honestly," George said as he wrapped his scarf around his neck, "I can walk to the High Street and there's bound to be a cab."

"Nonsense." Briers grinned at him. "I'll give you a lift. My Austin may not be a sleek warhorse like your Armstrong but she's got her advantages."

"Oh yes, I see that." George gave Miles a sly look. "A proper family car. Thank you."

Briers jingled his keys in triumph and had just turned to unlock the car door when the door of the Crane house opened and Elsie came stumbling down the steps with the baby in her arms. She looked very different from the glossy happy young wife she had been when they had last passed the time of day with her.

"Mr Carstairs, Millie," she gasped. "I'm sorry – but I don't know what to do. Sidney hasn't come home tonight, and he's always home by half past six. Dinner's all spoiled, and I rang his office and – and they told me that I had telephoned this morning to say he was ill and wouldn't be into work today. I didn't, I swear it. I just don't know what's happened."

"Where's your maid – Colette?" Miles demanded. He went to Elsie and put his arm around her. "It's very cold, couldn't she mind the baby while we sort this out?"

"It's Colette's day off." Elsie began to sob. "And she didn't come home to help with Baby's bath. I'm afraid – afraid she and Sidney ..."

"Nonsense," Briers said his heart sinking. "Sidney thinks the world of you. He would never stoop so low. George, why don't you come with us too and we can get this sorted out."

They trooped across the road, Miles taking the wailing child from Elsie's arms so she could accept Briers' arm. She hung onto it as though her legs wouldn't support her weight and Briers exchanged worried glances with Miles. This was a development neither could have foreseen but that didn't stop Briers from feeling responsible.

Inside, they set about organising Elsie. "You need tea," Briers informed her, "so take George to the kitchen and he will help you make a cup. Millie will change the infant, because I suspect it needs it, and I'll see if I can find out what's going on. Maybe those fools in Sidney's office got the names muddled."

As soon as Elsie was out of earshot, Miles glared at Briers. "I'll change the infant? And what makes you think I'm any more qualified to do that than you are?"

"If the skirt fits …" Briers said with a smirk, but he did get directions to the nursery from Elsie while he helped Miles to wrestle the child into submission and puzzle out how to apply a clean napkin. Once he was clean, the baby was more cheerful and Miles sat him on his hip and accompanied Briers on a foray to Sidney's study, which was in apple-pie order with no visible causes for concern.

"Busy man," Briers said, eyeing the filing cabinets and book cases where texts on hydraulic engineering rubbed covers with more general works on physics and history. "Even if something were missing, we wouldn't be able to spot it."

"Not without going all through the files. Shall we see if Josephine has left anything in her bedroom?" Miles suggested.

Back upstairs, they explored the top floor and found Josephine's small chilly room. With the baby safely deposited in the middle of the bed, they opened drawers and cupboards.

"Clean sweep," Briers said. "She's taken everything bar the gas mantle."

"Waste paper basket?" Miles asked. "Secret plans in the po'?"

Briers grunted a laugh and got down on his knees to peer into the chamber pot under the bed. "Not a sausage. No, wait, there's something fallen down behind the bed leg." Just the corner was visible; a greenish card printed in black. He teased it out with a fingertip, grabbed it and sat back on his heels. "It's a ticket. Quite new. Look, no dust so it can't have been there long." Briers tilted the scrap of paper towards the light, the better to read the tiny lettering.

Miles stooped to look over his shoulder then took the ticket to the window to inspect it more closely. "I recognise this bus line. They're based in Southend. A threepenny ticket. Now who would Josephine be visiting near Southend?"

"I could hazard a guess." Briers slapped his hands together, startling the baby into a yelp. "Sorry, old man," he said to it and gathered it up gingerly.

They carried child and bus ticket downstairs and presented one to George and the other to Elsie.

"George has been telling me that the office may have made a mistake," Elsie said, "and that Sidney might have been sent across town to check on the pumping station in Southwark. But the man who holds the diary would have gone home by this time of night with the keys, so they can't check." She didn't look happy, but the panic had receded from her eyes and she had smartened herself up. "I'll give him such a telling off when he comes home."

"Oh, you know men and pumps," Miles said. "One sight of all that glossy machinery grinding away and all the common sense goes out of their heads. He'll come home contrite and flustered, and you can get him to take you up West for an evening to make it up to you. I don't suppose you have a map? Of Essex?"

"Sidney has maps in his study. But what do you need a map for?"

"Oh, Brian and I are looking for a place out that way and wondered about somewhere near Southend. Sea breezes and all that."

Leaving Miles to keep Elsie talking about mythical house-hunting plans while she drank her tea and fussed over the baby, Briers and George raided the study to obtain the map. They spread it on the dining room table and tried to calculate how far a threepenny bus ticket would take Josephine from Southend.

"Plenty of farms," George murmured. "And much of this area was inundated in January. If you're looking for derelict and abandoned rural property, I wouldn't think you'd have to look much further."

"What do you think?" Briers glanced over his shoulder to the drawing room and caught Miles' eye.

"One moment, Elsie," Miles said and went to the table to join them.

"We've narrowed it down," Briers said, "and think it's somewhere around here. Now, I don't think it's a good idea for Elsie to stay on her own. Do you think you could keep her company, Millie, while I drop George off at the taxi rank and then I'll go and investigate?"

"I have a better idea," George said. "Miles – er – Millie can stay and look after Mrs Crane while we *both* go to Southend and try to trace the bus route." He gave them both a meaningful look. "I believe that time could be short, even if it's not already too late. This is a two man job."

"Then I should go." Miles' hands on the back of the chair displayed white knuckles. "George, Elsie is more likely to listen to you and so is Broadway House if you ring to try and get hold of Naylor. He needs to know about this development. Also, there may be some running involved and I don't mean to be insensitive, but …"

George grunted a grudging agreement. "Charlie Naylor. I'll give him a call for you. Just tell me what you want me to say."

"Tell him you're ringing on behalf of Brian and Millie Carstairs," Briers suggested. "Crane missing, Josephine missing, bogus phone call to Crane's place of employment, bus ticket, we've gone to check it out."

"Also, it occurs to me that the police station in Southend may have a list of derelict and abandoned properties," Miles said. "They'll be more inclined to let us have a copy if someone official has warned them in advance."

"I can do all that. And Briers, take care of – of Millie." George shot his little brother a glare that combined concern with affection. "Don't want anything to happen. I don't think our employers have anyone else who speaks that dialect of southern Croatian."

"Thank you for caring," Miles said, and went to try and sort out Elsie.

Elsie vetoed Miles' suggestion that she go over to the Merrill house and enjoy the company there. She plainly didn't want anyone else to suspect that her husband had run off with the nursery maid. George rolled up his sleeves and said, "In that case, we need to make some supper while Brian and Millie go to Southwark to find out what's keeping your husband, and bring him home if necessary."

"Oh, I do feel a fool," Elsie said as she accompanied them to the door. "But Sidney always, *always* telephones if he's going to be late. He knows that I worry so."

"We'll find him," Miles promised, gave her a peck on the cheek and hurried out of the house.

They took a moment to fetch coats and hats and to retrieve the maps from the floor in the parlour. They called out to Mrs Merrill to excuse themselves from supper then went back out to the car.

Briers gave Miles a stern look as he started the engine. "You do realise we've no guarantees that Crane will be alive. If he saw something he shouldn't, Andrija will have bumped him off."

"I know." Miles opened the map with an efficient snap of paper. "But we couldn't tell Elsie that, could we?"

They took the fastest route east, avoiding the heavy traffic on the main roads, with Miles navigating along residential avenues. It was quicker to go north and around the East End, they agreed, than to risk getting into the warren of streets, but it was still very late when they reached their goal. Briers parked a little down the road from the police station and they both hurried inside.

"Good evening," Briers said to the desk sergeant. "My name is Carstairs. I believe you may have some information for me?"

"Evening, sir, madam." The man's smile was polite rather than enthusiastic, his walrus moustache twitching. He stepped out from behind the desk and led them to a large scale map, framed and mounted on the wall. "A threepenny bus ride, you said?" He inspected the ticket closely then nodded. "Assuming that the traveller embarked at the bus stop closest to the railway station that would take him – oh, about so far." His nicotine-stained finger described an arc. The surface of the map shone greasily as Miles and Briers leaned in to peer at it.

"Are any of these buildings derelict or deserted?" Miles asked. "I understand the flooding was very bad here in the winter."

"Yes, miss. The sea walls breached. Some of the farmers lost most of their stock and a few gave up and have rented out their land to other people. There are some empty houses. Not many that are habitable."

Briers could feel the sergeant staring at them, probably wondering what on earth they needed to know this for, and worrying that there was something he hadn't been told but that he should know about.

"Could you give me directions?" Briers asked.

"I can do better than that, sir," the sergeant said. "I made you a copy of our list. Our men keep an eye on them when they are on their rounds." He frowned at them both. "Is it permissible for me to ask why? You see, I have men out there now and if there's something going on … ?"

"I'm afraid not, sergeant," Briers said. "The fact is that it's a security matter."

The policeman grunted and fetched a paper from the desk. "Thought as much," he said. "I hope that it's nothing that might get one of my boys hurt."

Five minutes later, they were outside with Miles puzzling over the list and trying to match addresses to locations on the hand-drawn map. "That wasn't a happy man when we left."

"No, I don't suppose he was," Briers agreed. "But in some ways, it's better that he doesn't know what we're doing. A well-meaning copper blundering into a bunch like Andrija tends to gather could only end badly."

"Briers," Miles tilted the list and the map to try and catch the little light, "do you think Sidney Crane is still alive?"

"It depends." Briers slowed to take a sharp bend and used the time to consider his reply. "If his disappearance is just due to his having seen or heard something he shouldn't then, no, probably not. But if it's more than that …. If we were wrong in assuming Josephine was merely hiding out there and she was actually there to get some kind of information, then he may still be alive. But what information Sidney Crane could be privy to at the Water Board that's more important than what Ingram has to deal with, I can't imagine."

"The Water Board," Miles said. "Oh dear God, do you think they might be trying to trigger another flood? Detonate explosives at the reservoirs, or – or block the Thames so the water backs up into the city? You weren't here in January, Briers. The disruption was unbelievable."

Briers snorted. "They couldn't do that. At least, I don't think they could. I don't see how they could. Dammit, Miles, now you have me starting at shadows. No, Andrija is a nasty bastard but he has his specialisms just as we do, and miracle working isn't one of them."

"I wish it was one of yours," Miles muttered. "There are a lot of houses on this list."

"Then we work our way through them, one by one," Briers said, his tone grim. He glanced at Miles. "If we want to help Sidney, it's the only thing we can do."

The first house was a shell, its roof sagging and garden rank, with a restless tide behind it. They circumnavigated the property by the yellow light of a bull's eye lantern Briers kept in the car. The place didn't look any better illuminated and their footprints were the only ones marking the muddy ground.

The next looked more promising, but it had an agent's sign nailed to the gate, offering it for rent at a reasonable rate and with an address promising viewing by appointment only. They argued over that a bit, but the list was long and the gate was padlocked. So they went on to the third address.

A village address, close to the local pub. The fourth had no roof. The fifth looked as though it could slide into the sea at any moment.

Midnight had come and gone and Briers' heart was in his boots.

"Where next?" he asked.

"Great Wakering, there's a place within walking distance of the brick works. Just off a creek, too."

"That sounds something like it." Briers slowed to take a tricky corner. "Brickworks mean lots of workers, coming and going. They aren't all going to know each other. Vehicles, too. Is it big?"

"The brickworks?" Miles chuckled. "It looks massive on the map. But the house is a farmhouse with outbuildings. Some bad flood damage but the barns are sound."

"Promising." Briers put his foot down.

At first sight, the place appeared to be as neglected as some of the others they had seen, but the lantern showed them fresh tyre tracks in a gateway. The house and barns were a hundred yards down a track and partially screened from the road by trees.

"This is the sort of place that I would choose," Briers murmured.

"Do you think we ought to get closer?" Miles suggested. "It wouldn't do to call in the troops then find out that there's nothing going on after all."

"No, you're right." Briers turned to him and put his arm around Miles' shoulders. "Miles, I want you to stay here. No, listen. Get in the driving seat and if I don't come back, you can go for help. Andrija and his men are thugs and I'd prefer you not to have to be in a position to have to defend yourself."

Briers sensed rather than saw the tension in Miles body. His imagination could fill in the other details too – the flush of embarrassment, the tight lips and the gradual easing into grudging acceptance.

"If the defence called for a wounding memo, then I'm probably your man," Miles said. "Fisticuffs – probably not."

"It would be fisticuffs at the very least," Briers said. "So I can count on you to bring that charming desk sergeant and his cohorts to my rescue? That's a comforting thought. Oh, this wind is cold. Get back in the car."

"Be careful," Miles whispered and Briers found his heart thumping a bit harder than usual at the urgency in his tone.

"I always am," he promised and took a moment, a very self-indulgent but much needed moment, to stoop and kiss Miles' warm mouth.

Chapter Twelve

Briers was less confident that this was Andrija's hideout than he had allowed Miles to believe. There was the possibility that Miles had misheard or that they were in the wrong county. The ticket on the floor in Josephine's bedroom could have been dropped there by Elsie Crane or the previous maid, Mary. There was no point in raising the alarm, disturbing a gang of itinerant workers and possibly allowing Andrija time to move his operation. Much better to make sure.

He crept along the shadowed side of the lane, the cover down on the lantern. There wasn't much of a moon, it was only just rising, but the stars were bright where they weren't covered by clouds and, as usual, the sky seemed brighter where the light reflected off the sea. He could smell the marsh – damp and salty and slightly fishy – and a tang of petrol, and coal smoke.

Briers sighed with relief. The house was being used. Now it only remained to establish by whom.

He started with the house. Laying a hand on the door, he checked for give, peered into the darkness inside and at the path outside. There had been some traffic. Water lay in tyre marks. There was a boot print brimming with liquid mud. But the prints passed by the side of the house. Beyond, the barns stood dark and silent. Briers stopped, filled with prickling unease. There had been a sound, the barest clink of a chain. Had he been spotted? Was some legitimate night watchman, filled with righteous ire, about to unleash a bulldog? Or was Andrija, even now, levelling a gun at his head. Briers eased further into the shadows, wondering what had put him on edge.

"Hands up."

Lights blazed from one of the outbuildings, illuminating him mercilessly in his sheltered corner between the house and a ramshackle lean-to shed.

"Hands up or I will shoot you in the leg." The voice was speaking in excellent English. The accent was light but enough to assure Briers that he had found what he sought. Pity they had found him first.

Briers stepped out of the shadows, his hands clasped on the crown of his hat, narrowing his eyes against the light. His captors were blurs against the headlamps of a car, parked in the shadows of a machinery store. As his eyes adjusted Briers did a quick head count. Six, standing well back, plus the shuffle of a foot behind him. Too many.

The spokesman stepped forward, smallish, broad-shouldered. "Who are you and what are you doing here?"

"I'm lost. I hoped there might be a phone," Briers said. "My hosts will be worrying."

There was a short silence then a laugh. "Very good, very good. Nicely plausible and suggesting that you are expected and will be looked for if you are not allowed to go on your way. My apologies. That will not be possible. Lower your hands and put them behind your back."

"What?" Briers played the outraged innocent for all he was worth. "What are you playing at? Look – I'm on my way to my cousin in Colchester and took a wrong turn. Just give me the right direction and I'll be on my way. I was hoping to find someone with a telephone so I could call and tell them I'd be late. I'm not burgling the place."

"Put your hands behind your back." The order was delivered in a sharp rap and Briers judged he was wearing out Andrija's patience. But if one of his confederates was close enough behind Briers to bind his hands then maybe Andrija would be unlikely to take a shot?

"All right," he said. "There's no reason to wave that – that thing about." He gestured to the gun then whirled, ducked and punched the man behind him. He darted past the reeling figure and ran along the shadowed side of the road. Still no shots, but he was followed by shouts and pounding feet.

Along the lane, a car engine started and more headlights blazed; the familiar cough of the Austin's engine was loud in the stillness of the night. Briers vaulted the gate and darted to the passenger side of the car, only to draw back with a curse of dismay as a man levelled a shotgun at his face.

"Stop there." The voice was familiar even if the face was shadowed. Béla, damn his eyes, supporting Miles' drooping body. "Hands up or your lady gets it." A knife glinted close to Miles' face. "She doesn't need both ears."

Briers made no further protest, even when they bound his hands, just wincing at the bite of the cords.

They dumped Miles into the back of the car and Andrija got into the driver's seat. Briers walked back to the farmhouse in front of the car, the headlights making any attempt at escape impossible. But then, he couldn't go and leave Miles in the hands of these thugs. Even if Miles had been a seasoned operative, Briers would have had qualms. As it was, he couldn't countenance the thought of leaving Miles to Andrija's mercy.

They pushed him past the farmhouse to one of the outbuildings and down five steps into a long brick-lined cellar. It was damp and smelled of rot and sea water, but had been made habitable with a couple of tables and chairs and a rickety camp bed. A hurricane lantern hung from a nail in a rafter, casting a pool of yellow light.

"Sit," Andrija said, placing a chair in the light, and when Briers had done so they set about making him immoveable. Cords at wrist and ankle, lashed with care and tied in such a way that he couldn't reach them, reminded him again that he was dealing with professionals.

"Bring the woman," Andrija ordered and Briers craned his neck to watch as they carried Miles down the stairs and dumped him on the camp bed. His face was white, eyes closed, jaw sagging, and blood had poured from a gash in his hairline. Briers took comfort from the care with which one of Andrija's minions tied Miles' wrists and ankles. That meant he was alive.

Briers was determined to look on the bright side.

"She's secure, boss." The minion who had tied Miles straightened up but Andrija still checked the tightness of the bindings himself.

"Good. Park their car out of sight and go and get the lorry loaded." Once the man had gone about his business, Andrija turned back to Briers and looked down at him with a frown. Briers had seen the man from a distance on several occasions, but this was their first meeting face to face.

Andrija could have come from anywhere in Europe. Slightly weatherbeaten skin, brows and lashes a shade or two darker than his light brown hair, thin lips parting to show the rabbity teeth. Briers had seen any number of similar faces in bistros and tavernas, on docks and in offices, smiling in welcome or glaring along the barrel of a gun. But these eyes were different.

It was like looking into the eyes of a corpse. Andrija surveyed him with no spark of interest or compassion.

"I'm sorry," he said, though he didn't sound it. From him, the expression of regret was just a sound. "It may be as you say and you may be lost travellers. If so, that is bad luck. We will be leaving soon. If your lady regains consciousness, it may be that she will be able to free herself and free you. Maybe not. But, you see, I am giving you a chance. Goodnight."

"Wait." Briers tugged at his bonds. "What if she's too badly hurt? What if she dies? You can't leave her like that."

Andrija paused on the very edge of Brier's vision. "I can and I will," he said. "It may be that you will be able to free yourself. Or that someone will hear your shouts. Who knows? God may provide. If I were you, I would start praying."

With that, he was gone, and Briers was left fuming and testing the strength of the chair frame. Ropes were all very well but if the chair was flimsy, he could free himself in minutes. He rocked the chair to test the joints, cocking his head to listen for activity outside. The Austin's engine started again but didn't go far, just a few yards from the sound of it before it cut out again. Dust sifted down through the heavy boards overhead as the floor shifted. Briers coughed. He heard a man murmur something, then a feminine laugh. Josephine. Briers swore. If she came down and saw him, saw Miles, they'd be finished. Andrija would know what they were and a quick death would be the best they could hope for.

More movement overhead, footsteps, something being dragged. Voices, speaking in Croatian, he thought, though the floor was so thick the sense of it was muffled. An admonition to be careful? Another engine started, this one loud and running a little rough. Briers heard Andrija call a farewell, then the vehicle moved off. Had Andrija gone? Had he left orders for their disposal? Briers swore and rocked the chair again.

A movement from the bed distracted him. Miles shifted, moaning a little as he opened his eyes. He squinted against the light, and murmured something Briers couldn't make out.

"Millie," Briers hissed. "Millie, love. Are you all right? Come on, open your eyes. I need you to pay attention."

"What?" Miles did open his eyes, one just a slit because it was awash with blood from his head wound. "Briers? Oh God, Briers, I'm so sorry. I tried to get away but there were two of them and –"

Briers interrupted across the frantic babble, trying to sound confident and good-humoured. "If you'd got away, they'd have cut my throat and had done with it. This way we have a chance. Now, how tight are those cords?"

Miles struggled a little. "There's not much play," he whispered. "If I could get them to the front I might be able to chew through them or something. Or I could wriggle over there and undo yours."

"Maybe when it's quieter," Briers suggested. "At the moment, they are more interested in their own business than ours."

Miles struggled onto his side, blinking to clear the blood from his left eye. "What happened?" he whispered. "Did you see – you-know-who?"

"Yes." Briers nodded. "Listen – I think more of them are getting ready to move out."

They both looked up as more heavy things were dragged across the floor and Miles flinched as dust fell onto his face.

An engine started. "That's a lorry," they both said, then smiled at each other and at the coincidence.

"Snap," Miles said. "What could they be moving?"

"Furniture?" Briers suggested. He was anxious to keep Miles talking because that would take his mind off their extremely uncomfortable position. "Maybe they are going to break into the House of Lords and redecorate in chintz."

Miles snorted a laugh then scowled. "Oh God, my head hurts. You all-action types must be made of iron. I can barely think straight."

"Just hang on tight and I'll soon have you tucked up in bed with some aspirin."

"I'd sooner be tucked up in bed with you." Miles smiled and raised his head. Briers was pleased to see that, though obviously in pain, he seemed to be gathering his wits.

Miles looked down at his bound ankles and disordered clothing, then peered over the edge of the camp bed. "Not too far to fall," he said. "And I can wriggle across the floor all right. Tell me when and I'll have you free in a jiffy."

His smile at Briers faded abruptly and he craned his neck to see past him. "Briers, there's a body. Oh God, there," he nodded, "in the corner. I can't see very well. Do you think it could be Crane?"

Briers strained round to see the darker bulk in the shadows against the far wall. The stocky build, the slightly receding hairline – yes, Sidney

Crane lay crumpled in the corner. He wasn't moving but something about the way the body lay made Briers feel he wasn't dead.

"Another very good reason for us to get free. Ah, there goes the lorry. Not long to wait now. Let's hope they didn't disable the Austin."

"Fingers crossed," Miles said. "Or I would if I could feel them. It's bloody chilly down here."

"I'll warm you up when I get you home," Briers promised and they smiled at each other again.

The sound of the door bolts being drawn sent the thought fleeing. Hobnails scraped on the stairs descending slowly then ringing on the cobbles underfoot.

Briers mused that this could be the best or the worst situation he'd ever been in. On the one hand, he had a gallant and cherished comrade to help see him through it. On the other, the thought of watching Miles die made something inside him howl. He'd never felt this way about a partner before, and wondered if he was going soft.

Miles twisted round on the camp bed, tilting his head back to see who was there. His mouth opened a little, his eyes widening with the beginnings of terror.

A hand clamped on to Briers' hair, drawing his head back and to the side. The glint of a blade by his cheek made him flinch, then straighten in his chair. He could smell the man – a sharp throat-catching reek overlaid by sweat, stale beer and carbolic soap – could hear the harsh excited breathing. He flinched again as a cold touch against the crease of his jaw sharpened into pain.

"No. God – no, don't." Miles lips framed the words but Briers couldn't hear them over the thunder of his own pulse. What a damnable thing for Miles to see. What a damned shame when they had been so good together. It would have ended sometime, but it should not end like this.

"I'm sorry," he said. "Miles. I'm sorry."

"No," Miles shouted, his voice cracking as he struggled. "No, don't, please don't, no!"

Briers' captor grunted, a bare breath of sound but it betrayed an excitement that chilled Briers more than the touch of the blade. The man let him go and moved past him towards Miles. It was Béla, with his shirt sleeves rolled up, presumably so blood didn't spatter them. He'd always taken pleasure in tidying up Andrija's loose ends. He stopped between them looking back and forth.

"You say no?" He smiled at Miles, tongue emerging to wet his lower lip. "Maybe I let him go? Maybe I let you go? What you give me, eh?" The knife point flipped Miles' coat open and Béla inspected Miles' bound ankles with a grin.

"Leave h-her alone." Briers rocked the chair again, feeling the joints give.

"Is this your lady?" Bela laughed. "She shit ugly. I fuck her anyway and if she's good then maybe I let you both go?"

"Don't you dare," Briers spat. "Don't you touch her. Don't you …"

"Seems a fair trade to me," Miles interrupted, his voice shrill but defiant. "Of course I would prefer not to catch whatever this gentleman is carrying but –" Béla's slap rocked his head to the side. "Ah – you bastard."

Briers strained at the cords binding him as Béla struggled with Miles. Even while bound, Miles was putting up a good fight, thrashing and kicking and Briers felt a rush of pride in his spirit. This wasn't about lust. Béla intended to kill them both but intended to hurt and humiliate them both first. But they didn't have to make it easy for him. They could make the bastard sweat.

Miles was tiring and another slap made him cry out, a sharp shocked bleat of pain. "Be still," Béla ordered, settling over him. He reached down to cut the cords on Miles' ankles and set the knife aside the better, Briers presumed, to unbutton his fly.

Miles gasped as Béla pushed his skirt up his thighs. "Please," he murmured then caught his breath.

For one moment, Briers had an excellent view of Béla's gloating face slackening into blank disbelief and shock. Then Miles drove his forehead into Béla's nose.

Béla reared back, blood spraying as he roared his fury. He reached for the knife, but Miles slammed one of his little stacked heels into Béla's throat. Another kick, in the face, snapped Béla's head back and he collapsed onto the filthy floor.

"Bastard, you bastard." Miles was whimpering as he threw himself off the edge of the bed and scrabbled for the knife. He lurched to his feet and slammed another kick into Béla, whether to check if he was shamming or to relieve his feelings Briers didn't know, then he darted to Briers' side and knelt to put the edge of the blade to the cords.

"That's it, Miles. Oh, well done." Briers strained his wrist away from the chair, tightening the cords further. The knife was sharp and the cords parted in a couple of strokes. Once his arm was free Briers took the knife from Miles and freed his other arm then grabbed Miles' hands and slit the bindings between his wrists.

"You are a wonder," he said, and put a moment to good use by turning Miles to face him and kissing him soundly. Miles was icy cold and he was shivering; long, bone-deep shudders that made his teeth chatter.

"I think I – I think I might have killed –"

"Check Crane," Briers ordered, "while I cut the rest of these cords. Then we'll all get out of here."

Miles glanced at Béla again, mouth twisting with revulsion, but he went across to Crane and stooped over him.

"He's alive," he said after a moment. "Beaten, I think, there's blood on his face. But he's breathing all right. Heart's steady."

"Good." Briers got to his feet, wincing at the prickle of pins and needles. His hands felt cold and clumsy, too. He supported himself on the back of the chair, stamping his feet to get the feeling back into them, then straightened up.

"Come on, let's get him into the chair."

Between them, they lifted him up and Briers felt Crane's chest and around his head. There was a gash caked with blood on his crown and it looked as though his nose was broken. But he didn't look nearly as bad as Béla, whose nose was a flattened leaking mess on an empurpled face. His breath rattled thickly in his throat. Not dead but, if Briers was any judge, not long for this world. If he had been alone, Briers would have finished him off but he thought Miles had had enough shocks for one night.

"Miles – door," he said. "Just open it a crack and see if anyone is out there."

While Miles was climbing the steps, Brier's took the opportunity to go through Béla's pockets. He found and pocketed a sheath for the knife and a small notebook, but left the scatter of change and a well-used handkerchief where they fell. He was weighing the knife in his hand, contemplating the places he could stick it to most effectively finish off

Béla, when the man shuddered and stopped breathing. "Good riddance," Briers muttered and sheathed the blade before putting it into his pocket.

A low groan from Crane brought him to his feet in time to prevent the man from toppling from the chair. "Sidney." He patted Crane's cheek. "Come on. Snap out of it. We've come to get you out."

"Who ..." Crane raised a hand to his face. "Who are you?"

"Carstairs," Briers said. "From across the road. Remember?"

"Head's muzzy," Crane muttered.

"Never mind, then. On your feet, man, and we'll take you home."

"Home!" Crane got up readily enough, with his arm across Briers' shoulders.

Miles beckoned from the door. "Someone was over by the Austin a few minutes ago, putting something in the back of it. I assume they are going to use it. It's just a few paces. I think they've gone back inside the barn. They – they were laughing about Béla. Said he'd take his time."

"May he rot in hell. Well done, Miles, you succeeded where many others have failed."

"He's dead?" Miles face shone pale in the light of the hurricane lantern.

"And that's a good thing," Briers snapped. "He needed ending. Now, if we can get to the car and start the damn thing we'll take Crane home to his wife."

His sharp tone got Miles moving again. They eased the door open and Miles took Crane's other arm before they carried him across the yard to the Austin parked in the shadows of the machine shed. Miles helped Crane into the back of it, then fished the starting handle out from under the seat while Briers kept watch.

"No, you drive," Briers said, taking the starting handle from him. Miles' fingers were icy cold and trembling. "I'll start the car."

The Austin was a star – she started first swing of the handle, the engine echoing in the silence of the yard. Briers jumped in on the run as Miles swung the vehicle in a tight circle, and headed it down the rutted track. Behind them, they heard a couple of shouts but no shots were fired. Instead, Briers could see the men running towards the other barn.

"Dammit, it looks like they have another car," he said. "I'd hoped they'd kept this one to use."

"They were probably going to dump it with us," Miles suggested. "It would be simple enough to park it on one of the causeways around here so the tide could wash it off. Look out, the gate's closed."

Briers threw open the car door and jumped out to run ahead. "Dammit!" Not just closed, but chained and padlocked. He kicked the gate, gazing around for something to jemmy the padlock but Sidney Crane shouldered him to one side.

"Peg hinges," Crane said, weaving and unsteady on his feet. "Lift!"

Behind them they saw bright headlights bobbing as their pursuers followed, the roar of the engine ominously powerful. Briers grabbed the gate, and he and Crane lifted it off the hinges and heaved it to one side.

"No, don't drop it," Briers said as Miles drove past. "We'll put it back on – maybe they'll stop and unlock it."

Back in the car, and Miles took off with a spin of wheels and a scatter of gravel.

"Oh God," he muttered. "These roads are appalling. Can't get up much speed because the bends are so sharp."

"Stupid," Briers grumbled. He slapped his hand on the dashboard to brace himself as Miles braked and guided the car around the first bend. "Who on earth thought that was a good idea?"

"Drainage channels," Crane said. His voice sounded stronger. "They make a criss-cross pattern and the roads run alongside them. With the sluice gates, they can control the run off and reduce the risk of flooding."

"More flooding." Briers glanced back down the road where the headlights were shining so brightly. "Fast as we can go, now. Sidney, it might be best if you lay down on the back seat. These are the type of thugs who carry guns."

"I would if I could," Crane said, "but there's a load of stuff in here with me." Briers turned as far as he could and peered into the back as Crane rummaged around. He heard a metallic rattle and saw light glint on something in Crane's hands.

"Ah, so that's what it is." Crane sounded both shocked and resigned. "Carstairs, can you handle a Tommy gun?"

"A what?" Miles yelped.

"Keep your eyes on the road," Briers advised. "Crane, are you sure?"

"I was more used to Lewis's," Crane admitted, "but the magazines are pretty distinctive."

"Oh, good man. Pass it forward."

With the weight of the Thompson in his hands and a spare magazine clamped between his knees, Briers felt more able to deal with their pursuers, but Miles was obviously rattled. He took the next bend too fast, the tyres scattering the stones at the edge of the road before the car straightened and hurtled on into the dark countryside.

"I don't suppose you've got anything else back there?" Miles asked, his voice sharp with nerves. "A small tank for instance? A Sopwith Camel? The band of the Royal Scots Dragoon Guards? Because I can see their lights. They are getting closer."

"No." There was a tense tone in Crane's voice. "But I think I may have a box of Mills bombs on the floor behind the driver's seat."

"Grenades!" The Austin, already careening along at an unsafe 40 mph, jerked as Miles floored the accelerator.

"No, that's good." Briers laid a hand on Miles' thigh and patted, feeling the twitch and quiver of the muscle under his palm. "It explains why they aren't shooting at us for a start. All you need to do is drive. We'll take care of the rest. Crane, you know enough to recognise a Mills bomb in the dark. Any experience in that line?"

"Four years in the Signals." Briers could hear Crane shifting around. "I didn't see much combat but … there's another box here, but the lid is tied down."

"I think we have enough fire-power for an Austin Seven," Briers assured him.

"But do we have enough horse power?" Miles slowed to take the next sharp turn. "Look ahead."

The road lay pale and straight under the stars, a long mile where a large powerful car would have an advantage. Miles sent the Austin bucketing along it and Crane muttered a prayer. Briers looked back and watched the following headlights sweep around the bend and fix on them with the pitiless stare of a raptor. He disengaged the safety catch on the machine gun. It was the old model with the drum, but felt tight and well kept. Andrija wouldn't have it if it wasn't in good working order but could Briers justify firing the first shot? His Majesty's Government took gun-play on home ground very seriously.

"Oh Lord," Miles murmured. "This is it, Brie-Brian. Top speed. We can't go any faster."

The headlights behind were coming up fast. Briers could see one of the passengers leaning over the side of the car, something long and dark in his hands. The staccato chatter was hard to hear over the roar of the engines, but sparks kicked up from the pebbled road alongside them. Miles swore and swerved.

"Thank you, you bastards. Now I can shoot back," Briers said and wriggled round to lean out and return fire. The following car swerved but was coming on fast.

"No," Crane said. "No, I won't have it. They aren't getting their hands on your good lady again." He reached over Briers' shoulder and thumped a hard metallic lump against his chest. "If you won't throw this, I will."

Briers took the Mills bomb. A seven second fuse, and they were travelling at fifty miles an hour. He glanced back at the headlights, already appreciably closer, and decided that the maths was beyond him.

"I'm going to have to brake," Miles said. "I can't take the next bend at this speed. I'm sorry."

"Just leave it as long as you can." Briers set the gun and spare mag on the floor, then pushed the car door open. He turned in his seat, feet on the running board and leaned out to look back. The segmented shell of the hand grenade weighed cold and heavy in his hand. "All right. Steady does it. Brake when you need to. Let them get close."

"Briers, you can't," Miles voice sounded strangled. Briers looked back to see if Crane had noticed the name change but he was staring at the approaching headlights.

"No?" Briers watched the other car draw closer, too. "After what they tried to do to you in the cellar? I damn well think I can."

"Braking," Miles warned.

As the Austin slowed Briers hooked his arm around the door pillar and stood on the running board. Not the best footing but it would have to do. He waited – waited until the Austin had slowed and was turning into the bend – then bowled overarm. The pursuing car swerved, fishtailing as the wheels spun on the loose gravel, left the road and crashed down the bank and into the ditch. Miles accelerated out of the bend as Briers settled back into his seat.

"Three … four … five," Crane was counting.

"No need," Briers said with a grin. "They knew we had Mills bombs, knew we were desperate." He tossed the unthrown bomb up and caught it again. "Their imagination did the rest."

Miles' laugh cracked with relief and tension. "Thank God for imaginative anarchists." His laugh broke on a stifled sob, but he drove on towards the light and safety of Southend.

Chapter Thirteen

They paused very briefly on the way back to London, parking by a public telephone box so Sidney Crane could speak to Elsie. Briers spoke to George, then made a separate call to Naylor's number while Miles sat in the car and shook as those ugly moments in the cellar played and replayed in his mind's eye. Béla's knife at Briers' throat, the trickle of blood, Briers' stoic expression belying the desolation in his eyes. They were going to die, Miles' head had insisted, but something had woken in his heart to snarl, scream and fight against the knowledge. Then that fury had been enough to keep him going, but now he felt sick and exhausted and the tremor in his hands just wouldn't stop.

Naylor met them at the hospital, doctor in tow. His gaze went straight to Miles but Briers had cut him off with a terse, "I'll fill you in later. Not much of it's his."

Miles assumed he was referring to the stiffened patches on his clothing – Béla's blood. Throckmorton would have a fit; it was bound to leave a stain. He rubbed at a patch on the dove grey wool of his coat while the doctor checked the cut in Miles' hair, feeling around the clots and asking questions about vision and 'how many fingers'. Miles answered as best he could, but most of his attention was on Briers making his report. A list of personnel; numbers of vehicles; a guess at possible fire-power; a brief recital of how they had escaped. When Briers had finished, Naylor gave an approving grunt.

"Crane came to much the same conclusion about numbers," he said. "Cool customer. Did he tell you? He left some papers behind and returned home to fetch them just in time to see Josephine packing her suitcase into a car. He went to ask where she was going and one of Andrija's men panicked and coshed him. Then they seem to have batted him around on principle. He's lucky to be alive."

"How is he?" Miles swallowed and asked again, conscious that the first effort had been just a weak whisper. "Is he badly hurt?"

"Crane has three cracked ribs, a chipped tooth, two black eyes and a concussion, but the doctor says he looks a lot worse than he actually is.

They phoned his wife and have put him to bed."

"Good." Miles envied Crane the bed – he was more tired than he had ever been.

Naylor nodded, his expression sympathetic. "We have enough information to make the arrests. I'll set events in motion, you two need to rest. No arguments and I suggest you don't return to your lodgings in Camden. Siward, would it be possible for you to get into your own rooms without being seen? Your man doesn't live in, does he?"

"No," Miles said. He stood at Briers' urging. "I gave him some time off. I think he said he might go to Frinton. Or Bournemouth."

"Well, go home," Naylor said. "I'll arrange to have your effects recovered from the house in Albert Street. There are a few things we need to wrap up. Allerdale, meet me at Broadway House on Monday at eleven. Siward, well done. I'll want to give you a proper debriefing, too, but it can wait until you can keep your eyes open. Come along with Allerdale and I'll speak to you both. Now, go and get some sleep."

Dismissed like a child. Miles' heart was in his scuffed and muddy shoes as he followed Briers out of the room they had borrowed at the hospital and down to where they had parked the Austin.

"Faithful steed." Briers patted the bonnet. "Do you want to drive?"

"No." Miles got into the passenger seat and folded his coat over his knees. His stocking was badly laddered – beyond any darning. He was filthy, his clothes ripped, his body bruised. He focussed on those minor problems, considering how to put those right. Sleep, clean linen, of course, but first a long soak in a hot bath.

He picked at the crusted blood on his coat again and looked out of the window as Briers directed the little car through the streets. It felt to Miles like hardly any time had passed when Briers drove through the archway to the mews behind the terraced houses in Castle Lane and the wheels drummed on the cobbles. But so much had happened – so many changes. Last time Miles had been here he didn't have blood on his hands.

Briers parked the Austin next to Miles' Armstrong Siddeley. "What time is it?" he asked.

"I'm not sure." Miles stifled a yawn. "Three? Maybe four? I didn't notice."

"Bloody watch has stopped." Briers got out of the car and came around to open Miles' door. "If we're quiet we should be all right. If anyone sees us, we're friends of yours borrowing the flat for the weekend."

Miles stifled a protest that he didn't have any friends who would turn up as filthy and dishevelled as they were, certainly none who would do what he had done tonight. Instead, he took the hand Briers offered him and followed him to the back of the house.

"Spare key," Miles murmured, reaching up to the top of the door frame. "At least I hope there is."

"Let me." Briers reached too, his chest to Miles' back, his arm around his waist. He took the key down and unlocked the door. "Come on, Miles," he whispered. "Let's get you sorted out then we can both sleep."

"I can manage," Miles said, shrugging him off.

Inside, the house was dimly lit and very silent. They climbed stairs, crept along hallways and found the spare key to Miles' flat. Briers opened the door again and locked it as soon as they were inside.

"Bathroom to the left down there. Spare bedroom beyond it." Miles turned on the light, wincing as the sudden brightness hurt his eyes. "Shall I make you some coffee while the bath is filling?"

"Coffee is probably not such a good idea just before sleep."

"Cocoa, then?" Miles unbuttoned Millie's coat, removed her hat, and hung both neatly. "I believe we have some biscuits, too. We never did dine. This secret agent business is very good for the waistline. If you're hungry, it might be possible to make you something else. No perishables, of course, but Pritchard will have made sure all the basics are here."

"Miles." Briers' voice was quiet but he didn't say anything else. He went along the corridor to the bathroom and Miles turned to the kitchen to see what he could find. This was normally Pritchard's domain, but Miles had made it his business to know his way about. It was not reasonable to expect his man to hang around until all hours so Miles had familiarised himself with every part of it, including the bang-up-to-date New World gas stove that Pritchard said made life so much easier. Miles looked for the cocoa. There was a box of biscuits on the shelf – Rich Tea. Miles took them down and put them on the draining board. Somewhere there would be cups. And a plate for the biscuits. He circled on the spot, weary beyond belief, until a movement caught his eye. There was a mirror on the back of the door. Pritchard always looked just so before he entered the drawing room. Miles should have remembered that. But whereas Pritchard would be seeing the perfectly turned out gentleman's gentleman, Miles saw a haggard clownish creature in tattered women's clothes, with filth ground into his skin, blood staining his face and the bleak expression of a man who had deliberately killed another human being. He flinched away, lunging for the sink.

He must have made more noise than he thought because he was only heaving for the second time when hands fastened on his shoulders.

"It's all right, lad," Briers murmured. "Let it out, that's it."

Miles retched, sour slime spattering the sink and Briers turned the tap on, swirling the water around the bowl, then cupping a little into his palm to splash Miles' face.

"Done?" he asked and when Miles nodded, he put his arm around his waist and made him straighten up. "Bath," he said, "then bed. It's been a bloody long day."

Miles had no words. He couldn't even think of the right way to express his gratitude. He followed Briers into the bathroom and began the laborious process of getting out of Millie's skin and into his own. Briers, already in his shirtsleeves, helped and it became clear to Miles he wouldn't be having the bath alone. There was something about the idea he knew should have excited him but he didn't have the energy. All he could think of was Béla's snarling, groping, roaring, bleeding, and the ugly rattle as his breathing had stopped and Miles had realised that he was a murderer.

"Bath." Briers' tone was quiet but imperative. "Into the bath. Now." It made Miles feel as though he was about five years old.

He got into the water and sat where Briers indicated, then watched as Briers stripped. Again he felt he should have been more appreciative as that familiar, much desired body was bared, but tonight he looked away. There was a sponge on the shelf. He picked it up and dipped it in the water, feeling the dry rigidity soften between his hands. He dabbed at his face, grimaced at the rusty stains on the sponge, and scrubbed a bit harder.

"Let me do that." Briers settled behind him in the bath, one long leg on either side of his hips, and drew him back to lean against his chest. He took the sponge from Miles and soaped it, then began to apply it to his face and chest. "You're icy cold. Let's get you clean, then get to bed. I need sleep far more than I need cocoa. Unless you're hungry?"

The careful sweeps of the sponge stilled and Miles realised they wouldn't resume until he acknowledged the question.

"No, thank you," he said. "I'm not hungry. I – I'm only tired."

"Ditto." The sponge moved again, across Miles' shoulders and down his arm. Soap stung in scrapes and scratches Miles had no recollection of getting, but he did recall the four nail gouges on the inside of his right thigh, and Béla's chuckle.

He shrank away from the memory and leaned his head onto his knees.

"Good idea. I'll wash your hair through." Briers hands and the sponge swept from Miles head to his shoulders washing away the stains and slowly the aching tension in Miles' neck and shoulders began to ease.

Warm water trickled. The sharp familiar smell of the soap brought back memories. Bath times had occurred in many other places but always with the same Pears soap. Rosemary – that was it. The splash of water and the smell of rosemary were a constant even though the bathrooms had been in Sofia and Bucharest, in Athens and in Istanbul. And in Cambridge, where he had once, just once, taken the incredible risk of sharing a bath with a friend. Miles smiled against his knees. Tommy would have approved of Briers, he was sure. Briers, whose strong thighs lying lax against the sides of the bath brought back memories of intense pleasure, the sure touch of whose hands brought comfort.

"You're done." Briers squeezed the sponge over Miles head and patted his back. Miles stayed where he was but turned his head just enough to see Briers from the corner of his eye making hasty and efficient ablutions before putting soap and sponge back on the shelf.

Briers lay back against the end of the bath and touched Miles' shoulder. "Come here," he suggested. "A little soak before the water gets cold."

Miles turned, feeling awkward in the cramped space, but found his waist fitted neatly between Briers' thighs and his arm slotted down by his side. Briers guided his head to rest against his chest, wet hair tickling his cheek, and wrapped both arms round tight.

"Safe and sound," Briers murmured. "That's what we are – safe and sound."

Miles nodded, closing his eyes. Warm and surrounded by Briers, angular and bony though the embrace was, Miles began to relax. He could hear Briers' heartbeat, calm and unhurried, under his ear. He closed his eyes and listened. The steady thump was comforting. They were home, safe. They could sleep in peace. "Do you think we should move to the bedrooms?" he asked. "I'm going to go to doze off any minute."

"Bedroom." Briers' smile was audible. "You said you'd given your man time off and I'm not leaving you alone tonight."

Miles let out a breath, surprised at the relief he was feeling. "Bedroom it is, then."

They did a cursory clear-up before they retired, putting Millie's coat and hat out of sight with the rest of her clothing. Briers' suit they hung up, Miles promising to sponge the worst off it in the morning. The rest of Briers' baggage was in the spare room so he wouldn't lack for linen.

"I don't think I have any pyjamas that would fit you," Miles apologised as they turned back the covers on Miles bed.

"No need," Brier said with a smile. "I don't want to cut off the circulation in anything vital." He dropped his towel on the bedside mat and got into bed, settling with his arms behind his head. Miles smiled at him and turned off the light, feeling shy and a little ill-at-ease with this happening in his own very private territory. But he too took off his towel, draping it over the end of the bed to dry, before getting under the covers as well. Briers grunted a sleepy welcome and wrapped his arm around Miles' chest to pull him close.

"Sleep," Briers murmured, his lips against Miles' neck raising goosebumps. "Sleep and we'll talk it all through in the morning."

With that, all the memories came crashing back and Miles' eyes opened, Béla's death rattle in his mind again. He must have moved because Briers' arm tightened around him.

"Well, I'm going to sleep," Briers muttered. "Just remember, what you did tonight saved three lives – yours, mine and Crane's – and avenged a dozen others. Béla was a killer, and a particularly vicious one at that. Miles, you did what you had to do. You'd get a medal – if we were in the kind of business to get medals – but we're not, so, we'll have a good night's sleep instead."

Miles snorted a laugh. "I'll try," he promised and Briers gave him a tight squeeze, his hand resting flat over Miles' heart. The encircling arm gripped for another minute or so, then relaxed and Briers' breathing deepened.

What it is to have a clear conscience, Miles thought.

"How much sleep do you think Béla would be losing over you?"

Miles started at the whispered question, barely heard as Briers' lips grazed his shoulder.

"None at all," was the only possible answer.

"What else could you have done?"

"Nothing." From the moment he and Briers had been caught and tied, their fates were sealed. He had one opportunity to save them and took it. "It just seems a pity –"

"Because Béla could have been captured then tried and hanged for his crimes? Well done, you saved us and you saved the hangman a job. Miles, you need to sleep. Come here."

Briers shifted onto his back, drawing Miles with him to lie against his side, tucked in tight, with his head on Briers' shoulder. He felt lips brush the top of his head. "G'night," Briers muttered, his breathing already deepening.

"Good night." Miles smiled wryly as he felt his lover's body begin the slackening into sleep. A few well-chosen words, appealing to logic and common sense, couldn't rid him of the conviction that what he had done was wrong, but he did find it easier to drift off and his dreams were not as horrifying as he had feared.

Chapter Fourteen

Miles awoke warm and comfortable, though the air in the bedroom was chilly, nipping his cheek and his shoulder where the blankets had fallen away. He had a moment of disorientation as he registered that he was at home, rather than in Albert Road, but still had the pleasure of company. The gentle drift of a hand from collar bone to navel and back must have been what had awakened him. He stretched, his buttocks spooning into Briers' lap, and smiled as he felt a greater warmth rest between them. Briers had been right. A good night's sleep had done wonders for his morale. His headache had faded, too, and he was ferociously hungry. But that appetite could wait.

"Awake?" Briers murmured. On this sweep his hand continued past Miles' navel.

"I am now." Miles sighed as Briers smoothed across his belly, down his thigh and back up to cup his bollocks, thumb stroking up the underside of his prick. Already half hard, it filled and Briers gripped it with a purposeful tug.

"Want you," Briers said and Miles nodded and turned towards him.

Qualms about his early morning breath were forgotten as soon as Miles saw the look in Briers' eyes. They settled comfortably face to face, Briers hand encompassing both hot hard pricks, Miles sliding a hand under Briers' waist to get a good grip on his arse. A moment's stillness while they studied each other, then they moved, kissing and sighing as their touches, their closeness, increased their pleasure. Briers turned onto his back, carrying Miles with him. He pressed down, one large hand in the small of Miles' back while he thrust up against him, and Miles kissed him, grinding their mouths together, gasping at the harsh rasp of stubble against his lips. He drew back to see that Briers' mouth was red and roughened as well, then very deliberately ran his chin across his collar bones.

"Ah, you rat bag." Briers slapped him sharply on the arse then grabbed his head to take control of an even stronger kiss. They rolled again, back onto Miles' side of the bed, and Briers settled on top of him with a deep groan of pleasure. They took their time, but after a while, once Miles' heart was racing and his breath had grown harsh, Briers stilled and propped up on one elbow. Miles looked up at him with a frown.

"What's the matter?" he asked. "Why did you stop?"

"Because when I said I wanted you, this wasn't quite what I meant." Briers smiled, lopsided and rueful. "I really want to fuck you Miles, but – well, after what happened last night, I'm afraid it might be asking too much."

Miles stared at him and Briers shrugged. "There aren't many people I won't lie to, but I won't lie to you, not about this. I'm happy to carry on with what we've been doing, but I would really like to do the other and I think we could both have a good time with it, but I have noticed the way you've fended me off. Does the idea of it appal you? I hope you'd enjoy it – not everyone does – but … ah, Miles, I'd take care to make it good for you."

As Briers was speaking, Miles had been considering. The act itself didn't appeal and he knew he could say no and they would carry on in the usual sweet way, then on Monday they would most probably part. Depending on how successful Naylor had been about rounding up Andrija and his minions, and Miles wished them every success, Briers might be sent back to Belgrade. Miles would be sent back to the cipher rooms and this strange but sweet interlude would be over.

"I'd regret never having tried," he said, "but … Briers, it's a bit daunting."

Briers' expression was grave as he said, "We can stop – if you don't like it, I mean. I'm not a total slave to lust, you know."

"I know." Miles licked his lips and ran his fingers down through Brier's chest hair to give his nipple a gentle pinch. "I trust you," he added "but I can't promise not to swear a bit if it smarts."

"Fair enough," Briers said, "though if I have my way –"

"Your evil way."

"Yes, my evil way with you, you won't even notice."

Miles wouldn't have believed how quickly he was reduced to squirming and even giggling. There were practicalities to be observed that Briers described in the most comical terms, then supervised in a matter-of-fact way that robbed the situation of its potential to be embarrassing. The trip to the chilly bathroom was succeeded by a return to bed, still warm, where the tin of Vaseline Miles kept for more prosaic uses was pressed into service. Briers kept up a commentary on what he was doing and Miles' wary cooperation that Miles found both distracting and arousing.

"So, why have you never tried before?" Briers asked, the teasing press of his fingers making Miles' breath catch.

"When I was with Tommy, it never occurred to us," he admitted. "Friendly touches became loving ones. Neither of us knew what we were about, just that it was terribly wrong and must be kept secret. What we did with our hands and mouths worked for us. Then, after Tommy left, and I looked around for a new friend, I found – I don't know – it was expected of me. As though someone who looked like I do couldn't possibly be good for anything else."

Briers gave an annoyed grunt. "You don't think I feel like that about you, do you?"

"Well," Miles grinned at him. "Maybe just a bit at first. I'm finding it hard to imagine you letting me do this to you."

"Hah, that just goes to show what you know. You can have a turn later. Fair's fair. Right, let's give this a try."

A new position, on his side, knees folded to his chest. Briers spooned tight behind him. Miles reached back to put his hand on Briers flank and pat, then they both flinched – Miles at the discomfort of the intrusion, Briers as Miles' hand clenched.

"Ow," they both said.

"Not ready yet, then." Briers chuckled. "No matter. That means I can do this."

Miles laughed as he was flipped over onto his belly, hoisted up into what was, frankly, a ridiculous position and when he complained of the cold, a 'tent' was made to accommodate them both. It wasn't the best of tents; there were gaps letting in tendrils of cold air and two little triangles of pale grey morning light. Miles peered between his spread knees. There was Briers, or rather his legs and belly and the impressive prick that, Miles gulped, would soon be pressing its way into him. He wanted to try, no doubt there, but it looked big and one couldn't help but worry. Then all that fled his mind as he felt the rasp of Briers' stubble in the small of his back and the first of the most intimate kisses he had ever received. Miles rested his forehead on his wrists and tried to remember to breathe. He needed his breath because, try as he might, he couldn't be silent. Sighs became moans, and moans became gasps of approval.

"Better?" Briers asked at one point.

"Oh God, yes."

"Let's try this then."

The second attempt, made with Miles on his back with his ankles on Briers' shoulders, was far more satisfactory. Yes, it felt odd, a little uncomfortable at first, but the tense stretched feeling soon eased into one of pleasure.

"Better?" Briers asked again. His face was screwed up with concentration – they had long since lost the bed-covers – but he smiled when Miles nodded.

"Better. And I like that I can see you," Miles admitted.

Briers nodded and leaned down to kiss Miles then glanced around the room. "Do you hear much from the other tenants? Voices, movement?"

"The people upstairs are out of the country." Miles grinned. "Major Leach, on the ground floor, is Artillery so we don't have to worry about him."

"Good," Briers said. "Because I had more than enough of being quiet in Albert Road."

After that, it all went rather well. Briers moved carefully until Miles discovered he wanted to move, too, then they went at it like the Guards marching double time. The bed head thundered against the wall. Pillows went flying. Miles was delighted to discover his own ecstatic shouts were actually in a lower register than Briers', who seemed inclined to yelp in extremis. Either way it was a huge relief not to have to hold back. Their final yells as the pleasure peaked, made the windows rattle in their frames.

"Well, that got the job done," Briers said. He sounded pleased. Miles' eyes were closed. Sprawled in a puddle of their own making he wasn't sure he would ever have the energy to open them again. The mattress shifted and Briers grunted then dropped something damp over Miles' belly.

"That's my towel," he said. "Yours is over the foot of the bed."

"You don't expect me to move, do you?"

"We'll be sleeping on a soggy mattress tonight if you don't. Go on, lad. You're sticky from arse to tit."

Miles groaned and sat up to grab the dry towel from the foot of the bed.

He *was* sticky from, as his lover had put it, arse to tit. In fact, arse to chin. He dabbed at himself and the bed, dabbed at Briers, spread the dry towel across the rumpled and wrecked sheets and got back into bed, spreading the blankets and eiderdown over them both.

"That's better," he smiled as Briers' arm closed around him. "More sleep? You don't have to be anywhere, do you?"

"Just for a bit. There's somewhere I need to go where I hope there might be a message for me. It would be handy to have before Monday." Briers' arm tightened and Miles wondered if he was as distressed at the thought of their parting as Miles was. Not that one could ever show it, of course. It would be unfair, and coercive.

"Once you've collected it, perhaps we could meet somewhere?" Miles kept his voice as even as possible.

Briers chuckled and gave him a tight squeeze then turned his head to nuzzle the top of Mile's head. "All my baggage is here and, if you've no objection, I would like to stay. But Monday, I'm betting they'll want me on the first train back to Belgrade. I – I've enjoyed working with you, Miles."

Miles sighed. "And I with you. So tonight we'll make a party of it. I'll ring Fortnums and get them to send champagne and oysters."

"Lots of oysters, and maybe a restorative draught. Don't forget, we had a deal."

Miles laughed and flung his arm across Briers' chest, hitching up to look him in the face. "Scared I'll wear you out?" he asked.

Briers snorted by way of reply and hooked his hand around the back of Miles' neck to pull him down to kiss him. Soft tender kisses as Briers' hands smoothed down his back in a caress made Miles' insides clench with remembered pleasure.

"Good morning, sir, or rather sirs."

Not the best position to be in as the bedroom door opened. But not – oh dear God – not the worst.

They didn't have a chance to spring apart with a guilty mutter of, 'This isn't what you think'. And what would have been the point when it so clearly was? Briers went rigid, apprehension clear in his expression. Miles caught his eye, gave him as reassuring a smile as he could manage and turned to face his manservant.

Pritchard placed a tray with Miles' morning tea on the bedside cabinet.

There was another cup beside it – from the smell, a very fine brew of Arabica. He stooped to plump the pillows. "I have brought in your mail, sir, also a message that was delivered about half an hour ago. I refused to allow the boy into the house to deliver it in person and he gave in far too easily. Not very good security."

Pritchard gave them both an affable nod, his expression the usual bland and serene mask, but there was a distinct glint in his eye.

Miles sat back against the pillows, knowing he was pink with embarrassment from head to foot, but determined to pass the morning off as normal. "Thank you Pritchard," he said. "I – um – how did you know I – we were back?"

"I spotted the light on in the bathroom, sir." Pritchard went to the window to draw back the curtains, flooding the room with sere November sunlight. "Ronald had one of his turns and I was making him camomile tea. I have a good view of your rooms from my kitchen."

"Ah, I hope Ronald is feeling better." Miles accepted his tea.

"On the mend, thank you for enquiring, sir. It's my belief that it wasn't actually a 'turn', sir, but a bad pie. The theatrical crowd keep such irregular hours that he grabs a bite where he can." He offered Briers his cup too. "Shall I run your bath, now, sir?"

"Yes please, Pritchard and," Miles took a deep breath, "breakfast for two. I don't suppose you have kippers?"

"Unfortunately not, sir, but I can get some in for tomorrow." Pritchard placed the package of mail on the blankets over Miles' lap. "And how does Mr Allerdale like his eggs?"

Briers cleared his throat. "Side-by-side, please, Pritchard."

Pritchard's lips twitched. "Of course, sir, very good, sir. Bath in ten minutes, breakfast in twenty," he said and left the room.

"Well – bugger me," Briers said once the door was closed.

"Do you think there's time?" Miles asked, his cup rattling on its saucer. He put it down hurriedly. A great bubble of hysteria was welling up inside and he was finding it hard to breathe. "Because when Pritchard says ten minutes, he means ten minutes."

"Naaah, let's save it for later," Briers said his voice breaking on the last word as his control cracked. He set his coffee aside, shoulders quivering, then fell back against the pillows, gasping with laughter. "Oh God. Your *face*," he managed after a moment.

"Should have seen yours." Miles put both hands over his mouth to stifle his howls at the sight of Briers, face down, fists clenched on a muffling pillow.

It was a few minutes before they could be sensible. Sitting back against expertly plumped pillows, fine bone china brimming with their preferred drinks in their hands, mouths red with kisses, cheeks roughened with stubble burn, and still quite sticky in places – and Miles couldn't help but laugh again.

"Pritchard is a treasure." Briers sipped the coffee and gave a grunt of approval. "It's my considered opinion, Miles, that you don't pay him enough."

"Probably not," Miles agreed. "On the other hand, Pritchard has the old coachman's cottage in the mews. Ronald moved in with him almost immediately. Like Pritchard, he's ex-Monmouthshire Regiment. He's a dresser at the Palladium. Having seen them together, I've *wondered* but one can never actually *ask*, can one? I enquire after Ronald's health when it's appropriate, but otherwise I've accepted that Ronald is Pritchard's old army comrade and they are living together to make ends meet."

"Nicely put." Briers grinned. "I don't think you need to worry about Pritchard turning up with the police in tow. He has too much to lose."

Tea finished, Miles put his cup aside and picked up the message. "Ah, it's addressed to you. So that's how he knew."

"Miles," Briers said, taking the envelope from him, "if he was in the flat half an hour ago, all he'd have to do was listen. The interior walls aren't that thick and I seem to remember you shouting as though you were on a touch line."

"I seem to remember I had good cause. And you weren't exactly quiet either." Miles sorted through the rest of the mail. "While you're about town, I think I'll go and see Crane. Are you going to take the Austin?"

"No ... the Tube." Briers' voice was distracted. "Naylor says the farm was deserted, signs of hasty clearing out. But they did notice traces of movement between the farmhouse and the creek, so they investigated and found Béla and the body of an unknown woman." He read on, making a sound of disgust. "She'd been there a while, poor girl. From baggage and clothing in a back room, the assumption is that she was the Crane's

125

previous maid, the one Josephine replaced. The car was still in the ditch. It was a Daimler stolen last month in Muswell Hill so you did well to keep ahead of it. No sign of Andrija or any known associates."

Miles paused in opening a letter from his mother. "You know, I really felt off about having – having killed Béla like that, but now I do feel it was justified."

"It was justified, believe you me. Naylor also says the house in Millbank was still showing signs of activity last night, so they raided it. They picked up half a dozen workmen as they left the premises, all local men who had been hired, they said, to clear rubble from the demolitions and to shore up a damaged drain. They are helping with enquiries. Again, no sign of Andrija, though some of the workmen claimed their boss had only just left when the police went in." Briers tapped the paper on his knee then sat up and got off the bed. "I need to get to that letterbox." He stretched, ran his hands through his hair and looked down at Miles with deep sigh of satisfaction.

"You look debauched," he said. "I feel proud. Do you mind if I bathe first? Once I've had my coffee, I like to be up and doing."

"Certainly. My dressing gown is on the back of the door." Miles smiled. "While you're bathing, I've got to catch up on my correspondence – Mother has written five pages instead of her usual three. Something earth-shaking must have happened."

"In Bucharest? Dear Lord, I hope not." Briers shrugged into the robe and left the room. A moment later, Miles heard his cheery greeting to Pritchard. He smiled, put down the letters and lay back to revel in feeling debauched.

Chapter Fifteen

Breakfast was a cheerful affair. The bread could have been fresher but it had toasted well enough. It was served firstly with buttered eggs that were tangy with Worcestershire Sauce, then with butter and Dundee marmalade. The coffee, of course, was excellent and Pritchard kept it coming. He had even found time to sponge Briers' suit and press out the worst creases. But, Briers mused, maybe he was in practice? For all Briers knew, it might be a regular occurrence for him to enter his master's bedroom to find him *in flagrante*. Briers doubted it. Miles seemed too self-controlled and far too nervous, but Briers had been wrong before.

Once they had finished eating, Pritchard made a discreet exit to the kitchen leaving Miles and Briers to get ready for their day.

"I'm not sure I'm going to be able to meet you for lunch," Briers said. "If there's a message for me, I may have to follow it up. But I'll make sure to keep our evening free. Shall I come straight back here or shall we arrange to meet somewhere?"

Miles grinned. "I'm guessing you haven't got evening wear with you and I don't have anything you could borrow. How about I try to get something from George? He's pretty much your height and size. We could go to the Savoy?"

"Savoy? Great idea. I'll be back around six, then, to change."

"And if George hasn't got anything suitable, we could go to the Criterion again," Miles suggested. "We could have a couple of cocktails then come back here for dinner."

"Excellent. If I think I might be late, I'll let Pritchard know. There's no keeping to a schedule in this job. But I'm looking forward to those oysters you promised me." Briers folded his napkin, placed it on his plate and got up. "The sooner I go, the sooner I can get back. Thanks, Miles, that was a terrific breakfast."

"I'll tell Pritchard," Miles promised. He got up too and followed Briers to the coat rack, taking down Brier's coat for him and holding it while he slipped his arms into the sleeves. Millie had done that, Briers remembered, and was hit by a rush of affection for Miles that had nothing at all to do with his enthusiasm in bed. Saying goodbye was going to be hard.

"Are you leaving, sir?" Pritchard appeared, Briers' hat freshly brushed and looking as good as new in his hands.

"Yes. Thank you, Pritchard," Briers said, taking the hat. "I – um – will see you later, Siward. Give my regards to Crane."

For one moment, as Briers opened the door and looked back, he caught a wistful look on Miles' face. As though he would have liked more than a cheery grin and a promise of pleasure later. As though he felt it wouldn't have hurt Briers to go back and give him a kiss goodbye, much as Brian Carstairs had given Millie on the mornings when they had known themselves to be observed. Briers wished he had kissed Miles. He had wanted to, but Pritchard's presence, benign though it seemed to be, had unnerved him.

Briers promised himself to do better next time as he hopped onto a bus and paid his penny, then settled in his seat to review some of the choicer aspects of the morning. He particularly enjoyed the recollection of the shocked yelp Miles had given as Briers' tongue had breached him for the first time, and the moans that had followed it. Briers was looking forward to hearing the combination of sounds again, and possibly even making some himself. Siward had a wicked tongue.

Recalling that morning's fun saw him from bus to Tube, and then a fast walk along to the Grange Road baths where he hoped he might find a message from Falk. There was an envelope confirming Falk was back in London and the trip to Lowestoft had not borne fruit. Briers dashed off a quick reply and asked if there was a chance it might be delivered. The housekeeper shrugged and promised to see what he could do, and suggested Briers might like to use the facilities. Breathing in the peculiar mixture of carbolic, sweat and arousal, Briers decided he might as well benefit from some time in the steam room. He had muscles that ached pleasantly – though probably not as much as Miles' did – and asked for a masseur to attend him while he waited.

The masseur had hands like shovels but was deft enough, and Briers lay back and enjoyed the pummelling until he heard a murmured request, the chink of coin and the large hands were replaced by smaller, colder ones.

"Not looking for company, thank you," Briers said as they swooped down his spine to fasten on his buttocks.

"Not even me?" Falk was grinning when Briers turned over to look up at him. "Ah, I see why. That is a very impressive bite mark." He pressed a fingertip to one of the reddish stains close to Briers' left nipple.

"I thought so myself," Briers said, smacking his hand away. "I was going to leave you a message if you didn't turn up. Most of the rest of the gang are out of the picture but Andrija is still on the loose. If you see him before I do, have at it. Enjoy yourself. Nemanja, too."

"I'm not going to do your job for you," Falk said. "Not unless you provide me with a lot more incentive than a feast for the eyes."

Briers inspected his old lover with nostalgic stirrings of lust, then shook his head. "Not today, Falk. Frankly I'm whacked. It's been a rough couple of days and this morning I took my mind off it in the best possible way."

Falk grinned. "The wife's a bit of a goer, is she? Oh, it's not the new partner? You never persuaded him to roll over for you? Is he wandering around this morning in a happy daze with a newly plucked green carnation up his arse?"

"None of your business." Briers' grin was equally broad and equally insincere as he turned back onto his belly. "And don't spoil a beautiful memory with any more of your salacious imaginings – though I'll admit the idea about the carnation is appealing. Come on, Falk. Doesn't the thought of putting a bullet into Andrija get the juices flowing?"

"Right now, I'd sooner be putting something else into you." Falk's tone and expression were peevish rather than seductive so Briers knew his point had been made. After a moment, Falk's cool hands smoothed up his spine to knead the tops of his shoulders. "Just so I have something interesting for my next letter home," Falk said, "is there any truth in the reports of gunfire in a rural area not far from the coast? My grapevine is cropping rumours like you wouldn't believe. Anything to do with you?"

"I believe connections of Andrija were involved but the perpetrators were civilians, at least one of whom had been in the Great War and knew his way around a Thompson gun."

"Ah, yes, and a happy Saturday to you too." Falk's thumb dug into a spot on Briers' shoulder that he must have known was tender. "I presume you were miles away with witnesses to prove it. How's the little woman?"

Briers glanced at the wedding ring and smiled as he recalled Miles' ecstatic moans. "As well as can be expected under the circumstances."

"Does she know what a flaming queen she has married?"

"No." Briers chuckled. He had been called a lot of things but a queen was not one of them.

"Just as well, poor dear." Falk patted his shoulder and moved down to work on Briers' calves. "Andrija," he said after a minute or two of strenuous massaging that actually felt pretty good. "And Nemanja. Did you manage to account for the woman, Josephine?"

"No." Briers scowled. "We lost track of her too. She was last seen with Andrija and we're hoping to get her when we get him."

"You have to admire her – she is equally dangerous and twice as slippery. I'll see to her for you, too, out of the goodness of my heart."

"I'd appreciate that." Falk's hands were moving up Briers' thighs now and he decided enough was enough. "Excuse me," he said and sat up, draping his towel across his lap. "I'd better go. I'm booked in at the barbers then I have a dinner date."

"So you genuinely feel the danger is over?" Falk folded his arms and gave Brier a look of such disbelief it stung.

"Of course not. Not while Andrija is still breathing. But the majority of his men are under wraps, Béla is dead –"

"Hip hip hoorah," Falk interrupted. "I bet you enjoyed that."

"Not my handiwork, my partner's and, no, I don't think he did enjoy it much."

"He'll soon get a taste for it." Falk smiled. "Go on, you were telling me state secrets."

"I was telling you I need to get moving." Briers stood up. "And, I suppose, goodbye. I imagine I'll be sent back to my station within the next few days."

"Ah." Falk nodded then extended a hand. "We'll meet again. I'll see to it. And next time, may we both be free of encumbrances."

Briers shook his hand then laughed and tugged Falk into a brief embrace. "Keep your head down and your nose clean," he suggested.

"Oh Briers," Falk chuckled and pushed him away, "where's the fun in that? Go and get your hair cut and I'll see you in Belgrade."

Briers left the barbers with a distinct feeling of a good job well done, though in other respects, he was aware things were far from ideal. Andrija was still at large and that meant he was a threat. No matter how blithely the powers that be dismissed the threat, Briers knew Andrija would be trouble, always, somewhere down the line. Until he heard from Falk that the man had been neutralised, or better still had done it himself, he would not rest completely easy. However, the prospect of spending the rest of the day with Miles raised his spirits. And the thought of the night to come raised something else. He strode along the street, hopped on a trolleybus, paid his pennies and settled against a window with a grunt of satisfaction.

Travelling by trolleybus was a pleasure. Not as noisy as a petrol-driven bus and rather more comfortable, there was the added bonus of occasional showers of sparks as the gantry bounced over the connection in the electric lines. They were faster, too, since vehicles moved off the rails at the sound of the driver's bell. But today, there was some congestion and the bus slowed.

"What's the problem?" Briers asked, peering ahead to where the road seemed to be clogged with traffic.

"Just some road works sir," the conductor said. "Blimmin' Water Board. They've got the road up all along the Strand."

"Water Board?" Briers stared at the man. "Has this been going on long?"

The conductor shrugged. "Gotta be done though, innit? All the damage last winter. If it's a wet one this year, we'll all be knee deep and I don't mean in good old Father Thames, either. My brother-in-law works down the sewers. He says they can get from Ealing to Bow without ever coming up in the sunshine. It's just the worse bits where they have to open up the road. Them sewers been there since Roman times, he says."

"Sewers." Briers scrambled out of his seat, his memory filled with the stench coming off Béla's clothing. "Goddammit, the sewers!"

"Hang on, pal," the conductor hissed. "Ladies present."

"My apologies," Briers said and fled, jumping off the back of the trolley and hurrying through the almost stationary vehicles to reach the nearest work site.

It was Saturday, of course, so little work was actually being done. Three men in mud-caked overalls were standing watching a forth who was settling a metal manhole cover back into place.

"About done for the day, gents?" Briers asked.

They gave him the wary glances of men who suspected he might be authority in disguise, so Briers gave them a cheerful drunken grin and swayed a bit.

"It's past noon," one said. "An' it's starting to rain. Can't work safely down there in the rain."

"No?" Briers peered at the cover. "My mate, Charlie, reckons a good tosher can get from one side of the city to the other without coming up top if he knows his stuff. A man could use the sewers to get away from the coppers if he needed to."

They snorted and the same man replied, "Of course we could. But you need to know the safe places. Some dirty tea leaf would get lost, maybe drownded."

"Unless he had the plans," Briers suggested. After some grudging nods, the spokesman agreed it could be the case.

"Gentlemen." Briers dropped a half crown into the willing hand of the spokesman. "Have one on me."

"Thanks, mate. You're a toff."

"No, I'm not," Briers said as he hailed a cab. "But I think I know where I might find one."

As he hoped, Miles had gone to visit Crane in hospital. Crane was sitting up in bed, head bandaged and his expression surly. Miles looked to Briers as though he was rattled but determined not to show it, and his smile as Briers entered the room had quite a lot of relief in it.

"Carstairs," Crane said. "I can't believe it. Is what – er – Siward's saying true? Have I really helped to foil some kind of anarchist plot?"

"I hope so," Briers said, "but I have new information. Crane, what can you tell me about sewers?"

"Sewers?" Crane's surly expression faded as he sat up a bit further in his bed. "How long have you got? It's not a small subject."

"Sewers." Miles stared at Briers. "Do you thinking we've been barking up the wrong tree?"

"I don't know, but Crane here might be able to help. Am I right in thinking one could use the sewers to get to just about anywhere if one knows the right route to take?"

"Oh lor'!" Crane put his hand over his eyes. "My maps. I have maps at home. It was a hobby. I'd been involved in a scheme to replace some of the oldest drains with new more efficient modern piping, but the plans were so scrappy and out of date I began to draw new ones and – well, a job like that's only worth doing if you do all of it. I've got plans at home showing all the systems from the Roman cloaca onwards."

"Including the parts no longer in use?" Briers sat on the end of the bed.

"Well, yes. I felt it would save time when excavating if we knew what was down there already." Crane's eyes lit up with enthusiasm. "I know it's a subject some find distasteful but so necessary to the health and well-being of the city. And you think those horrible people may be using the sewers? To do what?"

"We don't know," Miles admitted. "We do know where they may have entered the system. Some flood damaged houses off Page Street in Millbank. We thought at first it was merely a hideout, but if Carstairs is right and they are using them for access, where could they go?"

"From Page Street?" Crane frowned. "From there, one could get to Buckingham Palace, though I believe the protection there is top notch. Likewise Downing Street. Whitehall. Westminster Abbey is a hop and a skip."

"King Charles Street?" Miles tilted his head. "It's only a little further."

Crane frowned. "That's the Foreign Office. Is there something going on there?"

"Not until the fifteenth," Briers said. "And it's the tenth today. We have five more days to find them and put a stop to whatever they have planned."

"Then you'll need maps," Crane said, and rang for a nurse.

Chapter Sixteen

"You do appreciate that one cannot take chances with head injuries?" Crane's doctor looked Miles and Briers over with obvious disapproval as though scared they would lead his patient astray. "In my opinion, Mr Crane, you should remain here until Monday."

"We'll ensure he gets home safely," Miles promised. "We have a vehicle outside."

"I do intend to follow your advice, Doctor." Crane was already dressing with Briers' help. "But I cannot help these gentlemen from my bed."

"If you insist this is an urgent matter, I suppose I must give in. However, I must insist that afterwards you go straight home. Bed rest for two days at a minimum and make an appointment for your own doctor to attend you on Monday. He'll need to check you over."

"First thing on Monday morning." Crane reached for his coat, ignoring Miles' offer to hold it for him.

That Crane seemed so standoffish with him was no more than he had expected. He didn't blame the man, but regretted it. Sidney Crane had appealed to Miles as a decent sort. His quiet pride in his work, his family and home exemplified what Miles' work was all about. Those hours in the cipher rooms, the weeks spent sifting through foreign newspapers, telegrams, letters and private files obtained in strange and probably illegal ways, were all designed to keep the Cranes safe and enable them to live their lives in peace.

The dirty tricks used to maintain the peace should be a secret. The Cranes of the world should never know the things people like Briers and Miles were prepared to do to keep ahead of the enemy. And if they found out, especially in as shocking a way as Crane had, they were bound to feel disturbed and threatened and as though their trust had been abused. The silence in the car was tangible and it wasn't until Briers asked a direct question about Crane's son that the atmosphere thawed. Miles drove on, asking for directions when necessary, and left the conversation to the men.

Even on a Saturday, the nation needed water so the offices of the Water Board were staffed.

"Crane. Your face!" The man Crane had called from a back room shoved out a hand in greeting and gave him a concerned smile. "What the hell happened to you? And who are your friends?"

"No time for introductions, Johnson." Crane shook Johnson's hand. "I need to get into the plan room."

"The plan room?" Johnson looked Miles and Briers over with as much distrust as the doctor.

"The key, if you please." Crane lowered his voice. "This is a matter of extreme urgency. Please. We will be saving lives."

"I'm not sure I like the sound of this, Crane." Johnson scowled but led them back into the depths of the building and down two flights of stairs. He unlocked doors as he went. "Which plans do you need?"

"Sewerage," Crane replied, fidgeting as Johnson selected yet another key from his bunch. "I need the central London plan, but I'm hoping there's still a copy of the one I made with the additional notations."

"Finally going to come in useful, eh?" Johnson opened the door and flicked on the electric light. Miles looked around in interest. The room was long and low, the ceiling supported by buttresses of whitewashed brick. All along both walls were stacks of plan chests, reducing the space in between to a narrow walkway on either side of the slanting drawing tables.

"You know where to go." Johnson jingled the keys. "I need to get back upstairs. Don't take anything away with you and please let me know when you're done so I can lock up again."

"Thanks, Johnson," Crane said, already on his way down the stacks.

The plan was where Crane had left it. Miles could see how proud the man was of it in the careful way he unrolled it across the table.

"I'm so glad I made this," he muttered as he clipped it in place. "The black printed lines show our current sewers. The unbroken blue, green and red lines show antiquated systems that exist but are not in use. Broken lines show where they once existed but have been filled in. As you can see, some of the outfalls are very ancient. The Romans built to last."

"We're still using Roman sewers?" Miles asked.

"They handled excess run off from storm drains mostly but, yes, they are there."

"If this scale's right, some of these pipes are huge." Briers traced one with a finger. "You could drive a tank along this one."

"You could," Crane agreed with a smile, "but there's no access. Now the area you're interested in is here. Millbank. The sewers were terribly damaged in the floods. Clogged with debris and some collapsed due to the pressure of the water stripping out the old linings. Teams have been in there, assessing the damage and making repairs on the usable parts. Some of the blocks will be cleared and new systems put in place. I assume that's where your – um – enemies have been gaining access to the system."

"Yes." Briers' finger stabbed the paper. "And look, from here they could get right into the heart of the City. Can we make a copy?"

"I see no reason why not. There are materials in the cupboards at the far end of the room. They may be locked … Oh I say!"

"We will pay for a new lock," Miles promised as Briers lowered the draughtsman's stool with which he had smashed the padlock. "Now will you draw it or will I?"

With the copy accomplished and carefully rolled, Briers and Miles accompanied Crane back to the desk and returned the keys to Johnson, then left the building.

"Well, I suppose I should be getting home," Crane said. "I'll get a cab. You two have work to do."

"Nonsense. Siward will give you a lift, won't you, Siward?" Briers smiled at them both.

"Well, of course." Miles frowned. "But where will I meet you?"

"I'll leave a message with your man. Crane, would you give us a moment, please, old chap?"

As soon as Crane was out of earshot Briers caught Miles by the arm. "Give me the map," he said. "I'm going to take it to Naylor. I need you to go home and wait for me. This is not your fight, Miles."

"Not my fight?" Miles stared at Briers, moving the map out of arm's reach. "In what context? Just what have I been doing the past months?"

"You've been observing, and you have been admirable, but this is a task for which you are not qualified." Briers' hand on his biceps had closed to the point of discomfort. "Yes, I know you are the one who prevented Béla from cutting my throat but you were lucky. Beginner's luck. Béla was expecting a terrified housewife. Instead he got Millie. Even so, what we will be doing tonight is killing work, pure and simple, and I do not believe even Millie could do that – not in cold blood."

Confusion silenced Miles' protests. He did not know whether to be hurt or furious. It must have shown on his face because Briers grimaced and gave his arm a little shake.

"Come on," he said. "You've been a Trojan, Miles, but tonight I'm going to be too busy watching out for Andrija to watch out for you and that worries me. You'd be vulnerable, and it would prey on my mind so you must stay away. Miles? Look at me. You know it makes sense."

It did – a horrible cold kind of sense that took no account of feelings, of the desire to help, of his need to be near Briers and guard him to the best of his ability. Miles knew Briers had a point but that didn't make it any easier to bear. He pushed the rolled map into Briers' hand and tugged his arm free.

"Go on then," he said, hearing and hating the sharpness in his voice. "Go and be heroic. You'll know where to find me if you come back."

Briers blew out his cheeks and shook his head. "I'm not trying to – to belittle what you've done. It's a different job. You don't get a plumber in to hang wallpaper, that's all. You have your specialisation and I have mine." His tone was firm but Miles could see the sympathy in his eyes. "I promise I'll be back. Champagne and oysters – remember? Even if it's at three ack emma."

"Even if it's late." Miles put his hands in his pockets and nodded. "Oh Lord, all right. I'll keep them on ice. Oh, here." He offered Briers his house keys. "You can let yourself in."

Briers pocketed the keys with a grin. "I'll look forward to it."

They parted – Briers to take a cab to Broadway House, Miles to drive Crane home – without so much as a shake of the hand or a slap on the shoulder. Miles reflected that, had she been there, Millie would have demanded her due. The kiss in the street outside the Dorchester was one of his most cherished memories and then they had only been briefly parted with no danger in sight. Now they exchanged terse goodbyes and Briers hailed a cab without a backward glance. Miles didn't look back either. He headed for his car with a purposeful stride and jumped in, nodding to Crane.

"Soon have you home," he said. "Warm enough? There's a greatcoat on the back seat."

As he expected, Crane did not seem in the mood for conversation. He was brooding, his elbow on the car door, chin in hand, wincing at the sound of the engine. Miles drove with extra care, trying not to jolt him, and tried to convince himself that Briers was right. What did Miles know about combat? All George had told him was that it was something to be avoided, but something in his face had made the warning doubly imperative. To fight, to kill, seemed a poor way of resolving differences. A boorish way. So much better to be forewarned and nip any signs of aggression in the bud with the careful leverage of diplomacy. But what if the other party was intent upon a war? Sometimes one had to pick up a gun.

Elsie must have been watching from the front window because she was opening the car door and reaching inside to embrace her husband even before Miles had cut the engine.

"Oh, Sidney," she was sobbing. "I thought I'd never see you again."

At Crane's invitation, Miles followed them into the house, and stood in the hall, cap in hand, while Elsie cried on Crane's shoulder and the baby wailed in the parlour.

"Now, my dear," Crane said after he had assured her he was not much hurt and that he was pleased to be home. "It sounds to me as though William needs changing and I'm sure Siward here would like a cup of tea as much as I would. Perhaps you could deal with those two things. I need a word with Siward before he leaves."

"Oh, oh yes," Elsie dried her eyes and headed for her child.

"In here," Crane said once the door had closed behind her. He ushered Miles into the study and closed the door. "On the way here, I was thinking about the map we've just made and it occurred to me it might not be complete. I made several versions, you see, as new material became available. If you don't mind, I'd like to reassure myself. Please, take a seat."

"I don't mind at all." Miles watched him rummage through the rolls of paper stored upright in a cast iron umbrella stand. "Though I wouldn't be surprised if you find the one you want is missing. It's pretty clear that while it was assumed Josephine was monitoring the Foreign Office fellow down the street, she was actually after your information on the sewer system. If we had realised earlier, we'd have saved you and your family a lot of worry."

"How would one guess?" Crane flicked the last of the maps and sighed.

"Such minds – ones that plan to maim and kill – are unfathomable to me. You're right, there's one missing. The final version with all the information collated but …" he held up his hand to prevent Miles from speaking, "I have copies. They are a bit rough with lots of my notes but legible."

The box file, once he had found it, was bulging and had the lid tied down with string. It was not the place that Miles would have looked for large scale maps, but it proved to be stuffed with folded sheets of onion skin paper. Crane dug out half the pile and handed them to Miles.

"They are out of order," he said. "I meant to file them properly but never got round to it. There should be dates on the outside of each packet. I think the ones we need are late nineteen twenty-two. Or maybe three?"

Miles left Crane at the desk and knelt to sort the stack of papers by year. "How many years were you working on this? You must have drawn the whole of the city."

"Pretty much, and in many different scales," Crane said. His tone had warmed a little now he was discussing his enthusiasm. "There are constant revisions. Ah, this one might be useful." He opened one sheet, the paper translucent gold in the gas light, and peered at the fine lines. "Lots of government buildings. King Charles Street. Whitehall. We had to buttress a couple of the sewers when they built the Cenotaph. The weight of marble on those old tunnels could have caused a cave in."

"And that would never have done," Miles said with a chuckle. "Just imagine …" His voice tailed off and he sat back on his heels.

"Imagine what?" Crane asked as he folded the paper to set it aside.

"Imagine the distress, the fear," Miles murmured. "Imagine the King, the Prime Minister, the leader of the opposition, ambassadors of friendly nations, all the heads of the armed forces, all disappearing into the depths as that monument to death falls to rubble."

"Tomorrow." Crane stared at him. "It's tomorrow. Eleventh November. Armistice Day. It's – it's the tenth anniversary."

"Oh dear God," Miles whispered. "Surely not. Surely they wouldn't."

They spread the sheet out on the desk and Miles fished his glasses out of his pocket to peer at it. "Here," he said, pointing. "And here. There would be room to pack in explosives and not obstruct the flow of the sewage."

"And here's a route one could take to get to them from Millbank."

Crane's finger traced another line. "And away again. There are access points every few hundred yards all the way to the Thames."

"Crane, dear chap," Miles said. "I'm going to have to ask to borrow this map."

"Of course, of course," Crane folded it briskly and slid it into a Manila folder.

"One further favour," Miles asked as he slipped the folder into his pocket. "Could you telephone and ask for this number," he scribbled it on Crane's blotter, "and ask to speak to Charles Naylor on Miles Siward's behalf. Tell him what we've found and say I'm on my way."

"Certainly." Crane accompanied him back into the hall and Miles reached up to remove his specs just as Elsie opened the parlour door. She stared at him.

"Millie?" she faltered.

"Ah, yes, Mrs Crane." Miles smiled at her. "Well spotted."

"But you were living at Mrs Merrill's – with that man." She took a deep breath. "Sidney Crane! How *dare* you bring such a person into our home?"

It felt like being slapped. Miles folded his spectacles and slipped them into the breast pocket of his jacket. "Thank you for your help, Crane," he said over Elsie's strident demands that he leave. "We owe you our thanks."

"Your thanks?" Elsie shrieked. "You almost got him killed. And you and that – other person dared to take tea in our house. Good grief, you touched my child! Get out or I'm going to ring the police."

"I think you had better leave." Crane opened the front door. "She's a bit overwrought, as you may probably imagine. All the waiting around for news. And while I understand that you did what you felt you had to …"

"Which do you mean?" Miles was aware his voice was sharp with anger but didn't seem to be able to moderate his tone. "Do you object to the fact that I killed a man to save all of our lives? Or that I wore a frock for a couple of weeks? Both were necessary."

Crane's bruised face flushed a deep and embarrassed red. "I would prefer not to discuss this deeply distasteful subject, especially in front of my wife and child. You have the information you need, so go."

Elsie's shrieks redoubled as the door closed behind Miles. Heart thumping, he paused on the steps for a moment to regain his temper then hurried to the car.

"Well, what did you expect?" It took two goes to get the engine started. "Elsie is a classic *News of the World* reader. She's bound to over react. Empty-headed, fluff-for-brains idiot."

Suspecting Crane might have his hands too full with Elsie's hysteria to make the call to Naylor, Miles stopped at the nearest call box and paid his penny to be connected. The duty officer seemed very disinclined to take the call seriously until Miles mentioned Naylor, and even then he just expressed regret that Mr Naylor was not available to take calls.

"This is very important," Miles pressed on. "Is there anyone else I can speak to? It's to do with – with Andrija."

There was a short silence then the man said, "If you will hold on a moment, sir."

Miles ground his teeth and checked his change – he only had one penny left – however, he was not kept waiting for long.

"Siward, I'm afraid Mr Naylor is out in the field. We have no idea when he will be back. I suggest you come in to the office."

"Very well," Miles said, hoping Naylor would be there when he arrived. "I'll be there in twenty minutes. Less if the traffic is kind."

Miles drove to Broadway House as fast as traffic would allow. His conviction that the danger was immediate increased with every mile of the journey. Armistice Day, the tenth anniversary of the ending of the war. At eleven tomorrow morning, the whole of His Majesty's Government and His Majesty himself would be vulnerable, exposed. An attack then could destabilise Europe for another decade. Security would be high, of course, but what defence could there be against a threat hidden deep underground in unknown passages?

Miles abandoned his car across the street from Broadway house, dashed through the traffic and entered the building at a flying walk.

"I rang earlier," he said to the man at the desk. "I must speak to Naylor. A matter of great urgency."

"Mr Naylor is not in the building." The man's tone was reassuring, almost avuncular, and with his beefy shoulders and well-kept whiskers he reminded Miles of his own uncle – a jovial man who had always had a bag of Mint Imperials and a couple of back numbers of Comic Cuts for a small nephew. "If you would go up to the duty officer's room, you can leave a message."

"Thank you."

Miles sprinted up the stairs, his leather soles loud on the marble of the first flight and not much quieter on the carpet runner in the corridor. He tapped on a door and barely waited for the summons before throwing it open.

"Sir, I – oh!"

Mortlake paused in filling his pipe. "What's the matter, Siward? Broken a nail?"

Miles scowled at the last man he had hoped to see. "I have some urgent information for Naylor."

"Naylor has already seen Allerdale, so is aware of the situation." Mortlake struck a match, lit the pipe and grinned at Siward through the smoke. "Allerdale doesn't look too distraught. I guess he made you keep your hands to yourself."

Miles couldn't remember the last time he had felt so angry so many times so close together. He swallowed down a retort that would probably have got him fired and tried again. "This is information Allerdale wasn't privy to. Something I have only discovered in the past hour. I fear there will be an attack tomorrow, on the Armistice Day ceremony at the Cenotaph."

"You fear? I can quite believe that." Mortlake made a note on a pad on Naylor's desk. "For your information, when they took the guns out of your car last night, they found a box of Mills bombs and another with fuses and blasting caps. Naylor had a tip off that Andrija has been spotted in Harwich trying to leave the country – presumably because the guns and fuses were missing – so Naylor's gone to get him. I can't say when he'll be back but there's nobody here with any authority to deal with your *fears*." Mortlake's grin took on a more sneering quality. "We need corroboration from a source we can trust. But I'll be sure to pass the message on, just as soon as I see him. Meantime, why don't you go and get your hair done?"

Shouting at Mortlake was satisfying, in a suicidal kind of way. So was slamming both hands down on the desk and making him jump. But pointless. As Miles retraced his steps, he reflected if he had told Mortlake that he was on fire, Mortlake would have burned while waiting for corroboration from a source he could trust. At the desk, he begged paper and pen and wrote a concise account of what he had discovered from Crane, adding a sketch of the concealed spaces under Whitehall. As a terrible breach of protocol, he handed it over unsealed. "Read it," Miles said. "Please. I insist."

The man took the paper with reluctance, began to read then went a little pale.

"I promise I'll get a message to Naylor. I should be able to contact him through Customs and Excise." He looked at the paper again then folded it, placed it into an envelope and got Miles to sign across the seal. "Will you be looking into this yourself, sir? Because between the security measures for tomorrow, the scare in Harwich and our normal commitments, we are spread thin on the ground. It would be a comfort to know that a reliable man was checking the facts."

Miles gave him a measuring stare but could see no trace of sarcasm in his calm face.

"It would be a comfort," the man repeated. "I have a friend, in the Guards, who will be laying a wreath tomorrow. I intend to be there as well."

Had there been a slight emphasis on the word 'friend'? If there had, the man had taken an appalling risk confiding in Miles and that showed how seriously he was taking the threat. Miles swallowed the advice to stay away. There was a calm determination in the clerk's eyes. His friend had been given a great honour and he would be there to witness him fulfilling it, just as Miles would be there for Briers if he could. Briers who was who knew where, still thinking they had until the fifteenth.

"Then I'll go now," Miles promised.

Miles had forgotten he had given his house keys to Briers. He pounded on the door of the flat and pushed past as soon as Pritchard cracked the door.

"Sir?" he said, smile fading as he took in Miles' state of alarm. "May I be of assistance?"

"I hope so, Pritchard," Miles said. "Do we still have those awful old flannels? You know, the ones I keep for working on the car?"

Pritchard grimaced. "I believe we do, sir."

"Then hoick them out, there's a good chap. And if you can rustle me up something equally disreputable for my top half, all the better."

Miles hung his coat and hat then hurried to his desk. A telephone was a luxury but Miles enjoyed the possibility of calling his parents from time to time, and right now he was glad of the comfort of being to make a call where he was certain of not being overheard.

"George? Look here, I need –"

"Miles!" George sounded outraged. "I've been worried sick. When Allerdale told me what happened –"

"Never mind," Miles said. "I need a gun."

"Don't be ridiculous," George said. "Of course you don't. Now what's all this about?"

"Ask your man to let me in the tradesman's entrance. I'm not going to look fit to come in the front door."

"Oh dear God, you'll not be in skirts? Miles, this is odd, even for you."

"I'll explain when I get there, George. Gun and plenty of ammo."

"I'm not giving you a gun! Even if I had one here, which I don't."

"Dammit." Miles took a deep breath. "Do me a different favour. Use some of those fantastic contacts of yours to get Naylor back to town, preferably with someone from bomb disposal in tow. I think he may be in Harwich."

"Bomb disposal?" George's voice sharpened. "Very well. Report and make it snappy."

"Disused passages under Whitehall, a lorry load of home-made explosives and the Cenotaph ceremony tomorrow?"

"Christ! No wonder you want a gun. Tell me the rest."

Miles spoke fast, explaining the web of conjecture and coincidence and hoping George would see a flaw in his reasoning. But George swore and confirmed that, at the very least, the situation needed a proper look.

"I'll see what I can do about Naylor," he promised. "Meantime, Miles, for pity's sake, be careful, and if you can't be careful, stick close to Allerdale."

"I would," Miles assured him, "if I knew where he was."

In the bedroom, Pritchard was laying out a selection of Miles' least attractive clothing. "Are you sure about this, sir?" he asked, inspecting a battered sweater.

"I am." Miles hastily threw off his outer clothing and reached for the oil-stained flannels. "And in a tearing hurry."

"Then I may be able to provide you with more than a set of singularly unappealing clothing."

"Pritchard?" Miles paused in buttoning his flies. "You don't mean to say –"

"I do indeed, sir." Pritchard offered him an oil skin bag. "Smith and Wesson, .38, sir, plus all the other accoutrements and two spare cylinders. Fully loaded I might add, since one never knows when one might need a reload in a hurry."

Miles hefted the cold and heavy object with distaste. "God knows I hope I don't need it," he said. "Where on earth did you get it?" It certainly wasn't 'other ranks' issue.

"I received it as part payment for a case of champagne in the last week of the war, sir," Pritchard said with a smile, "from an American officer who was a little short of cash. For future reference, I keep it in the kitchen drawer with the string, first aid kit and candles. It is in good working order, sir."

"I can see that." Miles grinned as he refreshed his memory of how to swap cylinders, the new one snicking home with a decisive click. "Thank you, Pritchard. Yet again you've saved the day."

"Let us hope you can do that, sir, without having to pull the trigger." Pritchard smiled. "And another thing – just in case. I – er – found these rolled up in the bathroom. Beyond repair I'm afraid." He held up Millie's silk stockings, discarded the worst damaged of the two and dropped a penny down into the toe of the other. With a twist of the wrist he flicked the coin into his other palm and held the stocking garrotte-wise at throat height.

"Good grief." Miles took the stocking and practised the little swing and catch himself. "Pritchard, you're a wonder. Did you learn that in the Far East?"

"Bless you, no, sir." Pritchard took it back, rolled the stocking up and tucked it into Miles' breast pocket. "Barry Island can get a bit rough during Miners' Fortnight. Will you be wanting a late lunch before you leave?"

Chapter Seventeen

Harwich. Briers had been with Naylor when the word had come in. A woman meeting the description of Josephine had booked in at a hotel and claimed to be waiting for her husband. There were many tall good-looking women with brown hair but only one with a passport in the name of Colette Fornier.

"She'd have to be mad," Briers pointed out.

"And we know she isn't but my masters insist I investigate personally anyway." Naylor paused in putting on his coat. "Look, Allerdale, it would be a weight off my mind if you would stay in town. Ingram is at home today and hosting a dinner tonight, so he should be safe enough. We went over the house in Millbank with a fine tooth comb and didn't find anything out of the ordinary. But this sewer business really bothers me."

"You want me to look into it." Briers blew out his cheeks in exasperation. "Not the way I had envisioned spending my Saturday night. Dinner and maybe a show, I'd thought. But of course I'll do it."

"Start at Millbank," Naylor advised. "At least we know that's where they broke into the system. Who knows where they ended up."

"Chilling thought, isn't it? An assassin with a rifle or a Mills Bomb could pop up anywhere."

"But you don't need two dozen men for that." Naylor picked up his hat. "There's something else – something we don't know. I have to go. The duty officer will take messages."

Briers took the tube to Westminster then walked down to Millbank, sparing a glance for the shop doorway as he passed it. Miles had been offended by Briers' dismissal of his help and Briers sensed he would have to work quite hard to make it up to him. That was a pleasant thought and it sustained him through the annoyance of making contact with Rawling, the man Naylor had left in charge of the house in Page Street.

"But the scare's over," he said. "We're about to pack up and go."

"Not until I've seen Andrija's head on a pike," Briers snarled, and pushed past him to get into the cellar.

Water had sat there for weeks before it had been pumped out, and had left brown and green marks up the slimy bricks. The part of the wall that had been taken down had been cut through raggedly and the bricks tumbled to one side. Above the aperture, cracks radiated across the wall and ceiling, and the timbers bracing the structure were bowed. It all looked as though it might come down at any moment. Beyond the wall was a rough tunnel some six yards in length, then a dark void filled with the sound of water. Briers had armed himself with a bullseye lantern and, by the yellow beam of light, saw well-laid bricks arching over a drain. "Amazing," he said. "Quite amazing."

"Aye, they built to last." Rawling leaned on the side of the tunnel, careless of the cracking brickwork. "Along there to the left we found their weapons cache. All good stuff, too. American-made machine guns, spare drums of ammo. Some rifles, mostly Czech-made G-98s, but there was one lovely Moshin-Nagant with a sniper scope." His voice rang with enthusiasm and Briers scowled down into the dark tunnel.

"Any explosives?"

"Couple of Mills bombs. Same type as the ones you brought in last night."

Briers tilted the beam of the lamp to scan the roof of the sewer, then down to shine on the water. "How far along the tunnel in each direction did you go? And did you check any side tunnels? I can't imagine why they would have opened up this hole just to hide some guns. They could have done that equally well in a suite at the Dorchester."

"Who knows why these bastards do anything. You've never seen such a sorry bunch."

"Yes, but they were only the hired muscle." Briers turned off the lamp and went back to the cellar. "Their boss, Andrija, is another matter."

"Ah, but he's on the run." Rawling paused to light a cigarette. "I heard he and that floozy of his were seen getting on the boat train at Harwich."

"Josephine may have been seen." Briers took the folded map from his pocket and opened it, trying to get his bearings. "That doesn't mean anything. In fact it makes them all the more dangerous. Andrija might hold back if she's in the picture, but once she's safe, all bets are off. He's a man who would burn down an orphanage to warm his hands."

"Bastard. Look, have you finished?"

"No. And I need to borrow those waders."

"You're not going down the sewer?" Rawling pulled a face. "We went along in both directions and there's nothing to see but shit and rats."

"Then you didn't go far enough," Briers snapped. The waders were a little too large but pulled up almost to crotch level. He buttoned his jacket, made sure he could reach his pistol and folded the map into a more compact package. Rawling watched in silence until he stepped through the tunnel into the drain.

"I'll let them know where you're going," Rawling said. "And I'll warn my relief not to shoot you when you come back. God speed."

Briers didn't reply. He could feel the chill of the water even through the waders, and the smell was a fierce combination of rot, damp brick and ammonia. The footing was slippery, too, and Briers found it easier to move by sliding his feet gently through the water rather than picking them up and setting them down. Even so, he made good and careful progress. There were signs of activity everywhere: scrapes on the walls, soot stains on the arch of brickwork above his head. He judged that many groups of men had made this journey before him but right now, the tunnels were deserted by all apart from the rats.

"I wish you could talk," he said to one particularly large specimen. It sat up, some piece of unidentifiable rubbish in its paws, and fixed its beady little black eyes on him. "I bet you could tell me what Andrija was up to."

The rat transferred the piece of rubbish – perhaps a bacon rind or a worm washed down by the rain – from paw to mouth and crammed itself into a crack between two bricks. Briers sloshed on alone. Soon he came to a junction in the pipe where his branch met another at a gentle angle, presumably to avoid the water backing up. This was a wider thoroughfare with a raised walkway along one side of it. Briers scrambled out of the effluent with relief and paused to consult his map. He should be close to Parliament Square. Here the walls were cleaner, the rats less plentiful and the brickwork was in better shape. But in one place he saw an impression in the mud – he preferred to think of it as mud – where a crate had been set down, and there was a soggy remnant of a newspaper tucked down behind a pipe running down the wall. He recognised the headlines from the paper he had read in Miles' flat weeks before.

"On the right track, then," he muttered, and flinched at the way his voice echoed. He would need to keep quiet. If there was anyone down here he wanted to know about them first rather than the other way around.

He traced the route of the sewer on the map and tried to imagine the ground above his head. He assumed he was in the storm relief drain, which probably explained why it seemed a bit cleaner and from the lines of the map he was following the river, which should take him directly under Westminster. The thought was confirmed by a soft rumble that stopped for a moment then started again. The Tube. He checked the map again and found the point closest to the station.

More certain of his location now, he followed the walkway at a faster pace, ducking when he came to low bits, and taking to the water when he had to. He walked for fifteen minutes, then stopped and frowned. The signs of Andrija's men had been fewer but more obvious – footprints, scraps of rubbish that seemed too fresh for the normal detritus – but he hadn't seen anything for some time. Surely he hadn't lost them?

While he paused to consult the map again, he heard a sound. A splash, a curse, a laugh. He covered the beam of the lamp and crouched by the wall, closing his eyes to adjust to the dark.

A rhythmic splashing – two men – and the rustle of fleeing rats. Briers opened his eyes to see torchlight dancing on the walls. They were coming from the north. Briers reached for his pistol.

"Are you sure about this?" The soft voice was horribly familiar. "I haven't seen signs of anyone."

"Honest, guv'nor, I been all through these tunnels and I know just the place to stop. It gets wider up ahead, you'll see."

Briers gritted his teeth and stood up turning on his lamp. "Siward," he hissed. "Stop playing silly buggers and be quiet."

"Oh, thank God."

A few moments more splashing and Miles appeared followed by a man in overalls. Miles was shivering, soaked to the waist, his tweeds hanging on him in folds, but his smile was bright.

"Briers," he said, hurrying to the ledge and pulling himself up onto it. "Thank goodness. I thought we'd never find you. This is Jimmy. I found him doing some repairs off Parliament Square and he agreed to accompany me." Miles looked more anxious than Briers had expected and rolled a warning eye to indicate his companion, who grinned at Briers and turned off his lantern. In a flat cap, coveralls and Wellington boots, Falk looked every inch the manual worker, though his soft hands and a suspicious bulge in the thigh pocket of his dungarees gave the game away to a discerning eye.

"Couldn't let the young gennul-mun come down here and get lost, could I?" Falk asked in a very passable cockney. "Even with this fancy map he's got, it's easy to get turned round."

"Map?" Falk was a problem to deal with later. For the moment, Briers was more concerned with the idiocy of his lover.

"Yes, that's why I'm here and so very relieved to see you." Miles scrabbled at his pocket and, God help them all, produced a revolver. White-faced, he levelled it at Falk. "Briers, grab him. I don't know who he is but he's certainly not English!"

Falk raised both hands with alacrity. "Briers? His hands are shaking, Briers. Please, take that gun away from him."

Briers had never seen Falk look so shocked, and couldn't resist taking a moment to relish the situation. Then he very carefully put his hand over Miles' and pushed the barrel of the gun downwards. "Explain," he said. "I don't care which of you."

"After our meeting," Falk said, smiling and dropping the accent, "I was in the Strand and saw some road works and thought that maybe the sewers might be worth a look. Then I saw this young man trying to lever up a manhole cover and offered my assistance. I thought if he turned out to be one of Andrija's men, I could kill him and leave him down here for the rats."

Miles' face had fallen. "You know each other? I had sort of planned the same thing if Jimmy turned out to be a wrong-un. But I needed him and his crowbar, you see, so I thought it worth a chance. That accent, pure music hall."

Falk glared at Miles. "Nobody else has had any complaints about it."

"Oh God." Briers lowered the trigger on Miles' gun before letting him have it back. "I suppose we need introductions. Falk, Miles knows because he's a whizz with languages and is one of the brightest sparks of the cipher division."

"An accomplished linguist?" Falk's head tilted in a respectful little bow. "No wonder Briers likes you."

"Miles, this is Falk, an operative from a friendly power with whom I have worked on occasion."

"And what an occasion that was," Falk murmured.

The implication was obvious. Miles flushed and stowed the revolver away. Briers resolved to have stern words with whoever had been daft enough to let him have it.

"Falk, then," Miles said. "Perhaps we could look at this map now?" From his other pocket, Miles produced a fine golden sheet that unfolded to astonishingly large proportions. "Sidney remembered he had made some later additions and we found Josephine had stolen the good copy he had made. But this one is complete, though it's a bit rough. Look." He tilted the sheet of paper. "Hold the lantern up, Jimmy – er – Falk, please, there's a good chap."

Briers tried to ignore Falk's grin as he peered over Miles' shoulder. "Where are we?"

"Here. No, here." Miles pointed to part of the map that had been overdrawn several times. "There's another run of tunnels that weren't cut into until nineteen twenty-two, an off-shoot of the Scholar's Pond sewer that had partially collapsed. They shored up some of it, but decided the rest of it wasn't worth saving. There should be a whole run along here, north from Westminster."

Briers shook his head. "Wouldn't that take it under the park? What's up there? Buck House?"

"Whitehall," Miles said. "The Cenotaph! Briers, tomorrow is the eleventh. All the great and the good are going to be standing there in the rain, listening to *Taps*. If Andrija is going to do something regrettable, wouldn't that be just about the most hurtful time to do it?"

It was all too horribly plausible. Feeling sick, Briers nodded. "Yes, that's Andrija's style all right. But how do we get from here to that line?"

"It's tricky. Sidney couldn't remember. He said the two systems ran parallel for a while with some links, then the other one goes off at an angle. Most of the links are blocked off but one or two will have been left open for maintenance. We've been checking all the side tunnels. That's why I'm so wet."

"Some of those offshoots are tight and some are full of water," Falk said. "I damn near had to grease him to get him up some of 'em."

Briers glared at Falk while he considered their options. He wanted to tell Miles to go back the way he had come and let him and Falk, as the two people best suited to fighting down and dirty in the dark, carry on with the search, but he couldn't think of any way to make Miles stay behind short of tying him up and leaving him in a place of safety.

"I've been following their tracks," Briers admitted, "but they have petered out. I think I missed where they left this stream. We'll go back the way I came and search all the side passages. But for pity's sake, you two, keep the noise down and be careful."

They crept on in the darkness, Miles leading the way and Falk bringing up the rear. It made Briers feel more comfortable to keep them apart, though the skin between Brier's shoulder blades cringed. He knew how dangerous Falk could be, but he was counting on the fact that Falk hated Andrija more than he might relish the chance of tripping Briers up into a foot of sewage. The cold was creeping into his bones, and he saw the map Miles was holding quiver. Was Miles shivering from cold or from excitement? Briers didn't know, but he was sure it wasn't fright. Miles' expression when he turned his head to whisper was filled with intense concentration and a little glee. He looked young and vital and determined, and Briers had to swallow the impulse to grab him by the collar and make him go home to his nice warm flat where he would be *safe*. Miles had no idea what he was getting into. He looked almost – Brier's jaw muscles bunched as he gritted his teeth – as carefree as though they were on their way to the fun fair.

"I think we can cross to the other set of tunnels here." Miles pointed. "Look – there's a ladder and it's marked here on the map. We go up and should be able to get into the off-shoot on the other side. If it's disused, it might be dry."

"That would be a mercy." Briers consulted the map, his hand covering Miles' icy hand to still the sheet of paper. "I think you're right." He caught a glimpse of Falk's sardonic eye fixed on their hands and turned away. "Let's alter the order of our march. I think I ought to go first, in case we meet something coming the other way. You can watch our backs, Miles. Falk, thanks for your help but I can't ask you to go any further. It would be most useful if you could go and raise the alarm with the authorities. Make them aware there are people in the tunnels at least."

"We did that," Miles said. "I left messages everywhere for Naylor and found a nice copper in Westminster Square. But, yes, Falk we can't ask you to go any further."

"Rubbish." Falk hefted his crowbar. "This might be useful yet and so might I."

Falk's smile was calm, confident, and Briers knew from experience that one never had any success in making Falk do anything Falk didn't want to do. The only thing to do was to give in gracefully.

"Thank you." Briers folded the map, having made a mental note of the relevant section, and handed it back to Miles. He clipped his torch to the front of his jacket, covered the light and began to scale the ladder. The icy chill of the metal made his skin crawl, but not as much as the greasy coating. He swore as his boot slipped. "Watch it – the rungs are slimy with God knows what. When they flush these pipes through, the water must be over our heads."

"Water – that's a more comfortable way of looking at it." Miles came to the bottom of the ladder and peered up, his face pale in the dimness. "Can you see anything on the other side?"

"I'm trying," Briers said. "Hush, I want to listen."

Beyond the top of the ladder was an angled tunnel a few yards long, dry and intact, though it looked as though it had not been wet for a long time. On the floor were plentiful signs of traffic – foot marks, and scrapes as though small but heavy things had been pushed across the gritty floor. Briers covered the lens of his light, closed his eyes for a count of ten and listened. No sound beyond the rush of water, and the beat of his own heart. It struck him that Miles was as still and quiet as Falk, like a pro. Brier's smiled and opened his eyes.

Complete blackness.

"Come on," Briers beckoned. "This is the place all right, but I can't see or hear anyone on the other side. I'll get down into the tunnel, there's no ladder that I can see, and give you a hand."

The change from one tunnel to the other was effected with minimum fuss, with neither Falk nor Miles offering advice or alternatives. The centre of the tunnel had a runnel of water a couple of feet wide, and the sides were lined with soft gritty mud deep enough to muffle their footfall but not enough to make the footing slippery. Briers made sure their torches were hooded, illumining a few feet of the ground at their feet.

"The glow will still show up but only if they aren't using their own torches," he explained. "There's no reason why they would think they had been discovered, so I'm counting on us seeing their lights before they see ours. One thing. I'd prefer it if there was no shooting. A muffled shout doesn't carry far and can be explained away, but there's no disguising gun shots."

"Probably just as well," Miles muttered. "I've only shot a handgun twice."

"Then keep back out of the way, and keep the damned thing in your pocket."

Falk chuckled. "I too would prefer you to keep it in your pocket. To be shot by the enemy would be sad; to be shot by an ally would be tragic."

Miles glared at Falk, his face red with embarrassment and fury – Briers remembered the feeling well. "I understand the principles and at close quarters it would be deadly. It's a .38."

"We could stand here all night comparing calibre sizes, but we're not going to." Briers gave Miles a gentle shove. "Thanks for bringing it. Let's get on."

They had only been walking for a few minutes when Briers heard a sound from the tunnel ahead and spotted the faintest of glows. It touched the wall gilding dry dusty bricks, jigging and bobbing in time to the movements of the man carrying it.

Briers' gesture was unnecessary; when he glanced back Miles and Falk were already shrinking back into the darkest shadows they could find and Briers, too, hurried to find cover.

The men approaching made no effort to hide. They marched through the slurry, boots splashing, torches swooping, and called back and forth triumphantly in exultant accented English. At first, the echoes made it hard to hear what they were saying but Briers could pick out a word here and there. They had finished. They were relieved to be leaving. They mustn't miss their train. Briers scowled and waited until the last man was level with him before he stepped out.

"Hands up," he demanded. "Not another step."

They turned on him with yells of fury but Briers levelled his pistol, and their hands raised slowly.

"Step back." Briers said. "Keep those hands up. Now – where have you

154

been and what have you done?"

One of them edged forward, his hands at shoulder level, one holding an old long barrelled Luger. His face was gaunt, eyes bright as fever under heavy brows. "There's only one of you and four of us." His English was clear but Briers scowled at the accent. Russian, so not one of Andrija's usual team. "You might shoot one of us but the others will get you."

"Then I'll make sure I shoot you first," Briers promised. "And I'm not alone. Come on, lads – disarm them."

The sound of Miles' Smith and Wesson cocking was clear and the movement towards Briers stilled.

"So, two," the spokesman said, and the group of men scattered.

Briers couldn't fault them for courage. In the poor light, with beams of torchlight swooping and the sheet of foul sand kicked up into his face, he had a job to hit anything he aimed at, especially since he feared two of the darting figures were Miles and Falk. But he shot the spokesman as promised, and went in pursuit of the others.

"Down," Falk yelled and fired twice, one shot echoed by a splash, the other by a shriek. Two more shots thundered, which were deafening in the small space, and there was another yell of pain.

"Miles," Briers called and caught his breath with relief at Miles' shouted reply.

"I got him but he's running, shall I go after him?"

"Don't you dare. And put that gun away." Briers sloshed across to the spokesman's writhing body, leaving Falk to check their other captives. "Let's see – who's this?"

The spokesman was rolling, clutching his leg, and gasping with pain. "Chyort! Chyort voz'mi." Red stained his hands, dripping from his fingers. He glared up at Briers. "Pizda," he muttered, his accent thick, then followed the obscenity with a stream of Russian curses that grew weaker and tailed off into gasps.

"Who are you?" Miles demanded in the same tongue. "What did you do? Tell us."

The man grunted and Briers realised he was laughing. "Too late. Too late." He laughed again and Miles gripped his shoulder to try and pull his head back. Abruptly, the Russian uncurled, grabbing for Miles' lapel. Falk blocked his lunge and gave Miles a vicious shove before hurling himself away. Briers too saw the rounded shape in the Russian's hands, pin glinting as it fell.

"Jesus Christ," he spat and, hand fast on Miles' shoulder, he almost yanked him from his feet as he ran. He counted in his mind then threw himself over Miles' smaller body, crushing him down against the filthy floor.

Chapter Eighteen

The explosion rocked the tunnel. Briers rolled over, scrabbling upright and wincing at a sharp pain in his shoulder. He reached back, felt a warm wetness spreading, but the pain was ignorable and his arm moved with no difficulty. The Russian was dead, his chest shattered. Briers reached down to haul Miles to his feet. Miles whooped in a breath and ripped out an unexpectedly ripe curse, his voice tinny and weak against the buzzing in Briers' ears.

"Mills bomb?"

"Something similar. Are you hurt?" Briers was still trying to control his breathing as he recalled the man's grab for Miles and how Miles' ribcage, too, could have been blown apart.

"Winded, that's all. Falk? Are you all right?"

"Here." Falk, emerged from the dark, dabbing at his face with his sleeve, bespattered with blood and worse. "I'm not sure where he ends and I begin. Ah, there. I caught my head, but I will live. Two others are dead also, the one Siward shot is still running, but he was limping, he won't get far." He looked down at the corpse. "You recognised him, of course."

"No." Briers found the torch, still shining despite its fall, and trained the beam of light on the ruined body. Miles gagged and turned away, his retches echoing off the brickwork.

The Russian's face was undamaged and oddly calm. Briers peered at it for a moment then nodded. "The only time I saw him, he had a full beard. He was one of Gregor Tamarkin's men. Andrija really has been recruiting all the crazies."

Miles had straightened up, white-faced but composed. "Tamarkin is a bomb-maker, isn't he?" he asked. "So, if all the others are dead or gone, hadn't we better find out where they have been? And what they left there?"

"Your little linguist is right." Falk got up and reached for his torch and crowbar. "Let us go."

They hurried on through the dark. Briers shook his head as the buzzing in his ears began to fade. Tamarkin had the reputation for not caring who he hurt, but his reasons were always impeccably along party lines. Andrija was a man for hire, but Tamarkin served only one known master and he had a very palatial office in Moscow. So, a state-sanctioned attack on the government of England? A coup camouflaged as an anarchist attack? Briers seriously considered trying to send Miles back to make another attempt to find Naylor and give him the latest information, but Briers didn't think he could chance it, not with a number of angry and wounded anarchists on the loose in the tunnels.

"Surely they can't have carried their gear much further?" Miles asked.

"We're getting closer to the surface. Listen."

A sharp rapping sound grew louder as they approached a void in the roof with the rusted ruins of a ladder bolted to the side of it.

"Hooves," Miles said. "And I think I can hear engines."

The clip-clopping died away and they walked on. Miles consulted the map again. "We must be close. Surely not much further."

"No, look." Falk pointed his crowbar at the wall of the tunnel. The bricks were in place, but stacked rather than mortared, and the wall and floor was streaked with greyish mud. Falk pressed on one of the bricks, making it rock in its bed, then they set to work to open up the concealed tunnel. It didn't take long to tumble the bricks out of the way, revealing a wall of planks with more material – bricks, clay and gravel – piled behind them almost to the roughly cut roof.

They shone their torches into the hole and Briers scowled as the circles of light displayed only more bricks and stone work. "Miles, if I boost you up, do you think you can get a better view?"

"I'll try," Miles said and folded the map into his pocket. With his foot in a stirrup formed of Briers' hands, he stepped up and slotted his shoulders into the narrow gap. "Oh yes, I see," he said. "Briers, all this is loose. It has been dug out and packed back in again. It's not a sewer. I think it's some kind of room. The walls are masonry. Well made. Falk, can you pass me the crowbar?"

With the implement in his hands and Briers' weight against his hip to steady him, Miles dug for a few minutes, spattering Briers with mud and passing back bricks as he loosened them. He worked until he could loosen the top plank, then the rubble moved more easily.

"Give me that crowbar," Briers demanded and found a place where it could bite. He and Falk threw their weight against it and more planks tore loose. Rubble tumbled as Miles hitched himself further into the space, pushing the loose stone and earth down with his feet.

"Can you see any better now?" Briers asked, still digging.

Miles turned over and scrambled into the darkness. His torch beam bobbed for a moment then steadied.

"Oh dear God." There was a distinct tremor in Miles' voice as he hurried back towards them. "Briers, there are boxes in there. A stack of them, and – and I can hear ticking."

"Can you see fuses?"

"It's like a spider's web. What shall we do?"

Briers and Falk exchanged worried glances. "I have not done a bomb disposal course," Falk admitted. "Have you?"

Briers shook his head.

"That is a pity." Falk sighed and shrugged. "Then I feel it might be best if we got above ground. You call the police and I will go about my business."

Briers grimaced. Getting out of this dark and horrible place seemed a very attractive option. "Well, when I said 'no', I've been kicking around mines for a year or two. I know a fuse from a blasting cap and when to keep them apart. I think I should stay and see what's what."

"Such gallantry," Falk said with a fond smile. "Miles, let us knock him out and I will help you carry him as far as the nearest policeman."

"Don't you dare," Briers said. "Falk, if you want to go, go now and I promise Miles will keep you out of our report. I need to do something about this if I possibly can. Miles, go with him. Find Naylor. At the very least you two need to get above ground and try to warn away as many people as possible."

"Falk can do that." Miles disappeared into the darkness again.

"Miles, damn it, get back here."

"No." Miles' voice echoed in the void beyond the rubble. "You two may not have done a bomb disposal course but I have."

Falk's shout of laughter rang in the tunnel and he slapped Briers on the shoulder. "So I will go to find a telephone, and you and your partner will find and disable the timer. I wish you both the best good luck." He lowered his voice and added. "And I wish you joy of him – if you both survive."

He ran off into the darkness before Briers found words to reply, so

Briers put him from his mind and crawled up into the hole, not sure whether to assist Miles or to strangle him. The sight of the stacked boxes linked with worrying numbers of fuses made up his mind for him.

"Bomb disposal?" he asked, playing his torch beam across the mass of boxes. "But you decided languages were more your thing?"

"No, they decided that a man who can speak half a dozen different Balkan dialects plus Russian shouldn't go to waste fiddling with whizz bangs." Miles sounded truculent but from the pallor of his cheeks, Briers decided his belligerence was his way of masking his fright. Miles clawed another brick out of the way, and set it aside carefully.

"I think the ticking is in this box," he said. "Now, do I open the box and risk setting the bomb off, or shall we try to expose the explosives and remove the blasting caps from each charge?"

"You're the expert," Briers said.

Miles' laugh was bleak. "Hardly. I didn't get a chance to do the really advanced stuff. Let's see what they are using," he muttered.

The lid came off one of the boxes with a squeak of nails and Miles grunted to see the canvas bag within. He opened it carefully, not disturbing the fuse, and said, "Ammonal or something similar. Easy enough to make if you can get the supplies and hard to make bang without a proper blasting cap."

"So we take out the caps?"

Miles sat back on his heels. "If we work quickly and there aren't too many boxes. But I'd better check the timer first. Oh God, I heard Andrija say something about timing being crucial."

Briers shook his head and began to open one of the other boxes. "I don't know about you, Miles, but if I were an anarchist bent on causing a maximum of disruption, I'd set bombs off wherever or whenever I felt like it just to add to the terror. But a stylish bastard like Andrija always likes to have a bit of extra show. His bomb will be timed to the minute. I'm guessing we've got 'til eleven tomorrow."

"The two-minute silence. Well, that gives us – God, twelve and a half hours. I hope they set their timer right." Miles was working fast, clambering from box to box, wrenching off lids, then inching out the blasting caps and setting them aside. His breathing was fast and his eyes wide, but Briers was relieved to note his hands were steady as he laid the caps down. Briers was working fast as well, but home-made explosives like this had to be coddled. One slip and the whole place could go up.

Briers had never been in London to see the annual ceremony at the Cenotaph but he had seen the news reels. The grey mass of the crowds lining the streets; the silent ranks of servicemen; the glint of dull sunlight on the bullion marking the uniforms of admirals and generals. The King stepping forward to lay his wreath of poppies. Briers imagined they shone brightly even in the sombre light of a November morning. As brightly as the blood shed on the fields of Flanders and Picardy.

"Oh God," Miles muttered after a while filled with anxious activity. His mind must have been running along similar lines to Briers because he added, "I hope they listen to Falk."

Briers looked at what they had done and what was still to do. There were so many boxes. He sent up a prayer to Saint Joshua, first of all the spies and a real hard case to boot, and wrenched off another box lid.

"I have to move the caps," Miles said after another ten minutes. "We need to get to the boxes at the back."

"I'll re-stack the boxes," Briers offered. "You get those caps out of the way. There's a shelf up there. Would that do?"

The defused boxes made a brave pile, slightly bigger than the pile left. Not that it would do them any good at all if the timer triggered.

Briers was moving the fifth box when he heard a scraping from the tunnel. He glanced back over his shoulder.

"Falk," he blew out a breath in relief. "Good man."

Falk scrambled into the cramped space and straightened up, his face calm though Briers could tell from the set of his shoulders that he was annoyed. "A conscience is an inconvenient thing and, in this case, it would have been better if I hadn't come back to help."

"I saw him," another voice grated. The man who scrambled from the shadows behind him had an automatic pointed at Falk's spine.

"Tamarkin," Briers said and raised his hands.

The Russian's teeth were bared, shadowed in his beard. Blood had soaked his mud-stained trousers and he favoured his right leg. "Back against the wall," he snarled. "Boy, you move too. All three of you back – back there."

Briers shuffled across the uneven floor, hands held level with his shoulders. Miles shrank away from Tamarkin and the gun until his back hit the ancient stone walls of the room.

"That's good." Tamarkin nodded and gave Falk a straight-armed shove to send him staggering into Miles. Briers caught Falk's eye and they closed up, offering Miles a little protection.

"There. Three in a row. Little eleventh hour heroes." The Russian snorted his contempt.

"Tamarkin," Briers said. "We've disabled your bomb. Some of it might go off but not all."

"It will be enough. If even one is left armed, the explosion will take the others with it!" Tamarkin smiled at the boxes then darted the gun towards Briers' face. "Do not think to distract me. I know what this means – death for all of us. You must know I consider it to be an honour to lay down my life for the cause."

"For Mother Russia?" Briers asked and Falk joined him in hooting with laughter.

Tamarkin shrugged. "The people who count will know what I have done. My friends will carry word home to our masters. My name will be remembered."

"Your friends? I hope you don't mean Andrija?" Briers shook his head. "He doesn't care how the bomb goes off as long as he gets his pay."

"He can still carry the message." Tamarkin's eyes shone with what Briers judged to be the holy light of utter madness. "This corrupt state will be left leaderless and then the honest working men can rise up against their oppressors and take their rightful place. When the revolution comes …"

"When the revolution comes, the place that is rightfully theirs will be taken by the usual silver-tongued rogues out to feather their own nests." Briers jerked his hands to the ceiling. "You don't think the average steel worker or coal miner has the time to lead a revolution?"

"Also, this is England," Falk interjected. "They had their revolution three hundred years ago and didn't much like it. I doubt they'll make that mistake again. They know what it leads to. Oppression by their peers, witch-hunts and the cancellation of Christmas."

Briers snorted. "British history, Falk? I had no idea of the depths of your knowledge."

Falk gave him a lopsided grin. "Know thine enemy!"

"Be quiet," Tamarkin snapped, gun wavering between them. "There is nothing to prevent me from shooting you all."

"I think there is." Briers glanced across at Falk. "Even with that automatic you won't get off three shots before one of us can jump you."

"No, but I can shoot two." Tamarkin's beard bristled as he grinned. "And one of you is too scared and too small to hurt me. I will leave him to last."

Briers tensed as Tamarkin levelled the pistol at Falk's face.

"No hard feelings," Falk said. "It would have been worth it to bring Andrija down."

"No hard feelings," Briers agreed, then blinked as a narrow length of pale fabric whipped past his face. The weight at the end of it struck Tamarkin in the teeth with a crack. Tamarkin flinched and the gun went off, the bullet spanging off the roof with an ugly whine, but Falk and Briers were already moving. They struck Tamarkin together. The lantern went over and a torch rolled, sending shadows swooping. The Russian was strong, vicious. Briers dodged a head butt, twisted aside from a jabbing knee, but couldn't avoid a blow from the pistol butt that left his left hand useless.

Then Falk wrenched the pistol from Tamarkin's hand and they bore him down to the ground. In the confusion of heaving bodies and thumping fists, Briers took an elbow to the jaw that rattled his brains but still managed to apply his forearm to Tamarkin's throat. Tamarkin roared, kicking and clawing. Falk ripped out a curse and struck a sharp jolting blow Briers felt through his hands, then again. Tamarkin convulsed once and lay still. Light flooded the chamber and Briers eased back on his heels, cradling his left hand in his right. Tamarkin's eyes met his in a glassy glare, one partially shaded by the brick embedded in his skull. Briers looked away and squinted into the light of the lantern being carried into the chamber.

"Naylor?"

"Yes." Naylor gave an approving nod. "I couldn't get a clear shot from where I was standing – too much of a risk of hitting the explosives. Well done, all. Now stand aside and let Barnet do his stuff."

"Excuse me please, sir." A pale-faced youth in army uniform scrambled past them and scanned the scene. He took a deep breath, removed his cap and knelt beside the box containing the timer. "Give me a moment."

"Just do your best, there's a good fellow." Naylor turned to Briers and smiled. "Barnet is a real expert. I was lucky to find him. Thank you for your messages, by the way. How badly are you hurt, Allerdale?"

"Sprained wrist, I think, sir." Briers grimaced as he moved his arm. "Though I'm not sure if it should be that shape."

"I need to assist Barnet," Naylor said, stooping to wrench the top off one of the remaining boxes, "so maybe Siward can get you to a – Siward?"

"He's hit?" Briers lurched over the rubble to where Miles was sprawled, his back supported against Falk's knee. "Dear God, where?"

Blood still dribbled from Falk's nostrils but his grin was cheerful as Briers shoved him aside and got an arm around Miles' shoulders. "No," he said. "Your little partner tried to pin Tamarkin's legs and got kicked back against the wall. I think he is just knocked silly."

"Twice in twenty-four hours, too. He's icy cold. Not good. I'll have to keep an eye on him."

Falk snorted then poked the muddy length of silk wound around Miles' fingers. "Is this what he used to distract Tamarkin? A lady's stocking with a penny in it?"

Briers smiled. "That old trick. Well done, Siward."

Naylor glanced over his shoulder at them, pausing in putting another blasting cap aside. "I saw," he said. "Breast pocket and used your cover to reach it. I believe you were right in your supposition that Mr Siward is wasted in the cipher room."

"I can assure you he is," Briers said, feeling the back of Miles' head and wincing at the bump he found there.

"It's a mercy he's more pocket-sized than his brother," Naylor said. "If he doesn't come round soon, it'll be easy to carry him out, but not perhaps until we have disarmed these explosives. How are you doing, Barnet?"

The soldier had set the box lid aside and was peering at the timer with a grim set to his mouth. "There's some complicated wiring, sir, but I'm fairly confident. If I could just concentrate, sir?"

"Oh, do, please. Allerdale, I thought this was a Balkan plot but now it appears that Tamarkin was involved? Could you have misunderstood?"

"I don't see how." Briers scowled and shifted Miles until he was leaning against his chest. "My informant is normally one hundred per cent reliable. I'll look into it when we get out of here."

"Well at least we have time to –"

"Sir." Barnet's voice cracked with tension. "We don't have time. I found another clock. Oh dammit, get out of here. One clock is set for eleven tomorrow, but the other is set for eleven tonight."

Falk looked at his watch. "Two minutes," he murmured.

"Do what you can, Barnet." Naylor said, sliding another blasting cap from its housing and setting it aside. "I'm staying to help. Allerdale, can you and your companion manage Siward?"

"Two minutes wouldn't give us long enough to get out of range," Briers said. "Falk, if you run –"

"And be caught in the tunnel by the blast? No thank you. I was buried once during the war. Once was enough." Falk offered his hand. "It has been a pleasure – in more ways than one."

"Amen." Briers shook his hand then glanced down as Miles stirred. Pity shook Briers for a moment. If they had to be blown to pieces or crushed under tons of masonry, it would have been better for Miles to have been unconscious. Then he saw the familiar frown, the belligerent jut of Miles' narrow jaw, and smiled. Typical he should come round fighting. He patted his cheek again.

"G'off!" Miles raised an arm to defend his face, opened his eyes and squinted up at Briers. "Oh, it's you." One of his cheekbones was marred by a weeping scrape and his eye was swelling, but his smile warmed and loosened the tight cold knot of anxiety under Briers' breastbone.

"It's me. We got Tamarkin."

Miles gripped Briers' lapel. "And the explosives? Did we do it?" he asked. "Did we, Briers?"

Briers looked across at Barnet whose hands were flying across the bunched wires of the timer. "Yes," Briers said, "we did it." And he drew Miles up to hold him close as Barnet reached for a knife.

Chapter Nineteen

It wouldn't have been possible to cut it more finely. As they took their places at the back of the immense crowd, the shrill, blare and thump of the military bands died away. The pound of marching feet stilled. It had rained and would rain again later but, for the moment, sun broke through racing clouds, scattering bright sparks on the brass on hats and sleeves. Flags fluttered or swung in the icy wind, their colours brave against the grey stone. The poppies were as red as Briers had imagined they would be.

"Thank you," Miles murmured to Briers. "I wouldn't have wanted to miss this."

"Nor me." Briers felt as battered as Miles looked and was taking care not to let his slung arm be jostled, but he wouldn't have missed it either. "And I'm especially glad to be here with you," he added and leaned a little so their shoulders touched – self-indulgent, perhaps, but permissible in this crowd. And after the night they had spent, Briers felt they had earned it.

After those first moments when, ecstatic with relief, they had all taken a turn to pound Barnet on the back and promise him all the beer he could drink, they returned to Broadway House, where they washed and had their hurts treated. Briers' wrist was broken, not sprained, and setting it had been no fun at all. He had also needed two stitches where the surgeon had removed a sliver of Mills Bomb casing from his shoulder. Splashing around in sewers was not conducive to good health, and they had been provided with a pharmacopoeia of ointments and bandages and were warned to take extra care over inspecting and redressing their wounds. Then they were provided with clean clothing and consumed probably the best beer and pies Briers had ever tasted, and had toasted Barnet's health until the poor man had to go and lie down. Once he was gone, Naylor brought them up to date.

Josephine had not been in Harwich, but a tall attractive woman with Josephine's passport was – a music hall dancer hired to act as a decoy while recovering from a sprained ankle. Naylor was incensed that Josephine and Andrija had escaped, but was confident he would soon get word of their whereabouts.

"So, it was not a completely successful mission but I think we can give ourselves a pat on the back." Naylor looked at his watch, scowled and got up. "Three a.m. I want to see you both on Wednesday, ten a.m. sharp. Make sure those grazes don't fester. I have to go and get Sir James out of bed and explain what has been going on. You two need to go home and get some sleep. Can I drop you off on the way?"

"Oh, please," Miles said, his eyelids drooping with weariness. Still damp from a much needed bath, with a purpling eye and in borrowed clothing several sizes too large, he looked like a schoolboy up long after his bedtime.

Pritchard had come to meet them on the pavement as Naylor's car pulled away then they had climbed the stairs to the tranquil safety of Miles' flat.

"Bed now, sirs," Pritchard suggested. "I'll be sure to wake you in good time."

"In time for what?" Miles had asked.

"For the ceremony at the Cenotaph, sirs." Pritchard smiled. "Since I surmise that there's no further danger."

They had made it, but only with seconds to spare.

The crowd stilled, stilled until Briers could hear the swish of the tail of a nearby police horse, then into that breathing quiet fell the first chime to mark the eleventh hour of the eleventh day of the eleventh month.

This was a time for remembering so Briers cast his mind back. It didn't feel like fourteen years since that uproarious descent on the recruiting office of his whole rugby side. Basic training had been a piece of cake. Such high spirits on the march to the front. A series of incidents he preferred not to examine too closely because sleepless nights were such a bore. Counting the cost in 1918 – they would have been able to make up a team for Sevens, but it hadn't really been played much then. It hadn't taken Briers long to find a man he knew had been in military intelligence and volunteer. Anything to prevent another four years like the ones they had endured during the war.

Reveille sounded, the bugle echoing off the stone walls of Whitehall. A police horse stamped, its rider's hand clapped against its neck. Briers glanced across, curious to see what was disturbing the beast, but its ears were slack, unperturbed, so he looked down at Miles' bowed head instead.

More recent memories bubbled up: of that little clerk in Naylor's office, tucked in and pink cheeked; of Millie glaring at him over the top of her specs; of Miles with his eyes screwed closed, teeth gritted with the strain of fending off his climax until Briers could join him. These were better memories to dwell on, but Briers didn't value those others less, for all they made his heart ache. One had led to the other, had made him what he was and had brought him here, on this rainy November Sunday, with this small gallant man by his side.

The bugle call died away in the hush of a thousand sighs as the waiting crowd put aside their memories and got back to business.

"You look sad." Miles' whisper barely carried but Briers had been looking at him so saw the shape of the words. "Who were you remembering?"

"One of the best fly-halves I've ever seen. Lost a leg in the last week of the war. You?"

"My uncle." Miles' shoulders shifted as he let out a breath. "MC, DSO, mentioned in dispatches twice, lost at Ypres."

"Too many were lost." Briers bumped their shoulders again and straightened up to watch the files of people with their wreaths.

Bands played, hymns were sung, as the glowing circlets of flowers were piled against the cold stone. As a guardsman, massive in great coat and bearskin, stepped back from the monument, Miles sighed and leaned against Briers. Bruising shadowed Miles' left eye and the graze had scabbed over, dark against his fair skin, and he looked as though his headache had come back.

"Do you want to leave?" Briers whispered.

"No." Miles' smile turned to a grimace of pain. "But I think I must. I'm sorry, Briers. You still have your key, don't you?"

"I do, but I'll come too." Their position at the back of the crowd made it easier to get out without incurring too many disapproving glares. Not that Briers cared. They could glare if they liked. He doubted many of them would have been as spry as Miles after disarming a heap of unstable explosives and being kicked in the head by a Russian.

Since the rain was holding off, they cut across Parliament Square and walked along Tothill Street to Broadway, sparing a nod for Broadway House as they passed, then spent a few minutes dodging raindrops in Petty France before turning into Castle Lane. As they mounted the steps to

Miles' front door, the heavens opened and they hurried inside.

"I hope Pritchard is here," Miles said removing his coat. "I've a thirst that you wouldn't believe."

"I hope he has aspirin." Briers grinned at him. "You look as though you need it."

Pritchard opened the door to Miles' flat before they could get a key in the lock, and Briers realised he must have been looking out for them. "Gentlemen," he said. "You have a visitor. May I take your coats?"

"A visitor?" Miles asked. "But who … Ah, George."

"Don't you 'ah' me." George was limping towards them, pointing accusingly with his cane. "How dare you call me up to demand the loan of a gun then disappear unarmed into the depths of the city. Dear God, Miles, your face! What the hell have you been doing?"

Brier's laughed and helped Miles to a chair. "Honourable war wounds, Siward. Don't give him a hard time. Your little brother is a genuine hero."

"Sit down, George, and stop flailing about," Miles snapped, in enough pain to be tetchy. "It's nothing, a headache, that's all. A boot in the head will do that to a man. Some aspirin and I'll be right as rain. And," he added, "I didn't need the gun because I borrowed one elsewhere. I must return it before too long." He glanced up as Pritchard stooped to offer a glass of water and two aspirin on a silver salver.

"One might hope, sir, that the use of said firearm did not prove to be necessary?" Pritchard asked once Miles had taken the pills.

"One might in that case be disappointed." Miles grinned like a monkey. "I did use it. Shot a big ugly Bolshevik right in the arse."

"Very good, sir." Pritchard was far too self-controlled to beam but Briers could hear the laughter in his voice. "If you would care to leave the item out I will ensure that it is thoroughly cleaned."

"If it's all the same to you, Pritchard," Miles swallowed the second pill with a grimace, "I feel I should clean it myself. I did get it dirty, after all."

"My baby brother," George said with a huff of disbelief. "All grown up. So, Briers, what was the panic? Are you able to tell me?"

"If you will excuse me, sirs," Pritchard murmured – but Miles reached for his sleeve to detain him.

"No, don't go, Pritchard," he said. "We all have secrets here and Pritchard is privy to most of them. I see no reason why he shouldn't hear the truth. I know it will go no further."

Briers nodded. "Absolutely, Pritchard. You must know that for the past few weeks Miles Siward and I have been keeping tabs on a group of anarchists from the hairier places in south-eastern Europe. With the assistance of a member of a foreign secret service, we tracked them to their lair and foiled a plot to detonate several tons of explosives under the Cenotaph at eleven this morning."

"*Duw Mawredd.*" Broadly Welsh with shock, Pritchard dropped into a seat and stared at them. "How many tons?"

"Once it was all over, the bomb disposal boys had a count and estimated that there were about six tons of home-made ammonal packed into boxes and lodged in a secret chamber under Whitehall."

Pritchard's lips pursed. "Six tons is a lot. That would have made a hole."

"It would." Briers seated himself beside Miles. "Not a large enough hole to bring down the Cenotaph, perhaps, but maybe enough to bring down the Government."

"And certainly enough to scare everyone stupid." George leaned forward, elbows on his knees. "Anyone I might know involved, apart from Andrija, of course?"

"Gregor Tamarkin," Briers said. "Now safely dead, thanks to Miles and a brick."

George let out a shout of laughter. "Well done, Miles."

"I can hardly take the credit." The glow in Miles' cheeks at his brother's praise couldn't have been more pronounced, in Briers' opinion, if he had been at Buck House accepting a VC from the King. "I wasn't the man to administer the coup de grace."

"Coup de brick," Briers pointed out. "No, that was the gentleman of my acquaintance representing a foreign power who was, at that moment, on our side."

"Ah, friendly enemies." George nodded. "Useful chaps under the right circumstances. Tell me, Allerdale, what next? Back to your posting?"

Briers was very conscious of Miles' attention as he replied. "I'm not sure. I told all my contacts I was home on leave and left it open ended. Naylor said he wants to talk it over with me later in the week, but I doubt I'll be sent back immediately."

"Good." George grinned. "It's rugger season. You'll have time to catch some matches, maybe even have a social life."

Briers snorted. "The whole point of our profession is not to get our faces seen," he pointed out. "But a couple of weeks rest and recreation would not go amiss. I'll see what Naylor says then make my plans."

"Speaking of plans," Pritchard said as he headed for the kitchen, "luncheon will be in approximately twenty minutes, gentlemen. Tea – coffee for Mr Allerdale – is on the fender."

"Oh, good show." Miles smiled and headed for the fireplace. "You will stay for lunch, won't you, George?"

"Good grief, is that the time? No, I have an engagement for which I am very nearly late." George shook Miles' hand and gave him a clap on the shoulder that made him wince. "I'll be in touch. Dinner one night, my treat, all right?"

"Thank you, George." Miles fetched George's ulster and helped him into it. "Have a good afternoon."

The flat seemed larger and infinitely quieter once Miles' brother had left. Miles provided Briers with his coffee, set his own tea aside after one sip and leaned back on the sofa with a sigh.

After a moment, Briers reached for his hand. "You look exhausted," he said.

"Oh, you know me," Miles muttered. "No moral fibre. This has been a tense few weeks."

"It has," Briers squeezed Miles hand between both of his, "but on the whole, I've enjoyed it. A lot."

"So have I. And a few weeks more, maybe, until you go back to Belgrade?"

Briers nodded.

"Then unless you have other plans, would you feel inclined to accept an invitation to share a well-appointed gentleman's residence? You'd have your own room, of course, and full use of the facilities."

"Facilities." Briers chuckled. "I like the sound of that and yes, I'd accept such an invitation with enthusiasm, as long as you don't think Pritchard would be put out?"

"Pritchard has already suggested it," Miles admitted.

"It's a deal then, but there's something you should know first." Briers leaned back against the cushions, inspecting Miles' hand and scowling at the abrasions on his knuckles, the torn nails. "I didn't want to say in front of your brother, but Naylor has already given me an inkling of what might be required. I may be here for longer than expected. I don't want you to feel you have to offer to extend my tenancy, much though I would like to stay here – with you." Miles' flush suggested he had caught Briers' meaning. "My employers will be told I've taken sick and a substitute will be sent out in my place. There are new radio techniques and equipment I'll need to master and a whole new set of codes to memorise. It's bound to take a few months and I can assure you that, if it meets your approval, I'll be a very poor pupil."

Miles expression lightened. "You will be very welcome to stay for as long as you please. Or as long as His Majesty's Government will let you. I'll be delighted to have you."

"The feeling is mutual. I haven't forgotten that we had a deal." Briers turned in his seat and glanced towards the kitchen doorway beyond which they could hear a promising rattle of crockery. Briers shifted still further and when he leaned down Miles' lips met his in a kiss that warmed him to the core.

It wasn't ideal. Briers' broken wrist meant he couldn't hold Miles as tightly as he would have liked to have done, and Miles' bruised face felt stiff and unresponsive although Miles was doing his best. For a long moment their mouths worked together, tongues stroking, then Briers tilted his head and chuckled against Miles' cheek.

"And if you fancy giving Millie an airing that's fine with me," he whispered. "Long weekend in Brighton? Or just about the house when you've had a bad day. Or if you happen to feel like it. I'd be delighted to see her."

"You mean it?" Miles stared at him, saw the answer in his smile and beamed in reply.

Their next kiss was more heated, hands roving, so the shrill of the telephone startled them both. Miles laughed, patted Briers' knee and got up.

"I'll get it, Pritchard," he called and went to pick up the receiver. "Hello," he said. "Who – what? How did you get this number?"

Briers moved fast enough to hear the reply.

"Well, I am in the business to find out information." Falk sounded amused. "Is Allerdale there? I think I can hear two sets of breathing."

"I am," Briers snapped. "What are you playing at, Falk?"

"Just saying goodbye," Falk said, "and sharing a little more information before I ship out. Tamarkin was a – what's the word? Cat's paw? Patsy? This was not what it looked like. Andrija was in another's employ. One that would benefit from greater antagonism between England and Russia."

"I see," Miles scowled at the mouthpiece of the phone. "You do realise that this telephone may be monitored."

"That would be good – save time. Just as long as you know that when seeking enemies of the state, it's not always necessary to look too far afield."

"Good God, man …"

"Either side of the channel will do." Falk cleared his throat. "Allerdale, and you, my *gnädige Frau*, it was a privilege to work with both of you. I hope that nothing occurs to put us on opposite sides in the future. Now I must go. *Auf Wiedersehen.*"

The phone clicked and Miles grimaced and put it back on the desk.

"Farewell, Falk," he said. "Enemies either side of the channel. I don't like the sound of that."

"Neither do I." Briers reached for his pipe and tobacco. "Nor what he said about opposite sides."

"But Germany is stable." Miles shrugged. "With Hindenberg at the helm, they are no threat. Of course, there are those clowns in the NSDAP but they are a joke."

Briers frowned. "Are they? Tell me, Miles, out of all those many languages, do you have any familiarity with German dialects?"

"No." Miles grinned at him. "Apart from a few words. *Danke. Guten Abend.*"

"*Zwei bier, bitte*, is about as far as I go," Briers admitted. "Miles, I have a feeling that we should learn. How long would it take you to be fluent?"

"Eight weeks," Miles said without hesitation. "Six months to sound like a native, maybe a year's intensive study to understand all the nuances in poetry." He reached out to grip and tug one of Briers' waistcoat buttons. "There's one phrase that I know already."

"Oh yes?" Briers moved closer, pinning Miles against the edge of the desk and slipping one hand under his jacket. He set his hand in the small of Miles' back, holding him close, and applied a little pressure in just the right place with his thigh. Miles took a sharp breath. "What's that, then?" Briers asked.

"Why, '*ich liebe dich*', of course."

The bright-eyed look, the teasing smile was wholly Millie, while the sinewy strength of the body in Briers' arms was gloriously Miles. "Ah, Miles," Briers laughed. "What's the German for 'me too'?"

Miles' mouth was warm and tasted of tea – a taste that Briers decided that he could bear as long as he experienced it under similar circumstances. After a moment, they both sighed and Briers dropped his head to press his nose into the hollow behind Miles' ear. They might not have long together but Briers planned to make the most of it.

"Gentlemen." Pritchard's voice sounded amused. "Luncheon is served."

About the Author

Elin Gregory lives in South Wales and has been making stuff up since 1958. Writing has always had to take second place to work and family but now the kids are grown up it's possible she might finish one of the many novels on her hard drive and actually DO something useful with it.

Historical subjects predominate. She has written about ancient Greek sculptors, 18th century seafarers but also about modern men who change shape at will and how echoes of the past can be heard in the present. Heroes tend to be hard as nails but capable of tenderness when circumstances allow.

There are always new works on the go and she is currently writing about the Great War, editing a contemporary romance and doing background reading for a story set in Roman Britain.

Manifold Press

Life in all the colours of the rainbow

For **Readers**: LGBTQIA fiction and romance with strong storylines from acclaimed authors. A variety of intriguing locations — set in the past, present or future — sometimes with a supernatural twist. Our focus is always on the characters and the story.

For **Authors**: We are always happy to consider high-quality new projects from aspiring and established writers.

Our 'regular' novels are now joined by the Espresso Shots imprint for novellas and our New Adult line.

Visit our website to discover more!

ManifoldPress.co.uk